IT TAKES DEATH TO REACH A STAR

Other Books By Stu Jones

The Action of Purpose Trilogy

Through the Fury to the Dawn
Into the Dark of Day
Against the Fading of the Light

Other Books By Gareth Worthington

Children of the Fifth Sun - 2017 London Book Festival Winner

Forthcoming From Gareth Worthington

Children of the Fifth Sun: Echelon

IT TAKES DEATH TO REACH A STAR

STU JONES & GARETH WORTHINGTON

It Takes Death To Reach A Star

ISBN: 978-1-944109-52-3

VESUVIAN BOOKS

Published by Vesuvian Books
www.vesuvianbooks.com

Printed in the United States of America

10 9 8 7 6 5 4 3 2 1

TABLE OF CONTENTS

For my mother—who always searches for the best in people.
~ Stu Jones

For my children—the only things I like about me.
~ Gareth Worthington

Everyone—pantheist, atheist, skeptic, polytheist—has to answer these questions:

Where did I come from? What is life's meaning? How do I define right from wrong and what happens to me when I die? Those are the fulcrum points of our existence.

~ Ravi Zacharias

MAP OF ETYOM

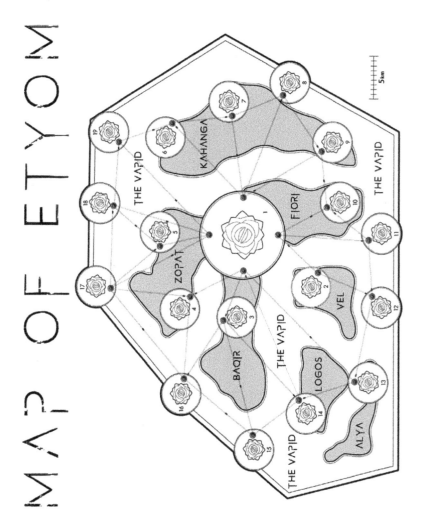

KAHANGA

FIORI

ZOPAT

BAQIR

VEL

LOGOS

ALYA

THE VAPID

THE VAPID

THE VAPID

THE VAPID

5km

CHAPTER ONE

MILA

No matter how badly I want it to be different this time, in the end I still die.

We all do.

I lie on the cot, cold sweat clinging to my skin, arms raised to my face, stuck like a marionette tangled in its own strings. The dream feels so real. Another breath—count it out. In, two, three, four. Out, two, three, four. My heart slows, my mind no longer caught in the grip of the terrifying dream: a battle in which I play a critical role, yet I'm no soldier. This nightmare stalks me night after night, and even though I know I'm dreaming, I'm powerless to prevent the inevitable—the coming of Death.

The alarm on my personal electronic device, or PED, chirrups three times: *05:00*. Not much sleep during the dark hours, again. I squeeze my shoulders, rubbing away the dull, muscular ache, and try to remember the fading embrace of a brother who now feels far away. A deep breath in, a slow exhale out. Get up already, Mila.

The frigid floor stings my bare feet. I shrug into a few less-than-clean garments and pull on my boots. The stale smell of the attire fills my throat. A shiver crawls across my skin. Sard, it's cold. Gotta find something warmer. After rummaging through a pile of soiled clothes that lie in the corner of my room, I pull out a short leather jacket, its collar lined with fur—though from what animal is unclear. Shaking it hard a few times, I stare at the fur lining. I know the lice are in there somewhere. No time to try and clean it now. The jacket slips over my shoulders, the ice-cold collar snugging up around my neck. It stinks like dead rat.

My PED and my precious collection of writings go into my satchel, carefully so as not to crush the worn old picture that lies at the bottom. I fish out the faded image of Zevry and me. I can be no more than eight-years old in this photo. He's grinning, as usual, with one arm wrapped around my shoulder. It was taken more than twenty years ago—yet little seems to have changed. Still have roughly cut short hair, now with a streak of color in the front. Still have a lean, almost boyish frame—though I've added some piercings and tattoos over the years in an attempt to distinguish myself. And then of course there's my scar—cutting its pink path across my forehead and left eye. Slashed deep into my face not long after this picture was taken, it's a permanent reminder you don't walk the streets alone in a place like Etyom.

No time for this. I stuff the picture back into my satchel and head out the door without locking it. Anything worth stealing is already on me—and it wouldn't take much to force the door to my closet-sized room anyway.

My boots creak on the rickety stairs leading into the bar below. It's quiet now, a far cry from the bedlam hours earlier. Smoke hangs lazily in the air, like the memory of an old ghost.

"Come on, Clief." I cough. "How do you breathe this stuff night after night?"

The man at the bar raises his head but continues to wipe down the counter. "Oh, it's not that bad. Sorta like burning plastic." He offers a tired smile. "Off so early?"

"Every day." Still pinching my nose and squinting, I make my way toward the door. "I'm serious. Get some fresh air in here. That botchi is going to scramble what's left of your tiny brain."

He huffs out a laugh. "And that out there? That's where you get the fresh air?"

2

"You know what I mean."

As I push open the door, the wind hits me like a frozen punch in the mouth. Going out in this icy hell never gets easier. The streets are dark and cold, shadows upon shadows concealing the horrors of Etyom. It's hard to believe this place was once considered a haven. Long ago, it was a vast, sprawling gulag-turned-mining community called Norilsk. Between World War III and the New Black Death, nearly nine billion people around the world lost their lives. Those who were left fled their homes and cities in search of someplace safer. For many, this barren hellhole was it. The conflict hadn't fully destroyed the city, and the New Black Death struggled to take hold in the brutal Siberian climate. Survival was possible here.

A mass migration followed; the Russian government was helpless to stop it. Outside Norilsk, organized social structure, at least the way people understood it then, gasped its final dying breath. And then, silence. Communications with the outside world went dark. Zev said anyone who hadn't died in the war succumbed to the New Black Death. It was then everyone here knew they were truly alone. They chose to isolate themselves, even renamed the city Etyom. My brother and I weren't born for another few hundred years, the descendants of those who fought to survive. *We're fighters, Mil. Survivors. Nothing can keep us down. That's why we're called Robusts.* But then why didn't you come home to me, brother?

I pull the jacket closer around my neck. Bilgi's place is only a block away, and it's a good thing, too, because with average temps below zero, the wind is cutting through me like a razor. I half run, half walk, down the quiet street, torn between wanting to get there fast and not wanting to bust my tail on the ice.

Six raps with my knuckles in the practiced manner and the rickety door immediately opens. Bilgi waits inside. His simple place is lit by a single oil lamp. It's barren and less than inviting,

3

but I'm not here to be pampered.

"Love me so much, you just wait for me by the door now?"

"If you would rather stand on the stoop a little longer, then be my guest," he answers in a clipped tone, ushering me in.

"Come on, let's do it already. I need to get my blood pumping."

The words are barely out of my mouth, my arms still stuck in the sleeves of my jacket, when he lunges forward. I see it coming, but the impact still throttles me as Bilgi's heavy hands encircle my neck and drive me against the wall. My hair scatters across my face. Bring it, old man. The jacket comes free, and with a flurry of punches and a swift roundhouse kick to Bilgi's thigh, I drive him back.

"Very good, young *krogulec*."

"I'm nothing like the sparrow hawk. I'm faster."

He smirks and comes again. This time I'm ready. Dodging to the left, I evade his attack. Parrying a second punch, I deliver a brutal knee strike to his midsection and a palm-heel strike to the side of his head—but in the process I've let down my guard. His spinning back fist catches me across the bottom of my jaw, snapping my head around.

I stumble back and collide with a short table before tumbling over it to the floor. Bilgi wastes no time bringing the fight to me. He tries to stomp on my head, but I roll to the outside and launch into a flying uppercut, which skims past his chin. Back and forth we evade and parry one another's strikes.

Bilgi finally raises his hand. Sweat beads on my brow, my chest heaving, fists still raised. The old man doesn't even appear winded.

"That's enough for now, Mila," he says, stepping away and fetching a small pot from the rudimentary stove. "May I offer you some krig?"

He only keeps enough of the strong, caffeinated drink to have some for himself once in a while. It would be rude of me to decline. "Of course, thank you."

He pours the krig and hands it over, the hot black liquid warming my fingertips through the tin cup. The ability to cultivate or manufacture sugar, in any real quantity, ceased long ago. My krig is taken black, like everyone else's.

Bilgi directs me toward the fire and offers a seat. I sink down by the hearth.

"Why sparrow hawk? Where did that come from?"

"You remind me of them—the way you move," Bilgi replies. His old, muscular frame shuffles back and forth as he pours himself a cup of the ink-colored stuff.

"Tell me. I have never seen one."

My mentor half closes his eyes, the recollection of some distant memory forming. "They glide, swooping in to take their prey. Fierce predatory creatures, they have the ability to dip and dive through the trees, riding the wind."

"Oh." How it must feel to be free. "I would very much like to see them dancing through the trees, or to see whole forests at all, for that matter."

"Hmmm." Bilgi holds the steaming cup to his lips.

I glance up from my drink. "Your son? How is he?"

"The sickness in his lungs seems to be getting worse." Bilgi's face bears no emotion. "Breathing too much of the spores from the deep mines below, I think." He gives a practiced smile.

"You're going to Fiori to visit him today?"

He nods. "Maybe my visits will help him recover."

"May Yeos see it so."

"And you, dear Mila, you still are not sleeping?"

"A little." I nod, but don't raise my head.

"Your vision returns to you. A specter of what once was. Or is it what is to come?"

What am I supposed to say? That Yeos speaks to me in dreams I don't understand? That I see Death?

"Well?" he presses.

"It's not that—"

"I believe it is, my dear. I can read it in your face. I recognize it because I understand it all too well." He's staring at me, waiting for an answer. "Mila," he begins, then seems to labor over some hidden thought. "I have been teaching you now for years. Many mornings we meet here, and we spar. You have hardened yourself and grown quite skilled in your chum lawk. I have taught you everything I know of it. I now have little else to offer you, apart from my charming personality." He flashes an enigmatic grin. "Mila, dear, I'm proud of you and your hard work. It's just ... it is a dangerous world out there, even when one doesn't go looking for it."

I take a slow sip from the steaming cup and wait for the inevitable lecture. The potent, bitter liquid warms a path down my throat and into my belly.

"No amount of training can protect you from yourself. Don't let your hate devour you."

"What are you saying?"

"Don't throw your life away, Mila. We have one life to live, one life to give in the service of the Lightbringer. Use yours to make a difference."

"Very poetic Bilgi, but—"

The old man gently touches my arm—an uncharacteristic gesture for him. "Just do something that matters with the time you've been given, Mila. Don't fade away, as so many do, out here among the ruins of the old world."

The words sink into my heart, stirring something deep within. Bilgi is right. Because he knows, just as I do, that all of humanity is dwindling—but most of all, our people, the Logosians, are fading fast. If we lie down and submit to the Musuls or the Graciles, or anyone else who decides we should cease to exist, then cease to exist we shall.

I slurp down the last of the krig, throw on my jacket, and get on with my day, giving little more than a simple farewell. Yet Bilgi's words follow me, clinging to the dark recesses of my heart: *We have one life to live, Mila. Use yours to make a difference.*

CHAPTER TWO

DEMITRI

The switchblade catches on the seam of my pocket but eventually frees from the twists and folds of the inner lining. Slowly and purposefully, I draw the razor-sharp edge of the blade across my naked forearm, dragging it with appreciable force along the well-worn furrow in my skin. The face in the bathroom mirror winces with the familiar burning—flesh splitting apart, hot blood erupting from within. The heat pulses in waves along my arm and into my brain. This is my body. This is my pain. This is my blood dripping to the floor, smacking these flawless white tiles.

Whining again, little zalupa? the voice in my head says.

"Please, not today." The hand towel is already saturated with my blood.

Every day, you pathetic kozel. *There is no escape from me—from us.*

"Just leave me alone, Vedmak."

I decided to give it, give *him*, a name a long time ago. It only seemed right. He is Vedmak, a creature who emerged from the concoction of horrors described in my many books on old Russia. Ghastly tales, from the very real Bolshevik war to horrible fairy tales told to children. I have never seen him, only heard his menacing voice. If he did have a form, he'd be a tall, thin man with cold blue eyes and colder white skin. He'd have long gray hair and boiled-leather clothing, wrapped in a heavy wool cloak.

8

Pah. Books? Always have your head buried in those relics. Why don't you use the neuralweb like everyone else? my demon rasps. His voice is like gravel being rubbed into the soft tissues of my brain.

"I have enough voices in here; I don't need to cram in anything more. Besides, you know as well as I do that if someone fished around in here, they might find you. Then we'd both be dead."

Defects of all types are weeded out of Graciles. Imperfections are diagnosed in the neo-womb or as a youngling, and then the being is erased. And by *erased* I mean euthanized. Murdered. *Axiotimos Thanatos*, the Leader calls it. We call it being Ax'd. Schizophrenia, dissociative identity disorder—whatever my affliction is, it will never be tolerated. It must be kept secret at all costs.

Such a little coward.

"Just go away, Vedmak." How juvenile.

"Mitya?"

Did someone call my name? The voice is muffled and distant.

"Mitya, who are you talking to?" calls the voice.

Damn. Nikolaj. He must have heard me through the bathroom door.

Vedmak snarls. *Tell him to get lost.*

"Mitya, are you even listening?"

He always calls me Mitya. A nickname, an abbreviation of Demitri from the old world. Thinks it makes him sound intelligent. My younger neo-brother, just two years my junior, is incredibly arrogant. Vedmak hates him.

In a practiced motion, I wipe up the blood on the floor with the hand towel and stuff the red-stained rag into the cleansing chute. I slather my wound in derma-heal gel, then roll down my sleeve. One last scan of the room for evidence of my injury, and then I slide open the bathroom door.

"Mitya? Are we going to the lab today or not? We're running late." Nikolaj's eyes flash angrily. He's already in his environmental suit. "You're not even listening to me, are you?"

"I am. And don't call me Mitya, *Nikolaj*. You know I hate it."

Ha. The sheep has learned how to bark, Vedmak says, cackling.

Don't listen. Just focus on Nikolaj. "Of course we're going to the lab. The accelerator calculations are still pending, and we're on a deadline."

"Good. Get your ass in gear. Put on your suit, and let's go." Nikolaj gestures toward the door and runs off to retrieve his helmet from his bedroom.

A moment later he returns, his wavy chestnut hair newly combed over his head and fixed into place with the usual inordinate amount of lacquer, his skin glowing from a quick cryorejuvenation blast. Just like me, he has almond-shaped hazel eyes, chiseled cheekbones, caramel skin, and a smooth jawline. Like all Gracile males, he stands an impressive two meters tall, with all the right muscles in all the right places. Neither of us needs to exercise to achieve our physique. We're the latest generation of Graciles— grown in glass wombs from carefully designed DNA maps. Our kind is constantly revised and improved. Initially genetic modification was so we could create immune systems that would resist the New Black Death, the NBD, but we're far past that now. These days, modifying our progeny feels like vanity more than survival.

Nikolaj wedges his helmet between his arm and his hip, then eyes me critically. "Sometimes I doubt we came from the same neo-womb, you know that?"

I know that. He tells me often enough.

"You should grow your hair out. Crew cut is so last year."

Why bother? I'll never be Nikolaj, never really be accepted. "C'mon. Let's get a move on. Can't be late," I call over my shoulder, fumbling with the door lock. Though I'm unsure if I'm talking to Nikolaj, Vedmak, or myself.

CHAPTER THREE

MIL∧

Perched atop a maintenance platform jutting out from one of the foundational support pillars of a Gracile fortress, my legs dangle precariously over the ramshackle buildings below. Had to ditch my jacket during the climb that brought me to this place, but now the wind is starting to cut again, sweat-dampened clothes chilling my skin.

The worn leather slides back over my shoulders, my hand fishing around in my satchel for a piece of hardtack wrapped in paper and my writings—a crumpled and poorly bound set of papers with meandering lines scrawled by my own hand. *The Words of Yeos.* I hold it to my chest in silent prayer, then set it aside in favor of my breakfast. The dense unleavened bread isn't good, but it's something.

Beneath my seemingly giant feet, Logos is alive—undulating like a sea of insects amid the many pathways and intersecting ruins. Norilsk was bombed during the war, and while some of the larger structures of the old city remain, much of it was replaced with dilapidated buildings stacked over one another in a jumbled mess. It's not unlike the favelas of Brazil long ago—or at least that's what Zev said. He knew everything. My PED chimes once. The janky old piece of hacked Gracile tech displays a single sentence:

Meet in the usual spot—20min ~ Gil.

Sure, twenty minutes. Like he'll be on time.

11

Though cobbled together from junk parts, the PED still wasn't cheap for me to come by. Took seventeen jobs to pay it off. The Graciles used this stuff long before the invention of the neuralweb and likely thought they'd be using them a lot longer, given the twenty-five-year batteries these things are equipped with.

Operating outside the Gracile neural network, jacked devices like these are perfect for discreet, untraceable communications. Unlike the haughty, self-absorbed Graciles, I won't be jacked with advanced internal technology.

I finish my breakfast, recheck the binding around my small collection of writings, touch it to my lips, and clamber to my feet. Reaching into my bag, my hand closes on a pulley and a T-bar handle. The zip line at my feet is the highest I've established yet, and just one in a series of lines I've rigged to speed up my own travel within Logos. It's not really safe—but neither is walking down the street in broad daylight.

The zip line is fast—a little too fast for my first descent on this line. Near the bottom of the line, after leveling out for more than ten meters, the series of intermittent cable bumpers are just enough resistance to slow my descent in bursts—except for the last one. It catches me by surprise, snatching the pulley from my grip, sending me sprawling.

My feet hit the tin roof first, and I launch into a forward roll to lessen the impact. It half works, but I can't regain my feet and end up sliding to a stop on my backside.

"Sard. Brake pad seven still sticks. Get it right already, Mila."

Cinching my sling bag down against my body, I start to run.

The shadows of the city bathe me in their coolness, the pristine interconnected Gracile towers above stealing the light of day. The gloom of a snowy day made infinitely worse by the structures above. No wonder so many die by their own hand down here. Who would want this life?

Dancing across the rooftops, my feet touch the flimsy structures just long enough to spring forward again and again. At the edge of one roof, I launch into the openness. I'm flying, just like a sparrow hawk. My fingertips find a concrete ledge, and I twist, pull myself up and over, and drop down the other side to the ground. Another forward roll and I'm on my feet again.

Three minutes early. Time to catch my breath before Gil arrives, assuming he's on time. Though timeliness is lost on Gil. He's an information broker and a lazy drug addict—but if you ask him, the world doesn't spin without his say-so. I wait.

Gil approaches from a darkened alley, his eyes glassy. He's almost four minutes late.

I fold my arms across my chest. "Glad you decided to show, junkie."

"Not today, Mila."

"You're an idiot, Gil. Do you know what would happen to you here if you got caught? Logos is stim free, yet here you are—"

"What part of *not today* isn't clear for you? You're a handler. That's all. Maybe you should shut up and mind your own business."

Something really is eating at him. Best leave it alone.

"Okay, Gil. You got it."

"Do you want the job or not?"

"Of course I want the job. I came all the way over here. Why wouldn't I?"

Gil doesn't respond but simply hands over an unmarked lead package. Judging from its size, it's a protected data stick.

"You have an hour. If you can't deliver it within the hour—"

"Destroy and discard. And I owe you the fee. Yeah, I got it." I take the package and slip it into my bag.

"And no accessing it," he says.

"This isn't my first time, Gil. Besides, I'm not overly fond of a bounty on my head."

"The address will be pinged separately. It's not anywhere you haven't been before."

"The deal pays in Etyom dollars? Or something else?"

"Dollars."

"Okay. I'll handle it." I nod and turn to walk away.

"Mila, I've got something else, but it's a little outside your comfort zone."

He knows being cryptic gets on my nerves. "Okay ... what exactly is that supposed to mean?"

"It means you're my best handler, and I need you to take it anyway."

"What is it, Gil?"

He sighs. "You know I can't tell you."

I turn to meet his bleary-eyed gaze. "Then who wants it transported?"

Gil appears to wrestle with the answer. "Opor."

"No."

"Mila, I need you to do it." There's genuine fear in his eyes.

"And I said no. I'm not leaving Logos to go deal with the resistance." I turn to leave again.

"The payout is big," Gil blurts out, stopping me in my tracks once again. "At least the value of eleven jobs. Consider it for the money if nothing else."

The figure is at least six months' rent. "I'm not making you any promises. Now stop wasting my time. I've only got fifty-five minutes left to make this delivery."

CHAPTER FOUR

DEMITRI

The bright-blue sky above the clouds is blinding. At least in the few milliseconds it takes for the photosensitive glass in my visor to react. I should be grateful, here in the heavens, to be free from the NBD, to not be hounded by the scum that scurries around in the crumbling city below.

Scuffing the floor with the soles of my boots, I follow Nikolaj across our lillipad—a gargantuan erection protruding from the old city below. Beneath us, its long thin stem reaches from the polluted ground to eight kilometers up into the atmosphere, then opens out into a circular podium nearly five kilometers wide. At its center, a huge lotus-flower-inspired building—the Pistil.

It's hard not to admire the Pistil's architectural magnificence. A metallic blossom fabricated of silvered glass, protecting me and my neighbors. The outer petals are formed of colossal solar panels. They fuel more than seventy percent of our needs: heating, lighting, and some hydroponics. But most of all, our work in the labs, think tanks, and schools.

A cold wind whips by and I shiver, hugging my body with padded arms. Enveloped in this hazmat pressure suit from head to toe, breathing apparatus pumping conveniently warmed air into my lungs, it's toasty. But watching the gust gather debris and fling it across the lillipad makes my skin prickle.

"Stop lagging, Mitya. C'mon." The voice crackles in my

15

headset.

"I'm just enjoying the view. The lillipads are pretty, don't you think?" I lie to him for the second time today. Perhaps I lie to him too much. Perhaps I lie to everyone too much.

Quit whining, zalupa. You're such a kozel, Vedmak jibes.

"What are you, a youngling? It's a HAP, Mitya, not a lillipad. A habitable aerial platform. You're a scientist; act like one." Nikolaj huffs and stomps ahead.

We pound across the sun-bleached tarmac, stepping over the fissures and cracks that seem to multiply every year. These structures were never meant for the purposes they now perform. Constant heating from the sun, poor protection from the thin ozone, and rapid cooling at night stresses the aging materials. The other lillipads come into view, glinting in the rays of the ever-climbing sun. At least the Pistils do. Just like my HAP, the others have gray tarmac surfaces. They were supposed to be stunning—sprawling gardens of green and brightly colored flowers. Nineteen lillipads spread out over more than 240 square kilometers.

As we approach the dock, the enormous helium-filled foil balloons sitting under Lillipad Three can be seen, sparkling an orangey, crinkled gold. This high up, the stem structures are flimsy, swaying from side to side. The balloons offer stability, and a safety feature—should a stem ever break, the lillipad won't fall and crash into the slums below. An elegant solution borrowed from the High Altitude Venus Operational Concept, a space program designed in the early twenty-first century. A time when we looked to the stars and planets, and wondered. Perhaps we should have been paying more attention to what was going on here on Earth.

Nikolaj glares through his visor. At least I think he does, but the photosensitive glass has transformed to an inky black. "For the Leader's sake, c'mon. I'm not getting any more demerit points on my license for being late because of you." The voice in my headset is garbled with snapping and crackling, solar radiation interfering with the signal.

Nikolaj turns and tramps to the edge of the lillipad, peering over the side.

Push him off. No one will know. See if the boring kozel is late then.

It's hard to remove the smirk from my face.

We wait at the dock for the cable car to come back from its first journey of the day. While I wish it would take hours, in almost no time it has already squealed and clanged into the station, the doors sliding back automatically, inviting us in. We used to have VTVs, vertical takeoff vehicles, but they weren't considered fuel efficient. At least for civilians. Now only the Creed use them—our peacekeepers. So every day we risk our lives on the swaying cable car at the edge of my HAP, held on a twisted steel rope by a single arm.

Peering down between the three-inch gap that separates the platform from the car, it's hard not to wonder what lies below the cloud line. What are the strange little Robusts doing down there— scurrying around in the dirt? Probably fighting or thieving, or pretending they're like us. Despite their inferior brains and physical stature, they still manage to do their best to emulate Graciles. Dodgy surgeries yielding crappy modifications. Still, Robusts do one thing well—narcotics.

My stomach knots. Dammit. Need some DBS—*dvoyuridnyy brat smert'*, "cousin of death." Though Evgeniy, my dealer, calls it *krokodil.* He says the skin of the Robusts who use it, due to their inferior genetics, becomes scaly and putrid. For me, it's something to shut Vedmak up for a while.

Patting my chest pocket, I can feel one capsule left through my thick gloves. I'll be able to take it when I'm safe in the lab, but I need to take a trip to see Evgeniy.

You won't silence me forever. Can't outrun your shadow, little boy. Vedmak's tone is low and menacing.

Nikolaj shoves his palm between my shoulder blades. I lurch forward, falling over the gap into the empty cable car.

"Dammit, Nikolaj."

"Get a move on, Mitya. *Bljyat'.* You're always in a trance. Snap out of it. The Leader is making inspections this week; it could be our lab next, and I want to impress him." Nikolaj's expression is hidden from me, but it's a good bet he's glowering.

I straighten my suit, stand as far away from the door as possible, and hold the handrail. My brother presses the button to close the door, then taps his finger on his leg impatiently as the cable car lifts away from the platform. As it sways in the thin atmosphere, we don't speak. Conversation has become harder and harder between us.

He's your brother, isn't he? Spit something from your lips.

With my head lowered, I whisper into my helmet. "He's a neo-brother, Vedmak. We came from the same genetic batch and were incubated in the same neo-womb, but that's it."

Vedmak laughs. *Just grow some* yaichki *and talk to him. Talk, or kill him. Actually, just kill him. I like that choice.*

"What do I ask him?"

Perhaps how it comes to be that you puppets do the work of a man who lives in his own palace, with private security, yet you have no idea why. Little Gracile puppets. Strutting around like a bunch of brain-dead peacocks. Do you even know what the other peacocks are doing up here? How their work is even related to your own pathetic little project? You're such a wretched little kozel, even for a Gracile.

"I don't know," I whisper as harshly as possible. "We just do as we're commanded. It's served us well. We're alive because of the Leader."

Hah. Afraid to ask him? Just ask him, little peacock. Ask him.

Ask.

"Okay."

"Okay what?" Nikolaj is turned toward me.

A cold sweat breaks across my brow. My stomach aches. "Ever … ever wonder what the other labs are doing? I mean, they keep our work pretty separate. I wonder how it all fits together."

Nikolaj grunts. "Why would you do that?"

"Do what?"

"Wonder? It's the Leader's instruction. We don't need to know the greater plan. We get paid well, our mods are discounted, and we're on a fast track to be on the council when we reach the designated age, rather than be recycled."

"You mean Ax'd." The thought makes my stomach hurt even more.

His helmet shakes, his index finger wagging. "I mean *recycled*, for the good of our people. Living beyond a certain age is just detrimental to our society and resources. Unless your wisdom and experience are great enough to lead the upcoming generations. And ours will be. You don't bite the hand that feeds you."

"Sure, I know. Just, with resources limited, don't you ever wonder why we put so much effort into our appearance and these experiments, but not much else?"

"Nope. And neither should you. Just be grateful. You could be living in the filth of the old city below, walking around in a pool of bacteria."

Of course I'm glad not to be trapped down in old Norilsk. A city at the edge of the world, dilapidated and broken even before the NBD. Grown and cultivated in crime and violence.

That was no answer. He twirls his tongue as the cow twirls its tail.

Damn, I wish he'd shut up. Need my DBS.

I nod at Nikolaj and peer out of the square glass window of

the cable car at the sky. Sandwiched between cirrocumulus and cirrus, our city in the clouds is surreal. Nineteen sparkling lillipads arranged in a spiral, Lillipad One at the center, larger and brighter than the rest. Yet something is wrong …

A boom. In the distance. Deep and reverberating. What the hell? A second boom, this time louder. The cable car swings in the aftershock. Gripping the rail, I hold my breath and peer out at smoke—a cloud of black ash billowing from a Pistil in the distance.

CHAPTER FIVE

MILΛ

The meeting at the designated drop point went as planned. Another brief encounter with another shady character in another dirty back alley. It only took forty minutes to make the delivery. It's possible this information will ruin someone's life.

It's not something to take pleasure in, but I do like to eat, and the somewhat shady nature of my job is just a fact of life—my life. The world changed, but the people in it didn't. The Robusts, at least, continue on as humanity always has. Deception, lies, betrayal, murder. There may no longer be any governments or major corporations in Etyom, but there is still every imaginable manner of trickery, falsity, and backstabbing. Information is still power—and money.

By midday my work is done. I take the time to go back and fix the bumper that threw me from the zip line earlier. A little sanding, a few adjustments, and it's good to go. On the way back home, I take a detour through the market's winding, narrow pathways filled with ramshackle stands and diminutive people to pick up some chiori meat, two smallish carrots, and a few herbs for dinner. It's simple but makes for an easy and fairly hearty one-pot stew.

A squat woman at a makeshift stand pushes a small cloth pouch toward me. "Krig? Krig for a good price?"

I take the pouch and offer her a thin gold ring that came as a speedy-delivery bonus on top of the payment for my last job. The ring is worth fifty times the value of this pouch—but I give it anyway. The woman breaks into a beaming smile, the dirt and grime on her face framing the toothless pink of her gums. This simple ring will feed her family for a month.

"You ... you are an angel, sent from Yeos Himself."

Don't linger, Mila. Don't care too much.

"Please. You come back anytime, dear. You can have as much krig as you want. Thank you."

The state of my people, and my inability to do anything about it, cuts deep. Slowly, without so much as a whimper, our way of life is dying. All of them cling to the most basic of hopes and dreams: to get back to someplace warmer, and maybe if they're lucky, into the embrace of someone who loves them.

This is my home. This is Logos—one of seven enclaves that make up Etyom. A small religious community, we are likely all that's left of those who have been instructed in the ways of Yeos, the Lightbringer. We aren't many, and we're surrounded by enclaves that hate us.

Outside Logos are six other enclaves. Each one is isolated and autonomous, protected by a wall fifteen meters high and many meters thick. Nobody planned it like this. It's the way people are, gravitating toward others who share their beliefs, their skin color, or their background. And in Etyom, by far the largest group is composed of Musuls. They occupy the largest enclaves: Baqir, Alya, and some of Kahanga.

Between the enclaves is a no-man's-land. We call it, the Vapid. It's a garbage-filled wasteland inhabited by Rippers, the outcasts of society. These people—the criminally minded, the violent, the psychotic predators of our communities—are expelled from their individual enclaves and forced into the Vapid because they can't be trusted to live inside the walls. Out there, they have turned to barbarism, the better traits of their humanity lost in an effort to survive.

The setting sun dips just past the edge of the westernmost lillipad as I push past the heavy wooden door back into the warmth of Clief's bar and the smell of flickering oil lamps. The botchi smoke is long gone, praise the Maker.

"Hey," Clief says as he emerges from behind a curtain in the back. Looking like he just woke up, he coughs a few times into his sleeve. "You got a minute?"

"Are you sick?" I can't help but shrink away.

"No, why?" he asks.

"You coughed."

"Relax, Mila. It's not the plague."

"You never know. What did you want?"

"I just wanted to catch you before you hit the stairs. Did you hear about that stuff at the mine today?"

"What stuff?"

"You don't know? Another two towl'eds got over the wall. Blew themselves up over by the entrance to the mine."

"How many did we lose this time?"

"The word is almost thirty people, but a bunch of the dead and wounded were women and children. The bastards attacked while those poor people were having lunch with their families."

"Yeos save us." That old familiar heat rises inside, my teeth working against each other. Damnation. "It'll never stop, Clief. Not until Logos is destroyed. You know that." I'm sure he can see the life draining from my face. It takes a concerted effort to fight the swell of hate, to remember the voice of my brother asking me not to be so quick to judge others for the acts of a few. I take a moment before answering. "Want me to make a donation to the Vestals? Contribute some aid money from the bar?"

"Sure, Mila." He nods. "Yeah, that would be nice."

"I'll take care of it." I'm at the stairs but can feel he isn't done. "Okay, cough it up. What do you want?"

"I uh ... I need you to ... fill in tonight."

"Come on, Clief. You've got to give me a little more advance warning."

"You're getting your warning now. I need you tonight, Mila. Go take a nap. It's gonna be busy."

"Yeah, sure thing, Clief. You got it. I don't mind working twenty-four-seven."

"You're a doll."

"No, I'm not."

Tired after the early morning with Bilgi and the job from Gil, the last thing I want to do is work tonight—but it's part of the deal. I need this place, and part of the arrangement is I have to fill in when Clief needs me to. Do my part, and he minds his business. It's a good arrangement.

The door to my room opens with a creak. My bag lands in the corner, along with my boots and jacket. The effects of sleep deprivation a physical weight upon my shoulders. I haven't even flopped down on my cot before my eyes begin to close. Just a couple of hours' sleep, please, Yeos. Maybe, just this once, I won't dream.

CHAPTER SIX

DEMITRI

Through two sheets of glass—my visor and the small window of the airlock door—the foyer of the Pistil looks as pristine and white as always, with large-leafed foliage strategically placed to add a feeling of serenity to the otherwise stark interior. Plants line the railings of each of the ten floors, rising to the top of the Pistil. A perfectly cylindrical screen fills the middle. On its surface, in extremely high definition, is our secretary of defense, Sasha Kaplinksi, talking with fervor, though it's not possible to hear what he's saying. Surrounding the screen is a throng of citizens. Some are huddled in small groups, like scared animals, while others run to and fro with no discernable destination. They just run.

The airlock hisses and the door pops open. I push through the opening and scramble to remove my helmet. The drone of conversation and murmuring in the Pistil is unbearably loud. Kaplinksi's voice is just audible above the din.

"*Once again, rebels from Lower Etyom have completed an act of terror on HAP Seven, though Robust terrorists have yet to claim the attack. Six of our people have lost their lives, including two younglings. Seven more are in critical condition. The Leader asks that you remain calm and focus on your tasks. The senate will discuss any countermeasure and how to improve our first lines of defense.*"

That doesn't make sense. There hasn't been an attack in years.

Nikolaj says that's because the Robusts need us for trade, to pay for their very existence, and that even the terrorists, their *resistance*, have figured that out. Still … if it is an attack, why Lillipad Seven? It doesn't have any strategic value I know of. It's just the mathematics lab. Full of guys whose brains work in a way mine never could. They imagine their universe, living inside a place of probability. As an experimental physicist, I prefer the definitive. At any rate, why would the Robusts want to destroy that facility? What value could that have? I don't even know anyone on—

My stomach cramps. Evgeniy is in that group. Oh, for the love of the Leader.

A wicked chuckling erupts in my head. *No more medicine for the little puppet.*

Vedmak is right. My stomach convulses and I drop to the floor, panting loudly. A gloved hand touches my shoulder.

"Mitya, you okay?" Nikolaj stares down at me, a genuine look of concern creased into his face.

"Yeah, it's just … just …"

Just no more drugs for the addict.

I ignore Vedmak and focus on lying to my brother. "I know someone on that lillipad. I hope he's okay."

Nikolaj slips his hand under my armpit and yanks me to my feet. "Let's find out, shall we?" He closes his eyes and accesses the neuralweb. "What's his name?"

"Evgeniy. Evgeniy Yarlov."

Why don't you look him up yourself, coward?

Concentrate, Demitri. Focus. "You got him?"

"Evgeniy Yarlov. Got him. Domiciled on HAP Nine, works on Seven. He's alive. In the infirmary over on HAP Eight, since the one on Seven was damaged in the blast."

Thank the Leader. "I think I'll go see him."

"Sure," replies Nikolaj. "But not now. We have to get to

work."

"Really? But no one else is—"

"We're not everyone else, or do I have to remind you? We're part of the engineering task force set up by the Leader himself. Next to be on the council and maybe even the senate. We're elite even among our kind. Pull yourself together. You can visit him after hours. Got it?" His hazel eyes probe into my own.

Stab him. Right in the eye.

Shut up, Vedmak. "You're right, Nikolaj. Let's go."

We filter through the throng of muttering citizens, all dressed in similar slacks and polo shirts, knee-length dresses, or skirts. No one ever deviates from these classic designs—flattering to our enhanced physiques, yet appropriately businesslike. Never in a bright color that would clash with our skin tone. The same caramel tone. Everywhere I look. They shoot worried glances at Nikolaj and me. As overall project supervisors, we're often looked to for advice in all manner of situations. I never know what to say. Vedmak usually has something vile to offer. Luckily Nikolaj is on hand with a grin and a handshake.

Nikolaj puts his arm out across my chest, stopping me in my tracks. What the hell? But now it's clear—the Creed.

Two peacekeepers stand in front of us in their standard royal-blue jumpsuits, wielding plasma energy rifles. They're not Graciles. They're not even remotely human. The Creed are geminoids. Fully autonomous androids perfected just before World War III ended. They were meant to be the soldiers to end it all—that is until the NBD did it for us. Nearly a thousand were recovered afterward and put to use as a sort of militia to protect us from Robust attacks as we built New Etyom.

The Creed's gaze is cold, and they have synthetic skin that lacks the luster of life. But this isn't what makes me uncomfortable about these machines. It's the fact they are made to look, walk, and talk like Graciles who have been Ax'd. Graciles who were considered to have been influential and socially important. Merely seeing Creed who look like them is supposed to give people the feeling of familiarity. Reanimations of our friends and neo-family. Thankfully, no geminoid has been modeled on anyone I have ever cared about. Who do I care about? Do any of us actually care about each other?

Such a child … always whining.

It's so difficult to hear over Vedmak's incessant nagging. Sard, I've lost track of the conversation.

The peacekeeper on the right is asking multiple questions of Nikolaj. Does he know what happened on HAP Seven? Did he see anything suspicious in the last few days? Where was he every day for the last week? Nikolaj recounts his movements, indicating we have been together the whole time. It isn't perfectly true. I often hide in my bedroom, surrounded by my old books. But this seems to satisfy the geminoid. He—it—nods and thanks us for our time before stomping off with its companion toward another group of people huddled around a carefully placed tree. Nikolaj marches off in the direction of our lab.

Eventually we make it to our workshop on the far side of the Pistil. Nikolaj punches a code into the panel at the entrance and stands rigid beneath the sensor just above it. The scanner beeps momentarily as it reads his iso-print—the DNA in his epithelial cells.

"Nikolaj Stasevich," confirms the computer voice, which is distinctly soft, female, and alluring. The door slides open and we shuffle in.

Our lab. Occupying a third of the Pistil, it's one of the biggest in New Etyom. But then it needs to be. The collider takes up half the space. Its simplicity and, frankly, brilliance makes me beam every time I see it. A huge, doughnut-shaped cylinder just over ninety meters in circumference, with narrow silver pipes running like metallic ivy over its surface and off into the adjacent wall. It's amazing to think these things were once nearly thirty kilometers long and buried underground.

I peel off my environmental suit and hang it up before taking a seat, then scan my station. The CPU wakes from its overnight processing—a 3-D image of two adjacent parallel beams contained within the doughnut glow green on the screen. The helium readout is stable, and the temperature of the magnets is absolute zero. It's been cooling for a day or two. I slip on the key gloves, which match my finger movements to commands, and within a few strokes, my two babies—my detectors—appear on the screen.

"How are our working girls?" Nikolaj asks without glancing up from his station.

I hate it when he calls them that. "They're perfect and ready to go."

ALICE and ELISA. When the collider is fired, beams of particles travel in opposite directions, smashing into one another. ALICE and ELISA tell me what pops out. ALICE—A Large Ion Collision Experiment—picks up particles from the beginning of the universe in a soup called a quark-gluon plasma. ELISA—my favorite, my Experiment at Light Speed Apparatus—detects a variety of different particles with a broad range of energies. Whatever form any new physical processes or particles might take, ELISA detects them and measures their properties. It's immensely satisfying.

Of course it satisfies you. You can't get a real woman, can you? Vedmak seems to relish that I'm alone.

Gotta focus on the task at hand. Talk to Nikolaj. "How's your little man?"

"Little man?" Nikolaj peers over his station. "You just remember, your girls couldn't even work if it weren't for THEO.

He's like their pimp."

"Their what?"

"Pimp. You know, like the Robusts have. A guy who's the boss of prostitutes."

"Don't call them that." Nikolaj's damn THEO—a Tokamak High Energy Output. THEO is one of two portable fusion reactors known to exist. He loves telling me how my work wouldn't happen without his. How his fusion reactor is the reason I can even run my accelerator.

And why is it used for this and not powering your stupid city? Ever think about that?

I had wondered that myself once. But Nikolaj explained that the solar power is enough for the city. Our work is prioritized over everything else.

"Okay, big brother, are you ready?"

"Ready." I love this bit.

Nikolaj scoots his chair on wheels across the room and over to a lonely desk at the back wall. The needle drops onto the spinning vinyl, the delicious crackle emanating over the twenty speakers lining the room. Eyes closed, I wait. Then, it happens: piano in C-sharp minor. The opening notes of *Quasi una fantasia*, Beethoven's *Moonlight Sonata*. The melancholic melody sends a shiver along my spine. Even Vedmak remains silent. I absorb the warm tones that can only be reproduced by a vinyl record. Despite this age of technology, we Graciles appreciate beauty in its purest form. The deck is one of only a few left in the known world. The Leader gave it to us as a gift when we began our work.

The music sets the tone for our labor: exploring the beginnings of the universe. I open my eyes and command the system to fire the beams, forcing the particles to dance to the melody, racing faster and faster toward the speed of light. My hand hovers above the trigger that will allow the beams to collide and

ELISA to do her job.

We wait patiently through the first movement with its sedate pace, and the second movement, slightly faster and lighter. Then it comes. The third movement explodes over the speakers, a near-frantic rhythm, and I press the button. The intersections open and the subatomic particles collide. It's how I imagine the birth of the universe, played out to the musical genius's glass-like piano notes. ELISA's readout begins to flood with information. Quarks. Muons. Mesons. The list goes on. Still not what we're looking for.

"Did you get anything?" Nikolaj asks, his eyes wide.

"No, I don't think so. I need to trawl the data, but I didn't see anything."

"Did you get the luminosity right? Was the velocity correct?"

"Yes, yes, of course. You need to be patient. We may not see it when we want." I hate it when he questions me.

"You've been distracted lately."

"Look, I know what I'm doing. We didn't get it. Maybe next time ... I'll tinker with the system." Why won't he leave me alone?

"Maybe I should check." He rises from his seat and strides toward me.

Before I can protest further, Oksana slides into the room. I didn't even hear the computer announce her. Dressed in a tight-fitting gray wool dress, she resembles every other Gracile female, designed to be aesthetically perfect according to our standards: long legs with perfect calves, tiny waist, full breasts. Yet the minute differences that make her unique also make her more beautiful. How her nose turns up slightly. How her chocolate-brown hair falls in open curls around her face and shoulders. The way she rests one hand on her hip when she's still. She ambles toward me, winking as she slips past, and kisses my neo-brother full on the lips, her arms locked around his neck. My gut knots again.

There she is, the only one you desire. And you let him have her.

31

You're pathetic.

I didn't let him have her. How can I let him do anything? He's him and I'm me. She chose him, because he's everything I'm not.

She chose him because she's a shallow slut.

Got to stay focused. Can't listen to Vedmak.

"Yeah, we saw the explosion," Nikolaj says. He's talking about HAP Seven. "Damn Robusts. When will they learn? You'd think they'd get that they need us to survive. Need the money we pay them to run their sad little lives. Can you imagine? Living down there. It's disgusting. I hear they don't even look human anymore. All squat and hunched, with eyes developed to see in the dark."

He's a scientist. He should know better. "That can't be true. Evolution takes a lot longer than that."

Nikolaj shrugs. "Either way, some of our citizens are dead. Mitya here knows someone over there who was caught in the blast."

Again with the nickname.

"Do you, Mitya?" Oksana searches my face for a response, those doe eyes of hers glistening. And now she's using that name, too.

"Yeah. A friend of mine."

"What are you doing with friends who work all the way on HAP Seven?" she asks. "Most of us can't be bothered to trek one, much less several, HAPs over."

"He's just a friend. I can't even remember where I met him."

"Well, clearly a good enough friend that it messed with your head this morning," Nikolaj says, gesturing toward our work. "Another zero result from the collider."

"Oh, that's a shame. Do you think you had enough luminosity?" she probes.

"I know what I'm doing. I don't need anyone to look at it." Just leave me alone.

"That's what I asked, Oksana. Here, move over, Mitya, and let me look." He steps toward me and reaches for the panel that controls ELISA.

"I said back off!" My voice reverberates around the room.

I know the words left my mouth. I felt my tongue make them, the air pass over my vocal cords. But that was not me. That was Vedmak. Did he just speak for me?

There's a long pause, and then Vedmak speaks in a voice deeper than usual.

You weren't going to do it. Pathetic kozel.

My heart pounds in my breast. That's never happened before. He's bugged me to say things. Pushed me. But never spoken *for* me. My seat is hot. Every fiber of my being urges me to leap up and run away, but I stay fixed to the spot. There's a cold silence in the room.

Dammit. Should have taken my last DBS hit.

33

CHAPTER SEVEN

MILA

To my genuine surprise, I don't dream of shadows and flame. Three hours feels like twelve. I'm a new woman, or might as well be. At least I'll be able to work tonight. Clief will be happy, and Clief being happy means a room for a while yet. I swing my feet over the edge of the cot and lower my head to whisper a short chain of rehearsed words. The Graciles abandoned faith long ago, but for us—for me—the power it has to sustain, to motivate, to generate hope, is more powerful than the evils at my door.

Mercifully the night goes fast. Bouncing at Clief's mostly involves avoiding flirtatious losers who should be at home with their families, or convincing a few of the soused miners it's time to hang it up for the night. Nobody gives me any trouble. Most of them know better. Before I know it, I'm helping Clief put up the chairs and wipe down the tables. We don't talk. There's no need, and we're both exhausted. Maybe I'll actually get another few hours of sleep before sunrise.

The door to the bar swings open, letting in a blast of frozen air.

For the love of … "Hey, how 'bout showing a little restraint there, jackbag? Heat isn't free."

Three men enter and shut the heavy wooden door behind them.

"We're closed," Clief says, wiping dry a ceramic mug.

34

"Good timing, then," says the dark-eyed man up front in a thick accent.

Musuls.

Two of the men make short work of placing the brace bar across the door. Somehow Clief still seems not to have noticed what's unfolding.

"I said we're closed. I'm going to have to ask you guys to leave. You're welcome back anytime during regular hours."

"We're not interested in the filth you peddle here." The man in front smirks, letting the words sink in. "Kapka wants his money."

"Kapka? Clief, what's this about?"

"Shut up." Clief keeps his eyes on his mug.

"No, Clief. Kapka? I know you didn't borrow money from Kapka."

"Shut up, Mila. You don't understand."

The man in front chuckles. "No, you really do not understand, girl. Best to mind your business and your fool mouth."

Only a severe glance from Clief and a little self-control keep me from coming unglued. Anger will get you killed right now, Mila. Stay calm. Be ready for anything.

"I need more time," Clief manages to say.

"They always need more time, don't they, boys?"

The two henchmen laugh and start to flank us.

"They're going to kill me," Clief says in a whisper as cold as the grave.

He's right.

"Hamza, take the hooker upstairs. We'll have a chat with Clief about what he owes Kapka. Then we'll join you to see what she has to offer."

"Hooker?"

Clief licks his dry, cracked lips. "Gentlemen, this isn't

necessary."

They say nothing as they close on us, each brandishing a large knife—the weapon of choice among most Robusts, especially Musuls. But I don't care. I'm still stuck on the insult.

"Did you really just call me a *hooker*?"

The solid henchman reaches out and grabs me by the arm. Before he knows how bad he's messed up, I'm already moving. Spinning into him, my elbow strike whips his head back and splits the bridge of his nose. He stumbles back. A violent kick in the chest sends him crashing against the wall, where he slides to the floor, out cold.

The head stooge turns on me, screaming. His knife comes in fast. I manage to twist away from the blade at the last instant, snagging a kiln-hardened mug from the counter that shatters across the thug's face. He howls in pain. My hands secure his wrist and torque the blade from his grasp. It clangs against the floor and slides under a nearby table. He comes again, blood pouring from his furious face. I launch a devastating kick to his groin, raise a chair as he's bent over, and slam it down, breaking it across his back.

The last one, who should have killed Clief by now, stands there stunned—probably wondering how some *hooker* whipped his buddies. Wide eyed, he searches for the door and makes a run for it.

"Now get the hell out of my place." Clief yells. "And you tell Kapka if he sends anyone else, we'll do the same to them."

The man, now hysterical, bumbles with the brace bar. "You're dead. Both of you are dead." He throws it off and in an instant, disappears into the ice-cold dark.

We stand there for a moment, sucking at the air. "I hate you, Clief," I say, moving to pull the door closed. I lean my back against it and nod at the men on the floor. "What do we do with them?"

"I don't know. Give me a second."

"What have you gotten me into?"

"*You* got you into this." He motions to the two unconscious men.

"That Musul called me a hooker, and who knows what they would have done to you."

Clief holds up his hands. "I know, Mila, I know, and you're right. Thanks for looking out."

"What in the name of Yeos made you think it would be a good idea to borrow money from the *worst* sarding criminal warlord I can think of—a Musul warlord at that?"

"Yeah, okay, Mila. I got it. I messed up." Clief hangs his head. "This bar is my life. I didn't want to lose it. I needed the money."

"Well, we're in deep now. Kapka is going to get the last word, even if he has to send fifty men."

"I dunno, maybe he'll hear me out." Clief offers a weak shrug.

"Clief, are you stupid? He's not going to hear you out. He's going to try to kill us. It's probably best if we both just lie low for a few days. Keep the bar closed until we can think of a way to raise some cash."

"Keep the bar closed? How am I supposed to live?"

"By not getting yourself killed by a gangster. Worry about your bar later."

We dump the men outside with a rudimentary sign hung around the head guy's neck that says "Violent Musuls." Outsiders aren't looked upon kindly, especially if they come to cause trouble. If the cold doesn't kill them, someone else probably will.

I help Clief clean up, then head upstairs to get my stuff. The desire to disappear, at least until we can figure this out, is nearly overwhelming.

What was that job Gil wanted me to do? Travel across multiple enclaves to carry a message for the Robust resistance? Not much out there could be more dangerous. Unless you've pissed off a big-time gangster who's planning to put you in the ground. Caught between a rock and a hard place, again.

No time to think this through. I fetch my PED and shoot Gil an e-message: *I'll take the job.* There's no need to specify. He knows which one. And he's probably smiling.

CHAPTER EIGHT

DEMITRI

With the clouds below the lillipad, the open expanse above is crystal clear—a purple wash as bright as freshly cut fluorspar slides over the orange of the evening. The world up here is calm and quiet, save for the rustling of my environmental suit as I shuffle along the tarmac on Lillipad Eight toward the central Pistil. The enclosure glistens, reflecting the emerging stars with such perfection that it seems like the whole universe is contained within a giant glass egg.

My heart pounds slowly, and my enhanced musculature tingles with each pump of fresh blood. Even Vedmak is quiet. These serene moments never last long. A pain in my chest spreads outward to my limbs, slowing my pace to an amble.

What's going on with Evgeniy? He's been acting weird. Only sending one reply to my thousand messages: *in person*. I quicken my pace and approach the outer door. A Creed peacekeeper stands at the entrance in full KOS armor painted in avalanche blue camouflage. I worked on their exoskeleton during my master's degree studies. Geminoids, while tougher than Graciles, are still relatively fragile and just as susceptible to puncture wounds inflicted by the outdated weapons of the Robusts. More than that, their internal servos are not strong enough to wield great weights. My exoskeleton upgrade, powered by Nikolaj's power pack, bears the weight of the system as well as ancillary mission equipment.

But I get no special treatment. To the Creed, I'm just another citizen to protect—or interrogate.

The geminoid pulls off its ballistic helmet. It's a woman. Or at least it looks like a woman. She's vaguely familiar. The robot raises a hand, signaling me to halt. The breeze whips her long auburn hair around her face, yet she never blinks. A placating, false smile sits awkwardly across her rubbery lips.

"*Good evening, Doctor Demitri Stasevich.*" The voice crackles over my headset.

Why use my whole name? It's just weird. "Good evening."

"*What is your purpose on HAP Eight this late in the evening, Doctor Demitri Stasevich?*"

"Just visiting a friend. Evgeniy Yarlov. He was injured in the attack today. I was busy at work and didn't get to come earlier. You know, on the collider …" She, it, doesn't need to know these things. Stop blabbering, Demitri.

"*Yarlov, Evgeniy.*" Her head twitches as she accesses the neuralweb. "*Yes, he is in the hospital section. Floor ten, ward seven, room five.*"

"Thank you."

"*You have thirty minutes left of visitor time, Doctor Demitri Stasevich. Please vacate Pistil Eight within this timeframe.*"

"Yes, I will."

She backs away from me and replaces her helmet.

I enter the inner airlock and wait patiently for the chamber to pressurize. The next door pops and hisses open. I climb through and close it behind me before taking off my helmet and wedging it under my right arm. The Pistil of HAP Eight is deathly silent, lit only with dim spotlights embedded in the walls. There's no one here except me. I'm alone.

You're always alone, little puppet, always. Except for me. I'll never leave you.

Vedmak. I thought perhaps I might have some peace.

There is no respite from who you are.

I tug at the zipper in my suit and yank it far enough down to reach the inner pocket. Using my teeth, I pull off my right glove—freeing my hand to fish around for my last hit. I find it immediately, and with a quick flick of my wrist, it pops into my mouth and slips down my throat. That'll take a few minutes to kick in. "Then you won't be able to bother me anymore, Vedmak."

I have infinite patience. You cannot escape what you have been dealt.

I just need to get to Evgeniy. He'll help me get more DBS. The foyer is silent save for a low hum from the cooling solar panels. The elevator door slides open. I should tell the computer floor ten, but for some reason, "Floor nine," spills from my lips.

The elevator hisses to a halt and the door glides open. The corridor is quiet and dim. My legs are rubbery and my head swims in a fog. The DBS is kicking in. I meander on absentmindedly, but it's an easy route. I've made this journey a thousand times and could navigate these corridors in my sleep—all the way to the neo-womb ward. Where I was born. Where we are all born.

The identity panel reads my iso-print. The same automated female voice responds, so loud the whole damn Pistil can hear it: *"Welcome, Doctor Demitri Stasevich."*

The door slides to the right, granting me access. The main incubator room seems to open up exponentially as the walls push back into the darkness. Only the low light from a thousand glass eggs penetrates the gloom. They hang, suspended in midair, row upon row, each holding a tiny fleshy embryo and a synthetic placenta fed by the same artificial blood supply and cocktail of nutrition.

The embryo inside the closest egg can't be more than a few months old. It has translucent skin and bud-like appendages. This

41

was once me. Designed. Engineered. No parents. No family. Who is this little one designed to be? What place in society has he, or she, been granted?

The eugenic youngling evaluator, or EYE, skims past my head and stops abruptly in front of the embryo I'm studying. The EYE comprises a metallic orb with a single black lens attached to a long robot arm with multiple joints. There's a low-frequency hum, followed by barely audible peeps and clicks. It's scanning. My heart hammers again. The EYE backs away a meter or so, then projects a thin red laser directly onto the glass. The fluid inside rapidly boils. The clear liquid becomes a pink sludge. The embryo is gone. Satisfied its job is done, the EYE slips away into the dark expanse of the room as fast as it came.

About four seconds. That's all it took for the EYE to decide this life was not worth sustaining. A waste of energy and resources. A genetic defect, maybe? Whatever it was, it was enough to deserve being Ax'd. My stomach knots, not for the little life that was just extinguished—but for my own.

How did I survive? Why was I not Ax'd in the neo-womb? Could the EYE not see me for what I am? Vedmak is silent. The DBS has quieted him for now. Somehow it's lonelier than ever. I storm out of the incubator room and into the elevator.

* * *

Evgeniy's room is dark but for a lamp by his bedside and a heart monitor blipping a neon-blue line repeatedly across a black screen. There are no wires, no tubes. A bioscanner monitors his status, waiting for when the effort to keep him alive is greater than his potential for society.

"I'm not dead yet."

My heart skips. "Dammit, Evgeniy, you scared the hell outta

me."

He opens his eyes and beckons me closer. "Come, young Demitri. Take a seat. How nice of you to visit."

I saunter in on unsteady feet, then pull up the rolling chair next to his gurney and sit. My helmet clunks to the floor. Despite this somber moment, the DBS has plastered a stupid grin on my face.

"Well, I had to see how you were. When I heard about the Robust attack, you were my first thought ..." My tongue slaps against the roof of my mouth, slurring my speech.

Evgeniy studies me. His brown eyes hold a cool wisdom, critical and unforgiving. As an older Gracile, some forty plus years, he's seen much. Perhaps that's why he's always been aloof and distant. It suits me fine.

"You've taken a hit, haven't you?" he asks.

"Ummm."

"You know how many times I've seen that look, Demitri? You can't lie to me."

My palms are sweaty again.

"Thought as much." He eyes me, then sits up in his cot. "And you panicked. With me dead, you wouldn't be able to get any more. Correct?"

Any answer is going to be a foolish one.

"Let me ask you this, Demitri: Why do you take it at all?"

The high of the DBS is snatched away. He's never asked me that before. What the hell? We had an understanding. "I ... I uh ... just need to relax sometimes. Work can be ... It's stressful."

"Indeed, work is stressful. Let me ask you another question. Do you believe the Robusts attacked my lab?"

"What?" Damn, my head is foggy. Did he just ask that? "What has that got to do with the DBS?"

"Answer the question." He fixes his gaze on me.

"I don't know. I guess. I mean. Honestly, I did wonder. Why they would want to bomb your lab. You're a theoretical physicist. But the Leader said—"

"Indeed. The Leader said." He sits back, a little more relaxed. "But still, you wondered."

"I guess." Is this a trap? I need Vedmak. He'd know how to handle Evgeniy's questions.

"You wondered. And that's why I chose you, Demitri."

"Chose me? For what? You chose me to be an addict?"

"No. I chose you because you have your own mind. Your own thoughts."

If only he knew.

"You take the DBS because you find our life—however privileged—hard, don't you? You need it for relief."

"Sort of." It isn't a total lie.

"I'm sure of it. Demitri, whether or not I am fit to survive, you and I both know I won't be allowed to live."

"Your injuries don't look that bad. You should be all right."

"My injuries aren't so bad. But I'll be Ax'd anyway."

What the hell is he talking about? "Why? What's going on?"

"Do you really want to know?"

"Yes, of course."

He smiles. "Good. To understand the truth, you have to go down to Lower Etyom. Go and meet with my contact, Yuri. He has the answers."

"Wait, why can't you tell me?"

"Because you wouldn't believe me if I did. You're skeptical, remember? Some things you have to see for yourself."

The DBS is fading fast, my euphoria evaporating. "You want me to go down there? Among those creatures, in the filth and rotting buildings? Not to mention the NBD. Are you crazy?"

"You want more DBS, no?"

He has me backed into a corner, and he knows it. "Yes, of course, but don't you have more up here? In a safe place, perhaps?"

"You think I just keep it lying around to be found?" He hacks a laugh. "I deal to order, young Demitri. Bespoke service. There is no more."

My buzz is almost completely gone. Adrenaline courses through me, wiping away the endorphins. "I can't, I mean, I couldn't possibly."

"Yes you can. And you will. You must."

That wasn't a command, it was a plea. "And if I go, I'll get more DBS?"

"Yes. But you'll also collect something else. A data package."

"A data package? Why isn't it accessible via the net?" As the question leaves my lips, I know the answer already.

Evgeniy's eyes are fixed on me.

"What do I do with the data package, once I have it?"

"Access it, and then give it back to the handler. Your heart will tell you what to do next."

"The handler? My heart? This is crazy talk."

"Is it?" Evgeniy replies. "We rely heavily on logic and reason. If studying the fabric of the universe has taught me anything, Demitri, it is that she has a personality—a will. You just have to open your heart to see it." He smiles and begins to fish around under his bedsheets.

"It was good to see you, Evgeniy. But I can't go down below. I just can't. And right now you're just rambling stuff that could get us both in trouble. My time is up anyway; I have to go. You'll be better soon, and we can resume business as normal."

Evgeniy flicks a small metallic capsule at me. I catch it in midair.

"What is this?"

"It'll help you get into my apartment. You'll find clothes and

45

equipment there to disguise yourself for the journey. It will also tell you how to get down and meet with Yuri. Tell him I sent you. Ask him about the package." He leans back into the cot.

I clench the object in my fist and pick up my helmet, then turn and leave for home.

CHAPTER NINE

MILΛ

It doesn't take long to get my stuff together, what little there is. A quick visual sweep and disposal of what's left is enough to sanitize my room. It's best Kapka's men think I've cleared out if they come looking again. Taking two steps at a time, I clomp down into the bar. Clief is on one of the stools. His face is stern, the stress eating away at him.

"Clief, you're going to be okay, all right? Just lie low, like I said."

He extends his arms. I give him a brief embrace and slap the side of his shoulder. He nods.

"Thanks, Mila. I owe you for sticking up for me."

"You don't owe me anything, Clief. Just stay out of trouble and out of sight for a while. You have somewhere to go? Somewhere they won't look for you?"

He nods. "My cousin. We're not close and not many people know we're related, but I'm sure he'll let me stay with him. For a few days at least."

"Good. That's good." I offer a smile. "When I get back, I may be able to help you out. Take care of yourself, you big dummy. Don't get killed."

"You as well, my friend."

Outside, the wind bites at my cheeks. The two goons we deposited outside the door are gone. A small dribble of blood on the ice at my feet is the only sign of their having lain here. If they were lucky, they escaped with their lives—at least until Kapka realizes they failed.

Bilgi's place is only a short detour on the way to Logos's outer wall. My knuckles rap on the rickety doorframe. Nothing. He's probably visiting his son. I open the duffel and grab the loaded satchel inside. Pulling the drawstring closed again, I slide the bag into our secret drop box under the stoop. When he finds it, he'll know it's mine. A short note clings to the outside:

> Bil: I'm taking a job that will send me out of Logos for a bit. If _anyone_ comes looking, _you don't know me_. Take care of yourself.
> — M.

A quick glance up and down the dark street, and I'm off for the wall on the northernmost edge of the enclave—the final meet with Gil before leaving the relative safety of Logos.

* * *

To my genuine surprise, Gil is already at the meet point. He looks far too relaxed. But then he would; he's an Easy user. One of the many stims available on the black market, Easy is a highly addictive concoction of synthetic dopamine, morphine, and various antidepressants. Life down here is hard. Becoming an addict is easy—literally.

"Well, well, I guess there's a first time for everything."

Gil just smirks, his eyes glassy.

"You're stimmed again? The Vestals would punish me just for associating with an active user, but you—you they'd hang over the outside of the enclave wall, just to make a point."

48

"Say what you want, Mila, but while I stay nice an' relaxed, you gotta go on a dangerous little errand without so much as some krig to keep you warm."

He's right. I'm about to take a ton of risk to make this delivery on time. Then there's surviving the meeting with the resistance and finishing the job unscathed. Neither a simple task. Gil, on the other hand, will take another hit of Easy, sit in some brothel in another enclave, and wait for the money to hit his account.

"Sounds lovely, Gil. Where am I headed?"

"Zopat. There's an abandoned warehouse. I'm told you can't miss it. It's on the southeastern edge of the enclave. It says 'Konistiva' on the side of the building. Your contact is a member of Opor. You can call him Yuri. Use all the normal precautions. Trust no one."

"Do you have an emergency button for me?"

"As usual." Gil produces a cylindrical device the length of a person's hand.

Along the outside are finger grooves for maintaining a positive grip, and on one end is a depressible blue button covered by a flip-top cap. A short-blast-radius electromagnetic pulse device, or EMP—it's not likely I'll need it against a mob of tech-jacked Robusts, but what's the harm in being prepared?

"Satisfied?"

I nod and stow the EMP in a hidden compartment in my bag. Gil continues with the briefing.

"Yuri will give you the package. You'll travel as quickly as possible to Fiori. There, you will meet a secondary contact in a sloop dive called the Forgotten Jewel. Ask for Lemmy. That's where the final transaction will take place."

This is gonna be harder than I thought.

"There's a catch though—"

"Gil, there are already catches. What do you mean there's a

catch?" Yeos, give me patience. Gil was born in Vel. Secrets are in his blood.

"Yeah, well now that I've relayed the job, you're on the clock."

"I'm always on the clock."

For the first time he looks nervous.

"What sort of time are we talking about here, Gil?"

"You've got fifteen hours."

"To get to the drop. Okay, and then how much to deliver?"

Gil's face is stoic. "That's fifteen hours to complete the job."

"What?" Is he screwing with me? "Gil, are you stupid or something? That doesn't allow me enough time to circumvent Baqir and make it to Zopat, let alone trek over to Fiori."

"I know. You'll have to go through Baqir."

"That's Kapka's enclave."

Gil shrugs. "What? You're not mixed up with him."

"Fifteen hours to do the job is not reasonable."

He glances at his watch. "You've got 'til late tonight at a push. Obviously you can't travel far when temps go negative, and Opor isn't willing to wait any longer just so you can hole up somewhere cozy. Fifteen is all you're getting."

"Gil, I'm not going through Baqir, got it? You'll have to find someone else."

"I've already confirmed your acceptance, and you know too much already. You don't have a choice anymore unless you want a bounty on your head."

There's already a bounty on my head.

I slam Gil against the wall. "Gil, you son of a ... You're setting me up!"

Maybe it's the Easy chugging through his veins that keeps him calm. Maybe he understands why I'm pissed. Maybe he simply doesn't care. "Mila, I didn't do this to you. You wanted this job. You knew it was going to be dicey."

50

Breathe, Mila. Work through this. Gil doesn't want to hold my gaze, but he does it anyway. "This was wrong, Gil, how you did this. You and I are going to have a heart-to-heart about it when I get back."

"If I were you, I'd get going."

Jackbag. He knows how dangerous this job is, and that if I don't make it back, he doesn't have to pay me my cut. I give a final shove, then release him and tab the countdown timer on my PED to fifteen hours minus the three minutes he just wasted. *14:56:59. 14:56:58.*

I hate crossing the Vapid. Leaving my enclave isn't a problem. As a resident, I come and go as I choose, but almost nobody ever leaves since the Vapid is dangerous and the other enclaves generally only let in specific traders. They exclusively travel the simple ruined roads that run between the enclaves and usually take a significant security contingent with them to protect their wares from Rippers, the raiders who have made their home in the wastes. These outcasts, driven to barbarism and cannibalism, no longer belong to any enclave, their brands removed by way of a flaming spike driven through the center of the palm. The object of many a scary bedtime story among Robust children, Rippers are the stuff of nightmares.

There's no time for this. Gotta get to the gate.

14:55:47.

CHAPTER TEN

DEMITRI

Breakfast. We sit in the food hall of HAP Three. Nikolaj and Oksana are fawning over one another. While all neo-births are strictly controlled, the Leader believes pair-bonding is a good thing, strengthening our society. But even this is controlled. Licenses have to be obtained, sanctioning the pairing according to an algorithm that determines if your match will be of benefit to the community. For many Graciles, it's become a sport: seeing who has the ability to correctly pick their mate. Nikolaj and Oksana were apparently correct. It makes him even smugger and only exacerbates my headache.

Coming down from DBS is never fun. It starts off slowly, the pain of the previous day pushing through my skull. Then Vedmak's voice, gritty and deep, initially echoing far away in the recesses of my subconscious, grows louder as the effects of the drug wear thin. Then all too soon, it's back to reality.

I poke at the vegetables on my plate and stare at the brilliant-white counter surface that stretches past twenty seats, lined up with twenty more tables just like it. I'm not hungry. Evgeniy was right. He said he'd be Ax'd. He knew it. His injuries didn't look bad, but he was Ax'd all the same. It must have been later last night. I went to see him early this morning—needed to see if his head was clearer and he was perhaps less cryptic. But there was only an empty cot. The

52

sheets were neatly folded and crisp, as if no one had ever slept there before.

But he was there, and now he's gone. What will you do? How will you survive without the DBS? Vedmak's needling is more abrasive than usual.

Breathe through it, Demitri. Concentrate. Nikolaj is bleating at Oksana again. He's talking about our work. At least he isn't clamped onto her face anymore.

"We're close, you know? We just need one collision," Nikolaj says. "That one perfect moment to prove the existence of other dimensions. And if it's true ... well, that's a whole other field of research with a plethora of possibilities."

"Why?" I'm not even sure why I ask. It will only start trouble.

Nikolaj glares at me. "Why what?"

"Why do we care about other dimensions? Shouldn't we be trying to fix this one?" As the words slip from my mouth, the question resonates in my head.

Indeed, little Demitri. Why aren't you doing something of actual value? Vedmak presses.

"That kind of talk will get you Ax'd. Why do you have to brood on things so much? Just be happy. Privileged as your existence is, everything we have is thanks to the Leader."

"Existence. Yes, but is it living? Evgeniy was Ax'd last night. Because someone felt his existence wasn't necessary anymore."

"We all need purpose, Mitya," Nikolaj snaps. "Evgeniy outlived his."

"I'm going to the lab. I have work to do."

"Are you sure, Mitya? Is it *worth* it?" Nikolaj fires back.

"It's better than sitting here listening to you smack your lips like a cow." I don't know where this inner strength came from. It wasn't Vedmak; it was my voice.

* * *

As I rub my temples, eyes screwed shut, trudging forward along my well-worn path, I slam into something—someone. A Creed soldier. Actually two. Larger than normal, they lack any empathy in their features. Neither resembles any Gracile I've known before.

"Gentlemen, let our esteemed colleague through. Do you not know who this is? Why, this is our very own Demitri Stasevich."

The Creed part and flank a man who steps through the breach. The Leader. My heart stops. The Leader has always shown Nikolaj and me special attention—a sort of father figure in a world where parents are obsolete. Yet he's always made me nervous. Though a little short at just under two meters, he seems to tower over me. His old but muscular frame exudes strength and authority. The breathing apparatus wedged under his nose, releasing the antibacterial mist, obscures his features just enough to hide whether he's smiling or scowling.

"Come, young Demitri. Tell me of your progress. How go the experiments?" He slips a long, powerful arm around my shoulder and guides me to the door of my lab. Without even pressing the identity pad, the door whooshes open, the voice overhead announcing his arrival in an overfriendly female tone.

"I, well, we … I mean to say, we've made little progress. The collisions are not generating the information we hope to find. Right now we have no way of proving extra dimensions."

"Indeed, Demitri. But I note that you are trying in here every day with your brother." His soft tones and wizened gaze are unnerving—his eyes a gray blue, not hazel. "This is what is important. May I look at your data?"

Without waiting for my reply, he dives into the electronic files at my station. Faster than I'm able to read, he flicks through each folder and document on the screen. In a few minutes, he's done. "Hmm, frustrating, I know. You seem to almost be there, but something eludes you …"

It feels like an accusation. "I guess, sir. Nikolaj and I, we are trying …"

His eyebrows raise. "I am sure you are. And where is your brother now?"

"Not back from breakfast yet, sir. But coming back soon, I'm sure. We have another run this afternoon."

"Excellent," he replies. "Most excellent."

Why does he suddenly seem as though every little thing pleases him?

"Of course, you don't seem to save your work to our servers, Demitri. You make me so curious that I have to come all the way here in person."

Was that an allegation? My stomach knots.

Tell him, puppet. Tell him why you don't access the neuralweb. Tell him and be free.

Not now—please, not now. My eyes must be as wide as saucers.

He should know, you coward. Why be afraid of this man? You know nothing of him; he's old and frail. Look at him.

I fake a smile and attempt to block Vedmak out, tapping my forehead with my fingers. "I um … I just think our work is important, I don't want anyone accidentally corrupting it." A lie—a bad lie.

He stares at me for an eternity before his stony expression breaks into a broad grin that can even be seen behind his rebreather. "Of course, Demitri. Whatever you need. Who am I to question the methodology of one of my brightest?"

"Thank—thank you, sir. Is there anything else, sir?"

"No, I don't believe so, though we should have dinner one of these days, my boy. I may even have a new vinyl record for your collection." He turns to walk away, but stops abruptly and looks back. "Actually, before I forget, I wish to offer my condolences for your friend, Evgeniy."

Of course he knows. He knows everything. My visit would have been logged. But how much does he know?

Vedmak laughs. *What to do now? Will he figure you out and Ax you right here?*

Shut up. I need to think. Keep it together.

"Demitri?" the Leader presses.

"Yes, I mean, thank you, sir. I knew him vaguely. We exchanged some thoughts on our work in physics, you know, as we work in similar fields and all."

"Indeed, Demitri, but still, it is great effort on your part. To travel to another HAP that far away at night. You must have been good friends." Again, his tone is accusatory.

Tell him you're a sad little addict who talks to himself, Vedmak rasps.

"Demitri, are you all right, my boy? You're a little pale ..." The Leader studies me. "Perhaps you should go home for the day?"

That wasn't a request. "Yes, perhaps, sir. I think the attack affected me more than I thought it would."

"Indeed. The attack. Those Robusts, a constant thorn in our perfect side. Every so often they get brave enough to climb out of their little hole and scratch us, but we will prevail."

"The Robust resistance claimed the attack?"

"No, not yet, but they will, I'm sure." He flashes a sympathetic look. "Time to go home, I think, young Demitri. Tomorrow is another day."

The same as yesterday, and the day before. And the day before that. Breathing in and out until you die. What an existence you Graciles have. The envy of all the multiverse.

Vedmak's laughing grows incessant. When he's this loud in my head, I can almost see him—those cold eyes, a cruel smirk, and long, lank hair whipping about his face in an imaginary squall.

Gathering up my environmental suit and helmet, I mumble an apology, then storm out and down the corridor. Near exit two, the force of Nikolaj tugging at my arm swings me almost 180 degrees. He grips me tightly at the elbow, but I shake free and keep walking.

"Hey, where are you going?" he calls.

"Home. The Leader gave me the day off."

"But home is through exit one. You're going the wrong way."

No, I'm not.

* * *

Lillipad Nine. I don't know why I expected it to look different from any other lillipad. Everything looks the same in New Etyom. There are no Creed guarding this Pistil. At least that's in my favor. Coming all the way to HAP Nine would likely be suspicious, and with Evgeniy Ax'd, who would I say I'm visiting? A new sweat breaks out on my brow. I just need to get the stuff. Go and meet his contact and get my drugs, then get back as fast as possible.

You can't control me. But perhaps I can control you, just like the little puppet you are.

The thought is terrifying. He's already spoken for me. What if he can control me? I need to get my fix. I tramp from the cable car, across the tarmac, through the airlock, and into the lobby.

Evgeniy lived on floor six, apartment nine, of HAP Nine's Pistil. It'll be easy enough to find. The elevator whooshes up and halts abruptly. I peer out, willing the corridor to be empty. Mercifully it is. I heave a sigh of relief and head toward his studio.

The metallic key Evgeniy gave me doesn't work. Dammit.

There's a low hum, then nothing. I grit my teeth, check the corridor, and try again. Again a low hum, then an electronic peep. The door slides open. I dart in and press the "Close" button before the open cycle has even finished. The door clunks shut and automatic lights come on, but they're low.

While the furniture in his apartment is much the same as in mine—functional and synthetic—Evgeniy, like me, has a collection of relics from the old world. Many of us came from the richest of the human race. Valuable items were dragged here before it would have been deemed resource inefficient to do so.

On a shelf stands a strange creature in bronze, composed of an elephant's body on ridiculously long stick-like legs. On the wall hangs a small abstract oil painting in shades of blue with splashes of yellow. The painter's expression is clear and vivid. I know it well. Or at least I know *him* well, a man who had a breakdown that resulted in the self-mutilation of his left ear and voluntary admission to the Saint-Paul-de-Mausole lunatic asylum. There he sat and painted, trying to figure out his own madness.

Why would Evgeniy want it? What meaning could it have had for him? My gaze falls upon a small placard with a quotation: "We take death to reach a star – Vincent van Gogh."

Perhaps death is the only escape for anyone. Focus, Demitri. Why are you here? The Creed have already been here, emptying his closets and drawers. What was it he said?

Vedmak snorts. *He told you the key would give you the information, you moron. Use that supposedly superior brain of yours.*

He's right. There, in his bedroom, sits a computer. I plonk myself at the desk and examine the machine. It looks like it's been recently tampered with. It's still warm. The key gloves slip over my fingers easily and the screen flickers to life.

To my surprise there is no password screen. It launches directly to his desktop. A bunch of files. Some photos and documents. Nothing special. I insert the metal object Evgeniy gave me, which I can now see is a data stick, into the multiport in the monitor. Immediately a program initiates, and a red low-power laser projected from a tiny opening next to a built-in webcam scans my face. A video window pops up on the display. It's Evgeniy.

"*Welcome, Demitri,*" he begins. "*You are watching this video, which means you're either intrigued by what I have told you, or your craving for DBS has gotten the better of you. Either way, you're one step closer to enlightenment.*"

Even in the video footage he seems jittery, glancing over his shoulder every so often. Where is he? I don't recognize anything behind him. A small cockpit, perhaps?

"*You're probably wondering how I made it back and forth to Etyom below. Well, this is your answer.*" He gestures to his immediate surroundings. "*An old VTV. Don't ask me where I got it. But it's the fastest and safest way to get down and back up.*"

"I don't know how to pilot that."

"*I imagine you don't know how to pilot this. Don't worry; when you get here, that won't be a problem.*"

Now I'm really confused.

"*Your bigger problem will be moving around Lower Etyom incognito. You will undoubtedly stand out, young Demitri.*"

That's an understatement.

"*In the VTV you'll find what you need to disguise yourself. But there is one ... specific piece of the disguise that will require you to use your nanobots upon your return. Again, you'll see what I mean when you get here.*"

"I don't have nanobots. For the Leader's sake, I wish he'd stop with the spy talk."

Vedmak laughs. *Afraid?*

"*To reach the VTV, go to HAP Seven and make your way to the edge facing away from HAP One. There's a large crack in the tarmac.*"

If you feel over the edge, there's a rope ladder that leads down to the vehicle concealed between the HAP and the support balloon." He glances over his shoulder again. *"You'll set down near an enclave— think of it as a village surrounded by a wall. The guard at the gate will ask to see your ID, which you'll find in the VTV. Make your way to a place, a building, called Konistiva, and ask to see Yuri. Tell him I sent you and you're there for the DBS."* He pauses and focuses on the camera. *"And tell him you need to know what was in the package I sent. You need to know what he knows."*

I hate this.

"Now go, Demitri. You may be of more value to this world than you know."

The video stops and the program ends.

Sard. What the hell is going on? There was no disguise here at all. Of course there wasn't. He wanted me here because only his computer could verify who I am. So the Creed couldn't find it. An empty feeling grows in the pit of my stomach. Now I have to make it to HAP Seven.

Don't chicken out now, Vedmak says. *You are so close to doing* something *vaguely interesting with your pathetic little life.*

Without giving Vedmak the satisfaction of a response, I make my way to the door.

CHAPTER ELEVEN

MILA

Standing at the base of the wall, I glance at the timer on my PED. *11:04:16.* Crossing to Baqir took far too long, but there's still time. After a rapid ascent, I'm atop the outer wall. Immediately my nostrils fill with musky, spiced perfumes, and my ears pick up the overly jovial conversation of the guards below, like the ones who laughed as they surrounded a defenseless young girl that dark day so many years ago.

Inside the wall, two of Kapka's men patrol with pikes in hand. They cross paths and take a moment to talk, snickering about who knows what. Now's my chance. I descend, feline in my movements. My boots thud against the icy cobblestones, and I immediately roll into the shadow of a nearby building. One of the men turns, searching for the source of the sound. He resumes his conversation.

Slipping across a narrow alley, I press myself against the wall. Like a black cat under the cover of darkness, I slink from one shadowy corner to another. It's a long and tedious process, testing the best of my patience—constantly having to flatten my body against the cold ground as a silk-laden caravan of traders passes or someone opens a door to throw out some murky dishwater.

The buildings here are different from those of Logos. Made of stone and mortar, the squat dwellings harbor a single living space for an entire family. All of them are like this as far as the eye can see, except for one: a massive structure, part of the old world. Kapka's fortress. From here, it's possible to see his guards walking the perimeter, carrying their machetes. Even from a distance, the place gives me the creeps.

* * *

Hiding in the shadow of another building, I'm much closer to the palace than I'm comfortable with. I hate this place. Mostly because of its governor, Kapka. A hard-line zealot who claims to descend from the terrorist leader who instigated World War III, he's a soulless monster. Part religious fanatic, part gangster, all warlord—the sort of man you don't want to meet and you really don't want to cross. It's true that he united the many segregated Musul factions under a single banner. It was accomplished by the sword. Get in line or be cut down. Political rivals, enemies, and any other opposition were quickly and viciously dealt with.

Why did Clief have to go and get me mixed up in this guy's business? It shouldn't be my problem, but now that I've dismantled a few of his guys, it is. Probably should have killed them—but that's really not my thing. Not unless there's no other option.

Over the snapping of the frozen wind, the moan of a child in distress reaches my ears. I crane my neck, trying to pick out its origin, moving as quietly as possible between the snowdrifts piled in the alleys. At the edge of a housing row, I crouch again and quickly peek around the corner into the alley ahead. Near the end, down on all fours, is a girl, probably nine or ten years old. Five of Kapka's guards surround the poor child, tugging at her robes and making barking sounds.

Not your business, Mila.

I slide down the wall to the ground, press up against the cold stonework, and reassess the route. About half a mile ahead of the mob of guards is the outer wall of the enclave—my way out. The child's sobbing grows louder. Breathe, Mila. She's not your problem.

There's another sound from the alley now—a scuffle. Another peek. A man struggles with the guards. Hitting him with their clubs and fists, they quickly subdue him and pin him against the wall. He screams, his eyes wide with fear as he reaches for the girl. Another guard holds her against the ground, pulling at her robes.

Don't do this, Mila. Don't try to be a hero. But I'm already climbing. There's no turning back now. I scramble up the side of the dwelling to the roof. These men do this because there's no consequence. No one to tell them they're wrong. Well, today there is—and the only language they'll understand, especially from a woman, is violence.

Yeos, lend me your strength.

Staying low, I fly across the rooftops, locking my sights on the fracas below. If I'm lucky, I can teach these jerks a lesson, hop the wall, and not drop too much time before getting the hell out of this place. This is beyond stupid. But there's no more ignoring this little girl. Not today.

Launching from the edge of the roof, I'm well into my descent before the first one sees me. Startled, he screams something unintelligible before my boots slam into his neck. His body flies out from under me as the force pushes him across the cramped alleyway and into a pile of garbage. I land and drop into a leg sweep, knocking another guard clean off his feet. He falls hard and strikes his head against the icy ground.

Two down. Savages. You had this coming.

Rising to my feet, the voices around me jabber in their native tongue. The one holding the girl glares at me and shouts at his friends. With a skip-step, my boot lands hard under his chin. He bites through his own tongue midsentence, blood spraying from his lips. Another comes at me from the left, his machete whistling as it cuts through the air. I duck the first swipe, catch him on the back swing, and trap his arm. Bracing it, my forearm slams behind the elbow, forcing the joint to separate. He screams in agony, drops the blade, and falls back against the wall, clutching his disfigured arm.

Something hits me from behind like a wrecking ball, striking me low across the side of my neck. My world spins, the ice and clouds and shouting men mixing in a swirling mess. I take another hard hit to the ribs followed by a heavy-handed blow to the head, dropping me to my hands and knees. A trickle of blood streaks down my cheek. My body shakes involuntarily, my head swimming with pain and nausea.

Stupid, Mila. You couldn't just mind your own business for once.

The young man and the girl run in the opposite direction down the alley.

Thank the Lightbringer.

The hood of my jacket is yanked back. The men gasp at the realization I am not only a woman, but a foreigner. Several of them swear. Another spits on my head.

"Logosian!"

Damnation, they've seen my brand.

The man with the severed tongue now stands before me, bearing a sinister grin.

"Joo whill rekret dish day, Yogosian."

"Don't—"

He kicks me in the teeth. The overwhelming blast of pain sends me tumbling backward into a black abyss filled with blood and spiced perfume.

Yeos forgive me. I'm as good as dead now.

CHAPTER TWELVE

DEMITRI

The cable car crashes into the docking station on HAP Seven. The doors slide open, and once again I stomp across the cold tarmac, the wind whipping and rustling the material of my hazmat suit.

It's no wonder we don't visit other HAPs, or have friends too far away. Who wants to do this every day? The walk should be a straight two kilometers, but the Pistil is in the way. I'll have to go around. That at least doubles the distance. Dammit.

The walk is long and monotonous. The worst kind of walk for me. Too much time to think. Too much opportunity for Vedmak to berate me—and berate me he does. A stream of insults and digs rattles around inside my head. I should be used to this, but he knows just how to gouge the deepest wounds. None more so than my loneliness.

At the core, it's the contradiction of being afraid of letting someone in, yet craving another Gracile's touch more than anything else in the world. A warm hand on my shoulder and a soft voice to tell me it will be okay. I felt close to Nikolaj as a youngling. My little neo-brother who had no concept of his own genius or place in society. He would stand by my side and defend me against other children in the educational clutch. He was invincible. When we were perhaps five, one child—Peter, I think he was called— tried to punch me. Nikolaj came from nowhere and took it for me,

65

square to the jaw, without flinching. Shoving Peter down, Nikolaj grabbed him by his ankles and upended him, then dragged him out of the class toward the airlock and threatened to throw him outside into the freezing cold. A teacher grabbed Nikolaj by the ear and marched him off to the Leader. His first encounter with the man. Now, it's different. *I am a burden to my brother—to our work. Any love he had for me has evaporated into frustration and annoyance.*

Much too soon, I'm at the outer edge of the Pistil. The wind howls outside my helmet. A thick layer of gray clouds covers the Robusts' domain below. What was Evgeniy's instruction? *A big crack in the tarmac; a rope ladder concealed under the platform edge.* Well, I'm at the edge, with what can only be described as a fissure some twenty feet long sprawling out beneath me to the outer perimeter. A particularly powerful gust knocks me off my feet, and I crash into the ground.

Vedmak snarls. *Careful, you simple idiot. You want to go flying off the edge of the world?*

"Sometimes, Vedmak. Yes, I do."

On hands and knees, I crawl to the edge and feel over the lip with gloved hands. How the hell am I meant to feel anything through this suit? But then, my hand touches something long and flexible. I shuffle forward on my chest, then dangle my head over the edge. My feet begin to tingle, and there's a gnawing pain in my stomach as vertigo kicks in. But just as he promised, it's there, bolted to the lip and disappearing around the curve: the rope ladder.

Frozen on the spot, I lie flat on the tarmac. The wind batters my head like I'm a rag doll.

Don't you want your fix? Don't you want to silence me for a while? He's laughing again.

"Why do you enjoy my suffering? Are you evil?"

What is good for a Russian is death for a German.
"That doesn't make sense. Evil is evil."
You would think that. When the masters are fighting, it's the servants' forelocks that are creaking.

He's talking in riddles again. But I understand his meaning. I haven't lived beyond the confines of New Etyom. I don't know all there is to know. But that doesn't change my current situation.

Time seems to pass in slow motion. The strong gale has a will of its own, pushing and shoving, attempting to peel me from the tarmac and toss me like garbage into the air. I grip the first rung of the rope ladder and hang on for dear life.

You think I'm going to let your cowardice put an end to us both, little puppet?

"What?"

Yes, a puppet. And like all puppets, I need only to pull on your strings.

My left arm jerks forward. My heart beats so fiercely it feels like it will explode through my chest. "What are you doing?"

Moving us.

"You can't."

Oh, but I can. Your panic makes you weak.

My arm jerks again. And now my legs. My vision is fuzzy and dark, as if my consciousness were draining away. I feel myself crawl in military fashion to the brink. One leg swings out over the edge. Then the other. My gut convulses as my feet dangle into the void.

Adrenaline surges into my bloodstream, electrocuting my neurons, and somehow I regain control of my body. I kick wildly, searching for a foothold on the next rung. Clinging with all my might to the ladder, I pin myself to the outer edge of the lillipad.

Now climb, puppet. Vedmak commands.

With my eyes screwed shut and the wind beating me against the lillipad, I move downward. The descent feels endless. Hand over hand, foot over foot, until my boot hits something metallic. I pry my head away from the wall and dare to glance down. And beneath me, there it is: the VTV.

Originally it would have been a sleek, rounded shape, with gull wings that open outward, revealing two rotor pods with more than three hundred horsepower. This one looks abused and disused, decidedly nonfunctional. How the hell am I meant to get in? I stamp on the hood and peer a little farther over the edge. It's sitting on a makeshift metallic platform, bolted to the side of the lillipad between the lip of the platform and the safety balloon.

Timing for when the last gust dies down, I drop with a clang to the roof of the VTV. Clinging with bulky gloves, I carefully slide over the top and drop to the platform, right beside the passenger door. The windows are covered in thick grime, and the once-blue doors are now a mottled mess of scratched metal. The door hisses and opens outward. Flailing my arms to maintain my balance, I stumble backward and off the platform with a shriek.

My descent stops as abruptly as it began. The initial euphoria of not plummeting to my death is replaced by a whole new fear. A Creed has me by the arm. My distorted reflection in the ink-back visor of its ballistic helmet stares, wide eyed, back at me. The Creed yanks me to my feet and, stepping back, pulls me by my forearm into the VTV. The door hisses closed.

Silence fills the air, but the Creed doesn't move.

Kill it.

How the hell am I meant to kill it? And what use would it be? It's connected to the neuralweb. By now it's already told the Leader I'm here. And then I'll be Ax'd. The Creed just gawks at me.

Kill it and let's go.

"You kill it. And why would you be encouraging me to go and get a drug that suppresses you?"

Even the wolf being fed enough nevertheless looks in the forest.

68

The Creed jerks to life. I hold my breath in anticipation. It clasps its helmet and, with a twist, pops it off. I finally exhale. It's the soldier from Lillipad Seven. The female geminoid guarding the Pistil.

"Good evening, Demitri Stasevich," she says in that strange monotone.

"Good … evening?"

Kill it already.

"Oh shut up, Vedmak."

She gives me a quizzical look, then reaches over and pulls an old flexiscreen from one of the inner compartments. Once it's unrolled, she slaps it to the cabin wall and presses a few touch-sensitive keys. It crackles and fizzes, but eventually a pixilated image forms on the clear organic-plastic sheet. Evgeniy looks at me once again from beyond the grave.

"Demitri, you have made it here. Interesting thus far, no?" He's smiling, again.

"What the—?"

"I see you've met my wife."

The Creed has a rubbery grin fixed on her lips.

"Her?"

"Well, at least a good representation of her. When they took her and gave a Creed soldier her face, I couldn't bear it. It was too painful. If the Robusts know one thing, it's how to jack our tech. Tatiana here has an entirely firewalled program running a personality algorithm that at least resembles her former self." His smile fades into an expression of pain. *"I can run it, and the Creed have no idea. It's comforting for a while."*

She wasn't guarding the Pistil, she was guarding Evgeniy— just long enough for me to visit.

He continues. *"I don't know if I'm still alive at this point, or whether you're fulfilling an old man's last request, but thank you anyway."*

"For what? I just need my drug ..." It feels like a lie, even to me.

"Tatiana here will fly the VTV to the drop zone and provide you with the disguise you'll need. It might ... hurt ... and you'll need to neutralize your nanobots for the duration, but you can switch them back on again later."

Nanobots? I don't have them. I never paid for them. Why would I need nano—

The robotic woman clasps my forearm and stamps the back of my right hand with something. Initially, there's nothing. Then, a searing pain burns through my skin and into my flesh. I pull and pull, but the geminoid's grip is vice-like. The acrid smell of blistering flesh fills my nostrils as I scream and struggle.

And then, it's over.

She lets go. Sobbing, I collapse, clutching my wrist and examining my tender hand. It shakes uncontrollably. A huge *Z* carves its way through my skin, red and weeping.

Evgeniy keeps talking. *"By now you've been branded. I'm sorry I didn't warn you before, my young friend. But if I had, would you have let her do it? That mark will give you access to the Robust enclave known as Zopat. It's the only way in. Don't worry, your nanobots will repair you when you return."*

I don't have any sarding nanobots.

No, you don't. Vedmak cackles. *How delicious. The little peacock has had some feathers plucked. At least now you look more interesting.*

There's no time to scream at Vedmak. Evgeniy is talking again.

"Your height will give you away."

"Oh, for the love of the Leader, are you going to break my legs?"

70

Vedmak erupts into a new fit of guffawing.

"There's not much we can do about it, you'll have to stoop. But I do have some exoskeleton components that attach to boots and will give the impression you've been jacked to your current height. We'll also need to cover your eyes. No Robust has eyes like a Gracile."

The geminoid hands me some blast goggles. They look benign enough.

"These actually have some functionality. It's dark down there— darker than you're used to. These have some night-vision capabilities to help you see better. Other than that, there are some clothes in the rear of the VTV for you to change into. That should do it."

What the hell have I gotten myself into?

"Tatiana will set you down in the Vapid, just outside Zopat. Do not hang around there. Make your way into the enclave and head for Konistiva. It's in the southeast corner. Ask for Yuri. Do not talk to anyone else. Do not stop. Do not deviate. It will not be worth your while, trust me. Tell Yuri I sent you. If I'm dead, tell him that, too. But most importantly, tell him you need to see what's in the package. Good luck. Take care of Tatiana for me."

"Wait. No rebreather? What about the plague?"

The screen blacks out, and once again it's just me and the geminoid. Is this really happening? What am I doing?

"What about my DBS?" No one answers. What if there is no more DBS? What if he lied? Is this just a ruse to get me down there? What does he want me to see so badly?

Can you afford not to go, little puppet?

If I don't go, Vedmak will eventually expose me, and I'll be Ax'd. If I go, I'll probably get eaten by a hungry Robust. I'm dead anyway.

Vedmak snorts and coughs his laughter. *Time to go. Don't worry—for a mad dog, seven versts is not a long detour.*

He's right about one thing: it's time to go. I need to move, before Nikolaj notices I'm gone. "Where're the clothes?"

The Creed points to a satchel at the back of the cabin.

"Can I get some privacy?"

"Of course, Demitri Stasevich. I will begin the descent. You may change clothes."

The robot turns away, enters the cockpit, and begins flicking switches and tapping panels.

"Can I get some derma-heal back here?"

"It is in the bag, Demitri Stasevich," she replies without turning.

I force myself from the floor, only to be thrown back down as the VTV jerks into life, pulling away from the platform. Whether I wanted this or not, I'm going down.

CHAPTER THIRTEEN

MILA

"I have to go. I have to do this," the man says.

"No, don't." I cry, grabbing at his jacket.

"We don't have a choice." He pushes my hand away. "Finish this, Mila."

The bomb detonates, flashing everything white.

In the darkness that follows, he comes. At first, nothing but a shadow, an imposter claiming to be human—but he's not. Fire burns in his eyes, and smoke stretches from his body in long snaking coils. He is the horseman—an ambassador of death. With agonizing slowness the image fades, and I'm alone again in the emptiness.

For what feels like forever, I hang there in the nothingness. Gradually the fear slips away, replaced by the warmth of better times—a time before the world went mad, a time when I still had people who loved me. I can see his face in this place. It's always clearer here. Zevry.

"Don't worry, Mil. I'm coming back. Don't worry for me. Okay?"

"Zev, I don't want you to go. I have a terrible feeling."

"Mila." My older brother looks at me with a scolding gaze. "You can't worry. It changes nothing and serves no purpose but to make you miserable."

"I can't help it. Something terrible will happen to you down there, I know it."

Zevry touches my cheek, dabbing away a tear with his scarf, his eyes twinkling like they always do. "Yeos will be with you, my sister. Do not fear."

Zev has enough to worry about with the mines in the condition they are. He doesn't need to concern himself with me.

"Okay, Zevry. I'll try to be strong like you," I say, casting my eyes down.

"I know you will, but what you don't yet know is you're already stronger than me, Mil. You're stronger than all of us."

"I'm not."

"You are," he says, lifting my chin with a wink, then embraces me—the assurance of his arms comforting even through my layers of clothing.

"Zevry. Come back to me, brother."

Silence. The hallucination fades. Then the distant cries of pain stretch out across the blackness and make their way into my ears. Trapped in a fog of discomfort and regret, my legs stir against a cold stone floor.

My eyes are open, but it's still dark. The air reeks of old taji beans. Where am I? Baqir? My body is constrained, a thick rope cutting into my wrists. A heavy burlap sack rustles over my head. I'm not naked, but they must have stripped most of my clothes off.

I wriggle again. The struggle sends a fresh streak of pain into my skull and down my back. That sarding jackbag kicked me in the face. I slowly work my tongue across my teeth, counting each one. At least they're all still in my head. I lick my lips, the flesh busted and swollen.

"I know what you're thinking." The voice is deep and menacing. "You're wondering why I haven't killed you yet." The accent is Musul, but there's something polished about the way he speaks. "Stand this groveler up."

Groveler. The slur outsiders use to refer to followers of Yeos. The rough hands of men grab me, pulling me up and sending yet another spike of pain into the base of my skull.

"Stand." The sack is jerked from my head, and I wince at the light in the room, however little there is.

The man in front of me is tall, with thick dark hair and a heavy black beard. He is dressed in an old-fashioned three-piece suit that clings to his muscles. He's got to be boosting on a stim like Swole or Jakked. Shouldn't that be against his religion?

The suited man nods to another at his side, a thin little goblin who is eagerly rubbing his hands. "That her?"

The jittery man bobs his head.

A twisted grin breaks across the bearded man's face. "The whore from the bar. Truly unbelievable. Here I was thinking I'd have to tear Logos apart looking for you, but instead you delivered yourself into my hands."

You've got to be kidding. The punk from the bar? I couldn't have worse fortune.

"Do you know who I am?"

"Yes." My mouth feels broken.

"And?"

"You're Kapka."

"And do you know *what* I am?" He waits for my answer with raised eyebrows.

"A religious fanatic who oppresses his own people? You make sex slaves of children, you brainwash men with opulence, power, and promises of heaven, and you murder others for the sheer enjoyment of it. Does that about cover it?"

"My dear, I'm a true believer. How many can say that about their faith?"

"Probably everyone who doesn't senselessly murder others in the name of their god."

"Well, at least we can skip the introductions." Kapka waves dismissively. "You know who I am, and I know enough about you. You're some filthy Logosian *streetwalker*, a groveling dog who believes she can cripple my men and move against my interests with impunity. Tell me," he whispers, stepping closer. "Where did you learn to fight like that?"

"I read a book on self-defense."

He chuckles. "Of course you did. And did you come here to try and kill me with your self-defense skills, Logosian?"

"No, but it's not a bad idea."

"No?" he rasps. "You attacked my men."

"You should keep your brainwashed animals on a tighter leash."

The guards around me squirm.

"My brainwashed animals." Kapka laughs. "I like you." He pinches my cheek. I instinctively jerk away. "Spirited like a wild horse—an animal that should be broken. Perhaps we should start by reminding you of your place."

The men laugh. Kapka leans in again, raising my chin with his finger. His eyes are remorseless—deep, black, and empty like those of a predator. He whispers as though telling me a secret. "Listen to me, woman. Listen closely. You should have minded your own business back at the bar. Before, I was only going to kill you. But now, entering my enclave? Attacking my men? For that—" He shakes his head, sucking air through his teeth. "You see, for that I'm going to ruin you, Logosian. Do you understand me? Do you know what it's like to feel ruined?" He smiles wickedly, a single gold tooth glinting in the low light.

I turn my gaze to the floor. Please, Yeos, not again. Just let them kill me.

"Oh, Logosian, I wish I could tell you what I have in store—oh, not just for you, but for your people, for all the filthy *kafirs*.

But for now, I simply want to look into your heathen eyes and tell you from my heart what it is I wish for you, inshallah." He leans in close, whispering again. "And what I wish for you, Logosian, is a world of endless misery and loss—"

"Kapka." a man cries, running into the room. "I could not stop him."

Kapka wheels on him. "You worthless insect. What do I pay you for?"

"I couldn't stop—" the man pleads.

"Who?" Kapka snaps.

As if in answer, the young man's eyes look to the entrance. They grow wide, and he stumbles back out of the way. A man enters the small room and shoves the stuttering Musul back to the right. Another man enters and moves left. They're huge—so tall in fact that both of them have to duck to clear the lip of the doorway. Each carries a slick metallic weapon that hums and pulses with blue light—bizarre, advanced tech the likes of which I've never seen before.

"Stand back and drop your weapons," they chant in perfect unison, their voices as cold and lifeless as their hazel eyes. Adorning these newcomers' perfect frames is a complex exoskeleton camouflaged in blue, black, white, and gray, with armor extending over vital areas.

Kapka nods, and his men obey, dropping their weapons on the hard stone.

Who is this that can tell Kapka what to do? The taste of dusty saliva and coagulated blood sticks in my throat. What the hell is going on?

A third man ducks through the doorway into the dimly lit room. By any reasonable standard, he is utterly massive—a towering figure of lean, hard muscle. His clothing is crisp and utilitarian, his gray hair slicked back over his head. On his face he wears a small device with a rubber seal that attaches to his nose and covers his mouth.

Their movements are too perfect. All of them are too perfect—almost sterile. The soldiers must be robotic. Creed, perhaps? But that would make the one in the middle ... a Gracile? What is a Gracile doing in Baqir? And why would Kapka stand at attention like a well-trained dog?

Kapka bows dramatically. "To what honor do I owe a personal visit from the benevolent Leader?"

The towering figure steps forward, still flanked by his guards, a look of mild amusement on his face.

Kapka presses—the formality all but gone from his tone. "What do you want? What is so important that you feel you should storm into my house and interrupt my business?"

"Your problem, Mr. Kapka," the silver-haired giant says with authority, "is you easily forget."

"You insult me now?" Kapka fires back.

The Gracile cocks his head but does not reply. His focus darts from one person to another, until it lands on me. With a look of disgust, he touches the device wedged under his nose, adjusting the small translucent cup covering his mouth. What is that? An air filter of some sort?

"We should continue this conversation in private," the Leader says, like he's addressing a stubborn child.

"This is as private as you're going to get. My men are loyal to the death."

"And this creature?" The Leader flicks a sickened glance at me, nervously pressing the device against his face.

"She is my slave. She will never again walk freely in this world. Even if she wanted to talk, it might prove difficult after I've cut out her tongue."

Yeos save me.

Apparently satisfied, the Leader gives a nearly imperceptible nod. "You received the instructions along with the last exchange?"

"Yes. It all went as planned," Kapka replies. "Just as all of our business has gone."

"And you read the attached information?"

"I said yes."

"Then why"—the Leader's voice suddenly rises in intensity—"has nothing been done?"

"What is it you want me to do? Drop my pants and lay it like a golden egg? It's a secret data package, not some bit of information I can have my men collect like trash on the street."

A secret data package. He can't be talking about my job, can he?

"Then you're not looking hard enough."

"You pay me to keep Opor and the rest of the Robusts distracted, not to be your errand boy."

"Mr. Kapka." The Gracile's tone takes on an icy edge. "The Robust resistance will be moving based on this information soon. I must know what they know, and I must know it now. If you cannot accomplish this simple task, then I will entrust it to someone who can." The Leader shakes with the words, his intensity rattling through the clear respirator—no doubt as an extra measure to protect him from whatever diseases he fears we carry. "You still draw breath because I allow it, and you will do what I pay you for. The bombings are no longer enough, and I will not have my grand design corrupted by Opor's meddling or *your* feeble-minded incompetence."

The room shakes with the final word, a single strand of silver hair falling across the Leader's furious brow. Everyone in the room stares at the two men.

By the look on Kapka's face, he knows he has no recourse. He holds up his hands and bows his head but says nothing. The Leader takes a deep breath, adjusts the nosepiece, and smooths his hair back. Inside the cold, dank walls of this room, the only sound is the distant dripping of water against stone.

This is unbelievable. The Gracile Leader controlling Kapka? I don't know which is worse—a gangster with no morals, or a Gracile with unlimited power controlling the gangster with no morals.

"Leader." Kapka's tone has changed significantly. "Maybe we can speak more of this in a more suitable setting. I'm sure we can come to an understanding."

"We already have an understanding," the Leader says, moving into the hallway. "Make it happen and notify me without delay, or else."

"Of course." Kapka seems withered. He rubs his hands over his face, breathing heavily through them. The Leader gone, Kapka jabs his finger at two guards. "You and you. Stay here with her and do as you've been instructed. The rest of you come with me."

He storms out, followed by the rest of the guards. The sound of his footsteps retreats. The two men left with me stand motionless, looking lost.

A third, more authoritative Musul enters the room and shouts at the two others. They nod, turning back to me. The one in charge closes in, smiling greedily and rubbing his hands. He begins removing his clothes as the others look on with lust in their eyes. My heart slams against my ribcage. Every fiber of my being stands on edge, ready to lash out. They will not have me easily. The one in charge steps close and with his knife traces the existing scar from my forehead, down my face and back toward my ear.

Oh, Yeos, hear me.

"*Hariq*," a panic-laden voice calls from down the hall. The men freeze, looking at one another. The voice continues to scream a cascade of Arabic I can't understand, except for a single word:

80

fire. The faintest smell of smoke reaches my nostrils. The guards freeze, partially undressed. More voices down the hall join in the screaming now.

"*Hariq.*"

"*Hariq.*"

The guards exchange terse words, and all but one flee the darkened cell. An instant later, a shadow enters and stops short, locking eyes with the last guard. Shouting, the guard grabs for his machete, but the shadow dashes forward and slams a dusty plank of wood across the side of my captor's head. The guard folds, knocking his skull against the ground, unconscious.

"Quickly." the shadow says to me. "You must come with me." His accent is the same as my tormentors.

"No. I'll find my own way out."

"You'll die." He reaches for my arms to check the rope.

"Don't you dare touch me, Musul."

He grits his teeth. There's a long pause. "If you do not accept my help, you will die. There is no other way." The man stoops and grabs a machete. I recognize him now—he's the young man from the alley, the one with the little girl.

"Why would you do this?"

He slices through my bonds. "Be quiet and get your things." He flicks his head toward the corner where my bag and the rest of my clothing lie. "We don't have much time before someone returns."

"They'll kill you."

"They'll kill us both if you don't come with me. *Now.*"

Rubbing my wrists where the rope cut into them, I quickly slip back into my clothes and sling on my bag, occasionally stealing a glance at my rescuer, who scans the exit to the hallway. A quick check confirms the package is safe in my bag's hidden compartment.

81

"Can you run?" he asks.

"Yeah."

"Then follow me closely. The fire will only keep them occupied for so long."

He slips through the door and veers hard to the right, taking one of three branching hallways. As we scurry close to the wall, a cry reaches out from the darkened hallway. It's not a Musul voice. Kapka has other Robusts in here. My rescuer realizes I'm no longer trailing him and comes trudging back. Is that anger on his face?

He stops centimeters from me, his eyes wide. "What are you doing? Do you have a death wish, Logosian?"

"I'm not leaving yet."

Another agonizing moan for help echoes in the dark corners of the madman's dungeon.

The Musul understands now. His lips purse, and he leans in closer. "You can't save everyone."

"There are other Robusts in here. If we escape, Kapka will be furious. They'll be tortured. I have to try." Turning and moving with purpose down the old hallway, I lock on to the faint cries for help drifting out of the shadows. We dash deeper into Kapka's fortress, at last descending an old stone staircase to the lowest level.

As the sobs grow louder, so do the pungent smells of urine and feces. Passing through a large archway, we come to the source of the wailing—at least ten prisoners chained to a rock wall wet with mold. They stir at our entrance, some coherent enough to recognize we're not here to hurt them. A glimmer of hope forms in their eyes. Others lie oblivious, too weak or emaciated to raise their heads from the cold stone.

"The guard. The one you knocked out. He must have keys."

The Musul keeps ducking out to search the hallway. "We don't have time for this, Logosian. My life debt is for you."

"Life debt?"

"Yes."

"If that's true, then I'm giving it to them."

His gaze follows my outstretched arm to the prisoners. "Look at them. They're already dead."

"A fighting chance is better than no chance."

He sighs. "You know we can't move as one. We'll be too obvious."

"Then we scatter. I'm not changing my mind. Are you going to help me or not?"

He holds my stare, then without a word, disappears back out into the corridor.

"It's okay," I reassure the terrified hostages. "We're going to get you out. But you have to be quiet."

Wide eyes gawk back at me. These people are from different enclaves, though many appear to be Logosians. Part of me hopes to find Zevry here, but I'm equally grateful not to see his face among them. They're probably traders and travelers, unfortunate enough to have been intercepted and captured by Kapka's men.

"You are Logosian?" a shadow of a man rasps from the corner.

"I am."

"Yeos has sent his angel here to save us."

I'm no angel. They're still probably going to die.

As if on cue, the Musul returns and tosses me the keys. "We must hurry, or we will not make it out of here alive."

I start on the right side, quickly working my way around the room, removing the shackles of the prisoners. "We can't guide you out. But we can give you a fighting chance. If you get out, run for the south gate of the enclave. Overpower the guards if you can and take your chances in the Vapid. Go to Fiori or Logos. They will give you shelter and aid."

"Thank you, sweet angel of Yeos."

"May He shield you from the enemy," I whisper, more to

myself than anyone else, as the shackles of the last feeble prisoner clang to the floor. "Now go, all of you. Run."

A few gaunt bodies rise and shamble toward the door. Others just lie there, free to go but unable to move.

"There's nothing we can do," the Musul says urgently. "If you have any desire to live, Logosian, you will come with me now. There is no more time." He tugs at my arm, pulling me into the corridor.

You're not the Lightbringer, Mila. You can't save them all.

With a heavy heart I follow him out, then down the half-lit hallway to the left. The prisoners flee to the right. Hopefully some of them will make it out. Back the way we came, the Musul runs the gauntlet of corridors, and I follow.

"Just up here, there is a door we can use to get out of this place," he whispers. "The guards do not monitor it."

Two more turns and we arrive out of breath at a heavy metal door. The Musul leans against it, cracking the icy seal. He anxiously surveys the immediate environment.

"What's the holdup?"

He glances back, but quickly returns to scanning. "It is afternoon. There are still too many people walking the street. You will stand out."

"I always stand out. *Let's go.*"

He shakes his head. "No. There are too many people under Kapka's thumb. When he comes looking for you, and he will, everyone will talk of having seen you with me and where we went. It is too risky."

"What then?"

He reaches into his jacket and produces a robe and head covering.

"*No.*"

"Yes. It is the only way we get out of here."

"No way. I'm not wearing that and casting my eyes down like a beaten animal."

He squints at me. "Your views are distorted, Logosian."

"I'd expect a Musul to say that."

He shoves the garments into my arms. "Now is not the time for this. Put it on if you don't want to end up back in Kapka's dungeon, waiting for his men to have their way with you."

It's either my life or my principles, and I need to get out of this place.

Two minutes later I'm briskly walking down the main drag, eyes down, my companion close to me, gripping the back of my left arm like he's securing a child in trouble.

Breathe through it, Mila. Do this and you survive.

Behind us a single thick column of smoke rises from Kapka's stronghold. Bells ring and men yell. I chance a look over my shoulder and see a handful of hysterical half-naked slaves making a run for the south gate. Kapka's men trail behind them, shouting.

As we approach the heavy, stylized door in the outer wall of the enclave, two guards step into our path. They eye us suspiciously. I want to drop the act and run in the opposite direction. My companion has a quick but dramatic exchange of words with the men, giving my arm another vigorous shake in the process.

Play the part, Mila, just a little while longer.

The men step aside and open the gate for us. A few seconds later we are through, and the gate shuts behind us with a clang, the crossbar sliding back into place. We shuffle off to the side, hidden in the shadow of the enclave wall.

I jerk my arm away and pull off my head covering. I should burn this oppressive trash. I take a deep breath, pull off the robe, and hand both garments to the Musul.

"You always keep a change of women's clothes on you?"

"They belonged to my mother—when she was still alive. I fetched them before I came to get you."

Well done, Mila. Change the subject. "What did you say to those guards?"

"I told them you, my wife, had brought shame and dishonor to our family by being unfaithful and that I was taking you outside the walls to stone you."

"Your culture is backward. You don't understand the strength of women."

"Are all Logosians this ignorant?"

"Not all Logosians have been at the mercy of your kind, so spare me the lecture." I turn away.

"Wait," he says, his fingers grazing the outside of my arm.

"The last guy who touched me without my permission got his nose broken."

He retracts his hand. "I apologize."

"What is this? Why did you do this for me?"

"Not all of us are like Kapka. He may call himself a Musul, but he only lusts for power, for the ability to dominate and enslave. He is a monster and a terrorist. I am *nothing* like him."

"You're all the same to me."

"If that were true, you would never have risked your life to save my sister," he says, searching my eyes, "and in the process, save me, too. I owed you a debt for my life. I owe you a debt still, for hers—regardless of the ancient feud between our people. My name is Faruq, and I am a man of my word."

"Words are cheap, *Faruq*, and yours aren't enough to erase the things I've been through at the hands of your people."

The Musul leans toward me. "Yes. I know. I've seen the atrocities this man has committed against my own family and against all of humanity—the men he brainwashes to die for him in the name of God, the women and children who are turned into sex slaves. He does not represent me, my people, or our faith. Please, it's important you understand."

I have no idea what to say to this man.

He just stares at me. Every step of the way, he's carried himself as if he were perfectly at peace—calm and balanced.

I swallow my pride and dip my head. "I'm Mila."

He nods. "Mila."

"I feel like I should say, uh ..." Why is this so difficult? "Thank you, Faruq."

"I still owe you, Mila the Logosian," he says with a small bow. "We live in a dangerous world. Be careful." He slips away, disappearing into the fading light of the afternoon.

Crouching in the shadow of the enclave wall, I reach into my bag, pull out my PED, and power it up. *05:37:16* flashes on the screen. Sard. No way I'm making it to Zopat and then Fiori in time. Maybe once I get to Zopat, I can bargain with Opor for more time. I'll tell them that if they agree, I'll also tell them what went down between Kapka and the Leader. They have to agree. Who else are they going to use? Nobody but a reckless idiot would take a job like this.

CHAPTER FOURTEEN

DEMITRI

The VTV descends through the snow-laden clouds, and instantly the shadow of the lillipads is apparent, stealing the sun from the sky. Although safe in this craft, I feel my skin prickle as everything shifts from a gorgeous blue heaven with a burning orange sunset to a muted gray sleet blustering between the great pillars that support my world.

Shuddering, the VTV drops like a falling stone. My scarred hand throbs, the fingers turning white as I grip the arm of my seat.

The engines whine as the vehicle banks sharply. My stomach convulses. I mash my eyelids together, willing the fall to stop—and just like that, it does. The complaint of the engines fades and is replaced by the howl of the wind blasting the craft.

"We have arrived, Demitri Stasevich," Tatiana says.

"Good. That's good."

Big brave Gracile. You're so disappointing.

"It is not, Demitri Stasevich. I fear we were blown off course during our descent."

"What? What is that supposed to mean?"

Don't cry, little kozel.

I need my DBS. Must focus. "Tatiana, what is that supposed to mean? Where are we?"

"We are ..." She pauses, her processors calculating our location. "We are outside Zopat, but farther out than intended."

"How far?"

"Six kilometers from the outer wall of Zopat."

"Well, that's just great. We can't fly closer?"

"We cannot," she replies. "The thrusters must first cool."

"Okay, then we wait."

The Creed shakes her head. "That is not an option."

My heart pounds a little harder. "Are you saying I have to walk through this Robust wasteland to get where I'm going?"

"No, Demitri Stasevich, I believe you will have to run."

"What are you talking about?"

"We are being watched."

"*Watched?* By Robusts?"

"It would seem so, yes." She points beyond the windshield to figures gathered on a nearby hill, their bodies and faces covered with heavy, bundled garments. In their hands, they carry crude weapons of every sort.

Oh, this is delicious. Let me out. Let me do what I was born to do.

"Shut up, Vedmak. I have to think."

Stop being a coward. It's not time to think—it's time to act.

"Shut up."

Tatiana swivels at me, looking confused.

"Not you ... not ... Just tell me where we need to go."

"We must go to the southwest—"

"No. Which way? Point."

Tatiana turns and points to the rear of the VTV.

"Okay. It's okay. I just need to—"

"Demitri Stasevich."

"What now?"

"The Robust humans are coming this way. My recommendation is we exit the ship and run for Zopat."

"You can't be serious."

The Creed nods. "I am serious, Demitri Stasevich. We should leave now. If they surround us, we will be trapped. They will disable the vehicle and get in. Eventually."

"There aren't weapons on this ship?"

Vedmak laughs hysterically.

"I have a plasma rifle, but this is a transport veh—"

"Okay, I don't care. Let's go."

Tatiana grabs her weapon, its vents glowing bright blue. She hits the release mechanism, and the door flies open with a *shunk*. The wind blast nearly knocks me over. I pull the ugly long Robust coat tight, slide the round goggles over my eyes, and follow Tatiana through the hatch.

Sleet stings my face. Darkness is falling fast in the shade of the lillipads. The only light amid the gloom is a distant glow—the lights of Zopat. I pull the lever to shut and secure the door, activating the electrical security system. If I'm lucky and these primitive creatures are superstitious enough, they may leave it alone after a few of them get shocked. Tatiana nods and takes off at a ridiculous pace toward Zopat. The howl of the Robusts echoes across the waste as I sprint after her.

"They have seen us exit, Demitri Stasevich," she calls over her shoulder. "You must stay with me."

I can barely hear her over the gusts of frigid wind.

Chancing a look back, I see some of the filthy beasts surrounding the VTV. Others chase us, their screams filling the frigid evening air.

Stand and fight them.

"I can't."

You disgust me.

"Just shut up, Vedmak."

Ahead, Tatiana opens her gait and rockets forward. Her head snaps right and left, scanning the environment for threats. The lights of Zopat grow brighter, streaming above the outer wall.

"Uff." I run full tilt into Tatiana, who has come to a dead stop, and bowl her over, falling on top of her. We tumble down a short rise. Immediately I spring to my feet and shake it off. "Why did you stop?"

Tatiana is already standing, scanning back and forth, her rifle at the ready. "We have been trapped, Demitri Stasevich."

"What do you mean—"

A large mass of Robusts waits ahead of us. In their midst stands one taller than the rest. He wears heavy garments adorned with jewelry and broken bones, and he's crowned with a primitive headdress. In his hands, he holds a pike with a long jagged blade at one end and what must be a tiny child's skull hanging from it. The others give him space.

"You," the big one yells out to us above the chattering and yammering of his minions. "You have intruded into my domain."

Tatiana is coiled, ready to strike.

"It was an accident. I just need—"

"You belong to me now," he shouts, thrusting his spear into the air. "Bring me the head of the Gracile."

"No. Wait."

Tatiana's rifle flashes again and again, blue bolts rocketing across the dark landscape, eviscerating the Robusts as they come for us.

"Please, please stop." Oh, for the love of the Leader.

Vedmak hisses. *You're going to get us killed. Let me do what I do.*

"No. I can't, I—"

A rock catches my heel, and I fall to my back. From the frozen ground, all I can do is watch as they swarm Tatiana. She moves with robotic precision, using her rifle to deflect blow after blow. But they are too many. A massive blade crushes the side of her weapon, rendering it inoperable. She clubs two or three of the brutes to the ground with the butt before it's pulled from her grasp. Tatiana's close-quarter combat programming takes over, and she launches forward, slamming her fist into the face of a savage. Repeatedly she spins and lashes out, pummeling the primitives. Trudging forward, she delivers a brutal stomp into the midsection of one and whips another's head backward with a perfectly timed uppercut.

Then without warning, the Creed halts her attack and looks down—a large blade protrudes from her torso. The Robusts converge upon her, their wild screams growing louder as they hack away with primitive weapons.

"Tatiana."

"Demitri Stasevi-vrrrrrrr," the voice says, distorted. "Run. You must—rrrrrrr." The screams of the savages drown out the robotic words.

"Vedmak. Help."

Oh, now you want my help?

"They're going to kill us."

I want to hear you say it.

The filthy, churning mass of men shifts and comes at me. "I want you to do it!"

And like an electrical breaker snapping, everything I've ever known as me ceases to exist.

CHAPTER FIFTEEN

VEDMAK

I hold his tiny head in my hands, the fear in his eyes is delicious. "Are you afraid, little one? Scared of the horror I have bestowed upon your comrades? Look, look at your leader. Yes, him. The one hiding behind his dogs, your brothers dead at his feet. You see how he doesn't come to rescue you? He is a big one. He should save you, no?"

He doesn't say anything, just whimpers as I squeeze his fragile skull.

"You bore me. Make yourself useful. Call out to your chieftain. Beg him to save you." My thumbs push through the eye sockets and into his head. The pathetic excuse for a man flails and screams, calling to his master. But I don't focus on the wailing creature. I am fixed on the big one, the overlord who stood back and watched me rip his men limb from limb with my bare hands. The screams stop, and the creature in my arms slumps to the ground, my thumbs sliding out of his skull with a satisfying sound. "Come at me. I challenge you."

He holds my gaze for an eternity. But I already know he won't face me in single combat this day.

"You are no king. You send your dogs to taste my blood, but you have not the stomach to spill it yourself. Come. Bring your spear and face me. Or are you a coward like the Graciles above?"

The feral chieftain's chest heaves rapidly—puffs of moist

breath escaping his gnarled mouth. He's large, the result of stolen drugs, no doubt. He should prove a sufficient challenge.

"Yes. Come and prove yourself against me. Are you afraid you will be stamped out under the boot of a superior creature? You should be bowing before me, worm."

The tribal chief grunts and levels his spear at my head. After a long pause, he shakes the weapon and disappears over the other side of the hill.

"Go then, but I will not forget this day."

It matters not. I'm free. Free of the chains that bind me. Free from the blithering idiot who keeps me inside. I am the master. Free to do as I choose—to kill if I choose. I'm alive again. It's survival of the fittest, raw and pure. And these dogs at my feet were not fit to survive.

This massacre was easy in this body. This engineered shell. Such power, such speed. If only the scared little puppet had known what this living engine was capable of. Instead, he hides and cowers inside his own head. Scared of that idiot brother and pining after the whore who hangs about his neck. They will be next. They'll soon bathe in their own blood, just like these vermin.

It's been too long. Too much time has passed since the glory days of old. Since the Red Terror. My brethren in the Cheka, they should be with me now. Imagine the pain we could inflict. We would not need the devices of our age. The boiling tar, or spiked barrels. In Gracile form, we could rip the limbs from the bodies of our enemies with our own hands. Yes, much time has passed, but the evil in the world remains the same. The Graciles. A class presiding over the working man. Separated now by biology—in a form they don't deserve. Centuries have passed, yet Mother Russia needs her Cheka, her Bolsheviks, more than ever. She needs *me*.

But my time is not yet. I must sit in the dark, between worlds, in a limbo that pulls me apart. Still, like a cancer, I grow stronger inside this pathetic Gracile. Soon I will consume him. Now his consciousness wakes. For now, I must slink back to the anguish inside. My own personal hell. But it won't be long. Fear weakens him and nourishes me. If you're afraid of wolves, you shouldn't go into the woods.

And you, little puppet, are deep in the woods.

CHAPTER SIXTEEN

MILA

I shuffle my feet to keep my toes from going numb. This doorman is taking his sweet time. The ornamental iron-banded door, covered in carved dragons and warriors, stretches up and up like a portal into some ancient mystical realm.

"Yah loh, you still want come in wat?"

"Yeah, if that door's not too heavy for you."

"You no funny la. Logosian no always welcome la."

"What did I do to you? Open up and I'll buy you a bowl of churri churri."

"No mah. You buy churri churri for you." The little man behind the door pauses. "You now give me money for singhi meat stick. Whole fam-i-ly mah."

"Jeez." I bite my lip. This little joker drives a hard bargain. "Okay, deal."

The door clanks and swings open just wide enough for me to enter. I'm faced with two little men. One jabs a short spear at me. "Play no funny business, lah."

"Okay, okay." I pluck a few paper bills from my pocket. "Enough for singhi meat stick, *whole fam-i-ly.*"

He snatches the bills from my ice-cold hands. "You go now mah. You go."

Zopat. You've got to know how to wrangle the locals in this bizarre enclave. Admittedly it's been a while.

With the sun now gone, the cold soaks through my clothes and into my bones. No matter how long I've lived in Etyom, there is no way to adjust to the cold that comes with the night. I hug my arms tightly against my body and roll my whole foot against the ground to keep up circulation.

Ahead, the lights glimmer off the snow and ice, giving the appearance of a winter holiday festival. A brief pause at an open-top fire barrel to warm up. A tingling spreads from my fingertips through my hand and into my arms.

"Oi, you no stand here. Fire no free, lah." A woman scrambles out of a doorway, shooing me off.

"Yeah, I got it." I make my way farther through the icy streets into the darkening enclave.

I still have no idea why that Musul wanted to help me. No, not just help me—risk his life to help me. Why would he do that? Sure, I helped him first, but people don't return favors like that anymore. Not in this world.

Another glance at my PED. Stop looking, you know you're late already. I'll just bargain for the amount of time I should have had in the first place. With the new information on the table, they'll have to extend my deadline.

The commercial district is hectic in the last hours of the working day. Signs flash in a never-ending gaudy display of drugs and other things everyone wants but few can afford. Who pays to run all the lights and strobing billboards? Energy isn't cheap.

A ramshackle health clinic juts out from the main drag. Past the ancient clouded glass of the windows sits row upon row of cots filled with ghastly, emaciated bodies. Caregivers in white move back and forth. The New Black Death has not been eradicated. Like humankind, it lingers on, even in this arctic hell. True cases are few and far between now, but we all still instinctively shrink away from anyone who breaks into a fit of coughing. Anyone could have the NBD, and no one would know until it was too late. It happens. And when it does, the bodies pile high outside, and the clinic shuts down. There is no defense but cold and isolation. Thankfully there hasn't been a bad breakout in a long time. Not since I was young and had it myself. That one was bad. Real bad.

Keep moving, Mila.

The street is full of bumping, milling people trying to sell that last ware or buy a bit of meat and a pinch of krig for the morning. There's a break in the cloud cover, and for just an instant, a few stars peek through to the evening sky. A gift from Yeos. Every step I take distances me farther from my near brush with death in Kapka's stronghold.

A large stone cathedral blocks my path. After my father died, my mother brought Zevry and me here in her trading caravan. The huge structure looms overhead. It's beautiful, strong, and ancient; the fortress-like stone arches stretch up, reaching toward the sky. With measured steps and great reverence, my feet ascend the snow-covered outer steps to the gaping entrance. I shouldn't waste time, but I'm already late. What's a few more moments?

The ancient doors rival the opulent entrance to the enclave. Stepping inside, I bow my head. Two fingers touch the founders' stone, then my forehead. Vibrant stained glass fills the windows and sets the large space awash with a purple-hued magic. It's silent here, inside the sanctuary. Even those who do not practice my faith respect this place, lowering their voices to whispers as they pass in the street. It's a testament to the endurance of my people. Still, it would be better suited in Logos than in this lurid dive. I whisper a hurried prayer, asking for the blessings of Yeos upon my journey and the protection of His omnipotent hand.

Outside, I make my way a few more blocks to the last of the street vendors. Old memories return with the smells of this place. My brother and I used to run between these stalls and down to the next block where the man with the funny hats always sold his wares. Mother would sell her knitted blankets here. She had a big heart and usually gave away more to the homeless than she actually sold. She said that was the way of the Lightbringer, the giving of a gift that cannot be repaid.

I stop at an unmarked intersection with a darkened alley. Why here? Of all the places, why did my legs bring me back? It was just a shortcut. I was just trying to beat Zevry and get back to Mother first. I couldn't protect myself … my purity. That was twenty years ago, Mila. Let it go.

The ice crunches under my boots as I reach the end of the alley, where it makes a dogleg turn and disappears into another snow-covered bend. The ancient ice-covered brick wall still sits there, the one I broke my fingernails on when clawing to get away.

I was just a child. Zev couldn't hear me screaming back here. No one could. Those monsters stole an innocent light that day and left the husk of a child in its place. My mother, heartbroken, refused to entertain it. She dismissed my pain and moved on. No one wanted to understand. No one was there for me. No one but Zev. Why did you leave me, brother?

Swallowing the lump in my throat, I wipe the stinging cold of tears from my cheeks. Get a hold of yourself. What are you doing?

Pivoting back up the alley, my body locks in place. Two figures block my exit. A tingling déjà vu washes over me. This isn't twenty years ago. This time they've got the wrong one. My fists clench.

"Wrong way dong lah. Lost girl? Shame, shame for wat?" The shadow has a small ax in his hand. Both men wear all blue and have bleached hair and shimmer contacts in their eyes. Gang affiliation. "You give us—"

Launching forward, I kick hard to the inside of the shadow's thigh and parry away a feeble swing of the double-bit ax. Spinning into the opposite shadow, I hit him with a flurry of palm-heel strikes to the head, dragging my nails across the flesh of his face. The man screams as the flat of my boot drives against his shin, scraping downward. Another cry and he falls backward, rolling down an ice mound.

The first man comes at me again. I deflect the ax, trapping his arm, and strip the weapon from him. Grabbing him by the hair, I bounce his face off the brick twice, rotate the ax in my free hand, and push the blade to his throat.

His friend struggles to pry himself from the ground.

"Try to stand and I bleed him." I give the ax man's bleach-blond hair a brutal jerk, eliciting a string of Zopatian cursing. The friend flops to the ground.

"Okay, okay, crazy girl mah," ax man shouts.

"Wishing you brought more of your stupid gang with you?" There's something about him. I spin him toward me and pin him to the wall, locking him down with an iron stare. "Shu?"

His face slackens at the sound of his name. "Let me go. How you know my name wat?"

I release him and step back, keeping my distance, the ax firmly in hand. "We used to sit together in front of the cathedral and share my lunch. There wasn't hardly enough for me, but you were hungry, too. We were just kids. Your mother begged for charity from the patrons of the temple."

His eyes grow wide. "Nooo wat? Mee-la. Long time ya? Why you back here, lah?" He opens his arms in a welcoming gesture.

"Did you just try to rob me?"

"Me? No lah. His idea." He flicks his head at the groaning friend. "I try to see you need help. I know it was you." He wipes a spot of blood from his cheek.

"I doubt that. Hey, tell your friend I'm sorry about the, uh …" I motion like I'm clawing my own face.

Shu laughs and helps his friend up. "Oh no, he fine."

The friend groans.

"Stepping up in the world from picking pockets? You were good, even back then. But this? Gang affiliation and robbery?"

"Hey, I stay hungry." He shrugs with a gap-toothed smile.

"You still don't know how to pick your targets, do you? You're lucky you still have both your hands."

"Lucky for long time, it called skill, mah."

"Sure." It's hard not to laugh.

Shu gestures back at me. "You, you come here for wat, lah?"

"Business."

His eyebrows rise. "Oh biz-ness. You have money?"

"Depends. Can you discretely show me where Konistiva is?"

"Dis-kreet? Cone-is-teev-via? Lo mah, for sure. Konistiva I take you fifty dollars."

"Twenty."

"Thirty-five."

"Twenty-five or I'll finish kicking your teeth out."

"Okay, okay, you bargain like you fight, Mee-la." He sticks his palms out toward me with a goofy laugh. "I not remember you so ruthless."

"Yeah, me neither. Get your friend and stick to the shadows. I've got a meeting to attend, and I'm planning on making an entrance."

CHAPTER SEVENTEEN

DEMITRI

My head hurts. It's still dark. Or at least dim—a layer of smog covers everything. My throat is dry and swollen. Need water. I clamber to my feet and stagger a few steps before finding my balance, then pull the goggles from my eyes. Dark shapes gouge troughs in the frosty powder that conceals the ground. Snow should be beautiful, white and glistening. But it's not. This is grubby and gray with soot, and spattered with ... blood?

Heaps of bodies are sprawled across the permafrost. Dismembered and broken, their insides seep from massive wounds, their heads missing or smashed beyond recognition. My stomach convulses, the watery contents spilling from my mouth onto the snow. They were massacred. Who did this? What happened?

The tongue speaks, but the head doesn't know. Vedmak's tone is uncharacteristically calm and more menacing than usual.

I did this. Or he did this, using my body. The snow is cold and wet, soaking through the fabric of my pants as I crumple to my knees. He used me to butcher them, and I let him. My palms are stained crimson; the thick, life-giving liquid is soaked into the sleeves of my jacket and cloak. I grab a handful of cold snow and rub frantically at my clothes, but it only turns to pink slush.

You cannot wash away what you have done, my little puppet.

"This is what *you* have done. Not me. This isn't me." Is it? Or is Vedmak just an extension of me? My subconscious brought to life. Perhaps I deserve to be Ax'd.

After taking off the head, you don't bewail the hair, child. Without me, you would be dead now. You willed this.

He's laughing again. But he's right. I let him through, and if I hadn't, we'd be dead right now. What was Evgeniy thinking? What does he want me to learn down here? How truly disgusting the Robusts are? To appreciate my Gracile life? Well, I do. It may be sterile, but it's better than this frozen hell. I need to get my DBS and get out of here. The VTV? Where's the VTV? And the Creed? "Tatiana? Tatiana."

From a few meters away, a muffled voice replies from under the snow. "Demitri Stasevich."

I sprint to the source and fall to my knees, digging until her face is revealed. Her head is intact, auburn hair strewn across her brow. But her body is broken, missing everything from the middle of her spine downward. Only her left arm remains. That fake smile still sits on her rubbery lips.

"Demitri Stasevich," she repeats.

"Yes, I'm here." I stroke the hair away from her face.

"I am broken, Demitri Stasevich."

"I know, Tatiana."

They pulled her apart in seconds.

"Bastards." Though, why do I care? She's just a Creed.

"Demitri Stasevich. Please tell Evgeniy I'm sorry."

What? She didn't use his last name; she just called him Evgeniy. "Sorry for what?"

"For failing, Demitri Stasevich. Tatiana loved him very much. She is sorry." The expression on the Creed's face freezes, and she says no more.

Did she just say that? Did the Creed know there was another

personality program in there? Was she aware of it? Was she … like me?

You think too much and act too little, Vedmak says.

A cold wind snaps at my face. It's dangerous out here. I need to get to the enclave. Placing the goggles back on my face, I swing left to right until the compass readout in the goggles points southwest. Got to move. I pull the hood of my cloak over my head and begin tramping in the direction of Zopat.

* * *

As Tatiana predicted, less than thirty minutes' walk and the huge walls of the enclave, stony and solid, loom out of the dark. They seem to have no end, the barricade disappearing into the fog in both directions. Above, the silhouette of the lillipads casts a cold shadow—the evening sky hidden from view. My fortress in the clouds comes at a cost for the people down here.

The door to the enclave is huge. Metallic, adorned with strange carvings, and studded with massive bolts. It seems impenetrable. I rap on it with frozen knuckles. A slot in the metal slides open.

"What you want, goondu?" says a voice without a face.

"I need to see Yuri."

"Jia lat, goondu. Yuri? Why you meet him here, la?"

What the hell is he saying? I only understand every fifth word. "Evgeniy sent me. I have business with Yuri. Let me in."

"He is lobang king, la. You must be important man to see him, no karung guni."

"Sure, important."

What is that moron saying? Vedmak grumbles. *Kill him and get inside already.*

"Through the door, Vedmak? Just let me handle this."

"What? Who you talk to, la?" the voice asks.

Damn. "No one, sorry. Please, I just need to get in, do my business, and get out."

"You have credentials, huh? You have pass?"

Pass, what pass? Evgeniy didn't mention—oh, he means the mark. I strip the fingerless glove from my hand and shove the scarred limb through the slot. For the sake of the Leader, I hope he doesn't cut it off. There's a clunk of metal. My hand is pushed back through the hole.

"Why you no say, la? Come, come in."

The door swings inward, and I quickly step inside. I figured it to be warmer, comforting. But it's not. The bite of the icy wind is dampened by the enclave wall, but that's the only respite. The portal clangs shut, and a little man dressed in poorly cut wool garments jumps and skits about my feet. He looks nothing like the Robusts from outside.

"Oh you no eh kia, la."

"What? *Eh kia?*"

"Eh kia, la." he gestures, pointing his palm at the floor.

"Oh, short. No, I'm no *eh kia*."

"Where you meet Yuri?"

"Ummm, Konistiva," I reply absentmindedly, wandering off in the direction I happen to be facing.

"Go stun, go stun."

"What?"

"Go stun," he repeats. "Wrong way. Konistiva is that way."

"Of course, thank you."

"You talk funny, la," he calls.

He talks funny, the stupid little kozel. You should have stepped on him.

Violence. Vedmak's answer to everything.

105

* * *

It's mesmerizing. The alleys and streets within this enclave are numerous and winding. The structures are high, yet unstable and ramshackle. Assembled from the carcasses of old high-rise buildings from a time long ago, held together with rusted sheet metal, and adorned with colored signs—the words formed from tubes of neon light in yellows, pinks, blues, and greens.

Despite the cold, people fill the street. Some have their heads hung low and sacks slung across their back. Others appear jovial, laughing and joking with friends, pushing and shoving and swilling some amber-colored liquid. And they don't look alike—at all. Some have dark skin, some thin eyes, some blond hair, and others beards as black as night.

I push through the crowd that grows denser the deeper into the enclave I venture. Even hunched, my shoulders are above many heads. And the stench, the smell of their drinks and their bodies, fills my nostrils—sweet and musty.

What is that? A doorway next to a neon-lit window. The sign simply says "Shop," though gives no indication of the wares for sale. I'm drawn to peer inside, where a lonely counter sits at the back of the room with no one in attendance. No items for sale line the walls. A shrill bell signals my entry as I push through the door, and mere seconds later a small, shriveled woman appears, seemingly from nowhere. She stands attentively behind what I can now see is a makeshift counter made of ill-fitting pieces of wood and corrugated iron.

"What will it be?" she asks, rubbing her hands together.

"Be? There's nothing here for sale."

"This is a bespoke service, my large friend. But look at you, you should know this. How much Swole have you taken? You're huge. The Graciles themselves would be jealous."

106

Vedmak laughs. *That's actually funny.*

"Swole?"

"Hmm, yes, perhaps not Swole for you. You look stressed. Maybe some Easy, yes, some Easy to calm those nerves, huh? I have a particularly potent cocktail, my own invention."

"Drugs. You're selling drugs."

"I sell dreams," the woman says softly. "You want to feel like Graciles, right? Of course you do. We all do. Imagine what it must be like to feel happy all the time. To be strong and confident. To feel beautiful. Whatever you want, I have the stim for you."

Is this how Robusts see us? Is this what they think it's like to be one of us? Maybe they're right. Maybe other Graciles do feel this way. Maybe it's just me who doesn't. Who am I to condemn them for this vice?

"Yes, yes. I'm not like other alchemists; I don't use inferior product. My stims are guaranteed," the old woman squeals.

"DBS. Do you have DBS? Krokodil?"

She studies me with faded eyes, the kind that may have once been bright blue, but time and suffering have drained them of life. "Krokodil? No one uses that anymore. It's dirty, not a clean high. Stims are the new thing in Zopat. A thousandfold more potent than natural endorphins and hormones, with an alchemist's personal touch thrown in, you see? Won't you try?"

She unrolls a cloth on the table and spreads out a dozen auto-injectors, each with a fluorescent liquid inside as bright as the neon letters outside her shop. Each one has black writing scrawled on it in indelible marker—"Easy," "Swole," "Hyper"—the names are strange. I have no idea what's inside, let alone if the needle is sterile.

"I think Easy for our stressed-out friend, hmm? Better than that nasty krokodil."

Vedmak, who has been silent up until now, barks in my head. *Or maybe it will kill you? Or make you invincible. Choices, choices, little peacock. Tick tock.*

Maybe it will kill me. I know DBS. It doesn't kill me. But still … if Yuri won't give me any, maybe I should take something. "I'll take some Easy."

"Good choice, my large friend—"

"And some of that," I interrupt, pointing at an auto-injector labeled, "Red Mist."

"Another good choice. I pity your enemies. A guy your size on Red Mist? Damnation. My old eyes would want to see that."

"How did you get into selling this? If you don't mind telling me," I ask, fishing in my pocket for some Etyom dollars.

"When you've been around as long as I have, young man, you learn the game well. If there is one thing that always sells, it's upgrades. Almost everyone down here is on something, except maybe the religious nuts. People always want what they think others have." She holds out an old withered hand.

"How much?"

"For you?" She tries peering past my goggles, frowning. Then she smiles, her eyes narrowed. "For you, two thousand."

It's crude to use plasticized paper money in New Etyom, but some of us still do, for nostalgia's sake. And clearly it's the way to go when trading with the Robusts. I pluck out two thousand and hand it to her. In turn she gently places the auto-injectors in my hand and closes my fingers around them.

"Enjoy them, my large friend. Everyone deserves happiness. Even a Gracile." She flashes a toothless, knowing smile, and disappears through a door into the backroom.

Everyone deserves happiness. Did she know? Am I not the first? I stuff the auto-injectors into the side pocket of my combat pants, leave the shop, and once more trudge down the street.

A woman grabs my arm, jolting me from my trance. She's short and petite, with thin eyes covered in dark makeup. Despite the freezing temperature, she wears only an untreated fur that drops to the ground and a garment that covers her pelvic area. Her exposed breasts look overblown, the skin stretched, the nipples hard.

"You a strong one, la," she says, attempting to drape her arms around my neck. "How 'bout you show me those pretty eyes, mister pretty boy." She attempts to pull on my goggles.

I reel backward and push her away. Her breasts feel cold and hard under my fingers. "Sorry, I'm sorry."

"You don't like merchandise, goondu?" she spits.

"Sorry, I'm sorry—" I back into a crowd of younger Robust males, who shove at me. These men wear all blue and have pale skin, white hair, and electric-blue eyes. They're brandishing some form of alcohol in one hand, and in the other they wield small axes with pronounced horns at both the toe and heel of the bit. One of them barks at me in a strange language, while another shunts me forward.

Let me defend you, Vedmak whispers.

My right hand balls into a fist.

"No. No, not now." I push the nearest Robust and tear out of the crowd as fast as my legs will carry me, the exoskeleton rattling with every step, until the last of the people have been left behind and the lights of the center are but a haze.

Traipsing farther along toward the southeast edge of the enclave, the environment becomes even more industrial. A series of abandoned warehouses pepper the dull-gray soil. Jagged and broken, they materialize from the darkness, their once-bright signs now dead and missing letters. Yet one building stands out. It has retained its original sign intact: *"конистижа."*

The heavy metal door reverberates with each rap of my knuckles. For a long while there's nothing. But before I can knock again, a rattle of keys and dull clunk signal the door's opening. A heavyset Robust peers out through the crack he's allowed. Thinning hair and piggy eyes belie his body language; he holds himself like a coiled spring ready to strike with either the twelve-inch blade in his hand or the antiquated, but rather huge, pistol on his hip. He says nothing.

"I'm here to see Yuri."

The man grunts. "There's no Yuri here."

"Evgeniy sent me."

"I don't know what you're talking about," he snaps back.

"Yes, you do. I ... I don't know the secret password."

The man laughs coarsely. "The secret password? Do you think this is a child's clubhouse?"

"No ... I don't."

"If you speak the truth, why did Evgeniy send you?" he presses. "Why didn't he come himself?"

"Because he's dead," replies a voice from the dark behind the guard. "You must be Demitri. Come, you mustn't linger outside."

The door swings open, allowing me in, then clangs shut. The guard begins patting my body and limbs, searching for something. I hope he doesn't find the drugs.

"He doesn't have any weapons," says the guard, halting my pat down.

Weapons?

"I doubt he would have needed any," the calm man replies. He turns to me. "Quite impressive considering what you did to those Rippers outside the wall, I must say. We've been eyeing you since you arrived down here. We may not have your tech, but we do have our methods."

Rippers? Eyeing me?

"I'm Yuri," he explains. He's shorter than the guard, and leaner. Sitting on his nose are wire-framed spectacles that are bent out of shape, and he has long graying hair, tied back. He must be well over fifty years old. Older than any Gracile I've ever seen, besides the Leader.

"I didn't do that to the other … people," I protest. "I mean, well …"

Tell him the truth.

Not now, Vedmak.

Yuri just observes me, a strange smirk on his face. "Evgeniy did mention you were a little odd. Come, come in. We don't have much time, and my handler is late." He turns and marches off into the expanse of the dimly lit warehouse. I duly follow.

Giant pieces of disused mining machinery stand in parallel lines, forming huge walls—enormous drill bits and circular saws more than three meters across, their teeth larger than my hands; gigantic mechanical arms attached to vehicles long since abandoned. Ancient light bulbs hang from the ceiling some ten meters above my head, each so far apart from the others that only pockets of yellow light illuminate the floor. Yuri briskly sidesteps into one of the makeshift alleys.

I'm prodded in the back by the guard, urged to follow. We turn the corner and enter a musty set of stairs leading up to a second floor or loft, the ancient wooden boards protesting loudly with each step. We exit into a smaller enclosed room occupied by more men. Below, the ancient machinery stretches out before us. We're now in the sort of place a manager might use to oversee the workers.

"Well, is this the handler?" one skinny man says, spitting through the gap where his incisors should be.

"No." Yuri shakes his head. "This is Evgeniy's replacement."

"Replacement? No, no, I'm just here for my DBS—"

"If he's not the handler, then where is he? We can't wait all day," another Robust interrupts.

111

How interesting; looks like no DBS for you. Vedmak breaks into raucous laughter.

"She," Yuri replies. "But you're right, she's late."

"I thought this handler was never late? We can't afford for this to be messed up, Yuri. It's too important," the toothless man says.

"I'll take it myself," volunteers another.

"Hey, about my DBS—"

"You ever handled a package before, Kristoff?" Yuri takes control of the small group. "No. If it were easy, anyone could do it. It has to remain secret. Only the boss can know what's inside, and frankly I don't trust any of you not to jack in and read it. Well, the boss and Demitri here." He waves his hand at me. They all turn to gawk.

"Look, all I'm here for is my fix. Evgeniy said—"

"No one cares what *Evgeniy said.* We're here to do business, so let's get to it—unless you all want to stand here stroking your egos all night."

Was that a woman's voice?

A female Robust steps out of the shadows. She's small and lean, almost boyish, but feline in her movements—her heavy boots never make a sound. Her hair is cut short, and her ears and nose have various piercings in them. An old scar runs down her face, but it's the fresh wounds that draw attention—her face is swollen and bruised, her lips split. She darts a suspicious glance at every person in the room, and my heart stops as her gaze falls on me. I get the longest look, but then she fixates on Yuri, who stands in the center of the room.

The guard raises his ancient pistol and targets the woman. "How did you get in here?"

"You're Yuri, I presume?" she says, looking to the small man.

Yuri gives a small dip of his brow in response.

"How long have you been listening? What did you hear?" another man snaps.

"And now you see why we need her." Yuri grins. "Gentlemen, this is our handler, Mila. Now, shall we get down to business?"

What business? What have I gotten myself into?

Vedmak just laughs and laughs.

CHAPTER EIGHTEEN

MILA

They just silently gawk. Probably judging my appearance or indulging in thoughts of sexual deviance. Dirty jackbags. All Robust men are the same—all of them except this one. My gaze drifts to the strange, stooping figure trying fruitlessly to hide near the back of the group. Something isn't right about this guy.

"Why are you so late?" an ugly squat man shouts at me.

Without hesitation, I point directly at my badly bruised face. "Sorry, I lost track of time while having a little too much fun out on the town."

"Don't waste our time, woman."

"You want to know the truth? How's this? I took a job from a half-cocked, super-secret organization that didn't give a professional enough time to do this job the way a professional does it. This resulted in me taking a dangerous shortcut, through a dangerous enclave, incurring unnecessary risk that almost got me killed—just so I could be 'on time' for a bunch of grubby resistance jackbags. That's the truth, and if you don't like it, *fat boy*, you can take this job and shove it directly up your fat—"

"Everyone, everyone." Yuri holds up his hands. "Please, let's calm down. It's been a long day for all of us, let's not do anything rash."

The ugly fat man's face is verging on purple, his hand closed around the butt of an old wheel gun at his side.

114

"Markov, please." Yuri motions for the fat man to take his hand off the gun. Markov continues to stare holes in me. Yuri moves his gaze to me. "Mila, are we okay?"

"Sure. We're okay. But you should tell your people if they ask stupid questions, they might not like the answers they get. Respect is a two-way street, is it not?"

Markov takes a step back and removes his hand from his weapon.

Yuri nods. "It certainly is, Mila. It most certainly is. But let us get down to brass tacks, shall we? You're late. Now you won't be able to receive this information and transport it to Fiori in time. That was the deal—no?"

"I understand that was the deal. But this deal was force-fed to me from the start, Yuri. People with my skill set do not rush a job like this. Doing it the wrong way always creates problems like the ones we face now. You should have given me more time."

"I'm sure you're right, my dear, but unfortunately time is not a luxury we can afford." He pauses just long enough to let the implication hang in the air. "Things are happening all around us, big things, as we speak. We all are but tiny players in this unfortunate game."

What in creation is he talking about?

"Mila, time is of the essence. The resistance needs to move this information, and I need you to move it. Can you do that?" I open my mouth, but Yuri holds up a gloved hand. "A simple yes or no will suffice."

"Yes."

"Good, but first, for my superiors to trust you again, I must see a show of good faith. This job is of vital importance to our people. We need to know you will complete it. What can you offer me?"

It looks like I have to play that ace up my sleeve. "I can offer

115

you information—something that will make your head spin."

Yuri smirks. "By the hands of Yeos?"

"I shouldn't have to swear by that—but yes."

"Okay. Well, let's have it."

"No. First we talk details. I'd be an idiot to tell you what I know without striking a new deal first."

Yuri folds his arms across his chest. "And?"

"My fee. It just tripled."

The group murmurs.

Yuri doesn't miss a beat. "Done. Anything else?"

"Yeah, on top of that, you're going to give me another twelve hours to complete this job."

More murmuring from the peanut gallery.

"I'll take it myself in twelve hours and save us a lot of money," Yuri retorts.

"No, you won't. I can see it in your eyes. You know too well what a Ripper will do to a person."

Yuri's face hardens. "Six hours."

"Ten."

"Eight, and that's my final offer. Any longer and I swear I'll see it carried myself and you'll be marked for death."

There it is again. Marked for death. No thanks. "Okay. Triple the fee and give me eight hours and you have a deal."

Yuri motions to a man standing in the back next to the hunched weirdo. The guy steps forward with a sealed package and hands it to Yuri, who accepts it and in turn steps forward, offering it to me with an extended arm.

"It's a deal then—plus the information that will make my head spin." I grab the package, but Yuri refuses to let it go. "Do not be late this time." His eyes hold no humor. I snatch the package from his pincer grip and shove it in my bag.

"Get this. Guess who's in cahoots—" A strange electrical

sensation prickles my skin. The hair on my arms stands on end. With an electrical snap the room is suddenly bathed in a blinding blue-white light. Frozen masks of shock and disbelief are cast on the faces of the men around me—all except Yuri, who has vanished.

"The Creed. Run," one man screams.

"No," Fat Markov shouts. "Don't move. They've already got us iso'd."

"They can't have us iso'd already," another yells back.

What is going on?

An eerily monotone voice booms over a loudspeaker. "You are hereby found to be participating in treasonous acts as defined by the authority of the benevolent Leader. This and other such acts will not be tolerated above or below the great nation of New Etyom. The penalty for your crimes is deconstruction."

The group fragments, men rushing in all directions. Markov screams something unintelligible and fires his wheel gun, which flashes with an earsplitting crack—but it's drowned out by a thunderous buzz from outside. A blue bolt arcs through the ancient glass windows, shattering them, and loops strangely, leaving wispy trails in the air behind it. The bolt hits the fat man with a thud and instantly separates his skin and fat from bone—flashing him into a fine gray powder that hangs in the air.

The fat man's dust sticks to my clothes and hair as I fling myself in the opposite direction. More thunderous booms from outside as the engines of some great airship whine louder. The men around me scream and come apart in powdery clouds of their own, the twisting blue bolts tearing gaping holes through the old building and finding their mark again and again.

Blind and desperate to get out, I collide with a wall and stumble back. No. It's no wall—it's a man who feels like a wall. The hunched weirdo with the welding goggles—who, while looking like he's going to wet his pants, has dropped the hunching act and is now standing straight as a board. And he's huge. No Robust is that big. At least two meters tall, maybe two and a half. He's got to be unbelievably jacked to look like that.

"Go." My words disappear amid the chaos. Can't hardly budge this guy. I grab his jacket and drop my center of gravity to pivot him around. "Move, you idiot. We've got to go, now."

"I … I just came for my … I just need—" he stammers.

"You're going to get me killed!" I scream, spittle flying against the dark glass of his goggles. No more words. I shove this weird guy forward, forcing him to gain momentum. Behind us, the small room comes apart under the impact of the concussive cannon fire.

"Cover your face."

"What? Wait, wait," he yells back over the din.

I exhale sharply as we head for the bank of windows before us. This big lug won't jump on his own. Thrusting my weight forward, I twist, crashing through the glass back first, my heavy jacket protecting me from the jagged glistening teeth lining the ancient window. Dropping through the opening, all my weight on his arm is just enough to sway his balance. His large frame crashes through the remaining cloudy glass of the window, and together we fall screaming into the dark below.

The fall is short, not more than ten meters. We slam into a pile of garbage and pitch forward into the snow-covered alley. The strange guy is muttering to himself and shaking his head as he raises himself to his hands and knees.

Above us, a hulking airship covered in avalanche-pattern camouflage hovers in line with the upper floor of the crumbling factory. It bears the exact same color scheme that covered the advanced exoskeletons of the Leader's bodyguards. The Creed. They must want the information I carry. The information Kapka couldn't get and the Leader absolutely must have.

The engines visibly shift, the craft whining as it spins ninety degrees to face another bank of windows. Snow and ice fly in all directions. The massive cannon slung against the belly of the ship opens up again, slamming away with rapid flashes of blue light. More screams from inside the warehouse. I have to get out of here.

The begoggled moron appears even more bewildered than before.

"Come with me, or die here. Your choice." Spinning on my toes, I tear away through the garbage-strewn alley.

As if directly tied to my movement, the monotone voice above responds. "Resistance fighters attempting to flee the target area. Acquiring lock on suspect location."

"No way." Cutting out of sight down a second trash-filled alley, I press my back to the wall. The weirdo rounds the corner and tucks in next to me.

"There's no way they can track my movement." I gulp air into my lungs.

"Yes, they can. We've been iso'd." He's not even out of breath, though he still looks like he's going to vomit.

"Iso'd?"

"Isolated." He swallows hard, glancing over his shoulder and back again nervously. "Their plasma weapons can isolate our genetic signatures and lock on to them. Like a heat-seeking missile."

"A heat-seeking what?"

"A missile. It's like a … It can follow your movement."

"Well, that's just great. How are they doing that from all the way up there?"

"You're shedding skin cells into the air all the—"

"I don't care about the science behind it, you giant idiot."

"My name is Demitri."

"Great, good for you." I take off again, making for the next darkened intersection.

This side of Zopat is run-down and desolate. What was a shadowy blessing before has now become a curse. Here, there's no swelling mass of people to disappear into, no businesses to enter and blend into, just street after darkened street. The huge freak has kept pace with me, but he's in the middle of the street.

"Stick to the shadows. You'll give us away," I yell back, but he's not listening. Instead he's muttering to himself again, his brow furrowed.

My hands lock onto his tunic and attempt to shove him toward the safety of the shadows, with little success. "What's wrong with you? C'mon."

"Look, it's no use. We can't outrun the Creed," he whimpers.

"Everyone can be outrun, you just have to know how to—" My body hair stands on end once again. Another electric snap of blinding light as everything around me becomes daylight. "Outmaneuver them."

The Creed strike ship whines overhead, searchlight swiveling.

"Robust human, do not make any sudden movements."

"What do you want?" I call into the light, my voice drowned by the droning of the engines.

"The data package you have in your possession."

"I don't know what you're talking about."

"It has been visually identified in your possession. Step away from the rogue Gracile, lie on the ground, then throw the package a minimum of two meters away."

Rogue Gracile? The petrified man at my side wrings his hands and chatters away under his breath. This guy? You've got to be kidding me.

"Please, just do it," he says. "There's no way out for us."

"There's always a way. As long as I'm holding it, they won't shoot. They don't want to risk damaging the information."

"Oh stop it, you're not helping us right now," he shouts.

"I'm the only chance we've got, so how about you shut up and—"

"No, not you. I … just …," he stammers.

I raise a hand to silence him and turn back to the hovering ship. "Okay. I'm going to get the package now. But I have to reach into my bag to get it."

"Get down on the ground first, Robust human. Move slowly."

I motion for the weird guy to get down, then stoop into the plank position and lower myself to the cold, wet stone—keeping my hands in plain sight.

"Now retrieve the package and throw it forward. Do anything else and you will be immediately deconstructed," the robotic voice commands.

How in Yeos's great creation do I get myself into situations like this? "Okay, I'm going for it now." I reach back into my satchel, my heartbeat pulsing in my ears. My hand touches the package, but glosses over it. That's not it. Where is it? "Do something," I call over my shoulder to the rogue Gracile. "Distract them."

"I can't."

"We're both going to be dead if you don't. Tell them they got it wrong with you."

This guy looks seriously distressed, but slowly he nods and starts to get up with his hands in the air.

"I'm sorry," he calls out. "You've got me all wrong. I'm no Gracile."

"You are," the monotone voice booms. "You have been isolated and identified as—"

"I've got it." Closing my fingers around the cylindrical device, I slowly pull it from my bag so Demitri can see it.

"Oh no, don't. That's—"

"Isolate this." I depress the big blue button on one end and heave the emergency device as far up the alley as possible.

Nothing happens.

Isolate this? That's the best I could come up with? And now—nothing. I'm going to murder Gil with my bare hands if I survive this.

"Robust female identified as Mila Solokoff, your noncompliance has resulted in necessitating your personal deconstruction."

The familiar crackle of a charging plasma cannon fills the air. This is it. I pinch my eyes shut and utter a simple prayer. But now there's a rapid snapping—and it's coming from the flashing strobe on my emergency button. The ship shudders, the engines faltering.

"Oh, Yeos, please."

"You have been condemned to deconstr-brrrrr." The loudspeaker breaks into a wash of static as the entire ship pitches forward and falls from the sky—right toward us.

I leap to my feet, grabbing the Gracile. "Sweet Moses. Are you completely useless? Run." He stutters something unintelligible as I shove him to the side, and together we fall into a short stairwell off the alley, tumbling into a groaning heap at the bottom of the stairs.

The ship above us spins and then, smacking back and forth like a pinball off the ancient structures, crashes and rolls before finally grinding to a stop in a ball of fire at the end of the alley. The Gracile is all tangled up with me.

"Get. Off."

"I'm sorry. I didn't mean ... You pushed me and then—"

"Just shut up and get off." I kick him away, scramble to the top of the stairs, and chance a peek at the burning ship. Inside, the Creed sit strapped into their seats, their mouths yawning wide as the flames engulf them.

"I can't believe that worked."

The Gracile rubs at his face in disbelief. "It shouldn't have. Not with a weak-pulse, homemade piece of Robust junk like that. I ... I can't believe you just destroyed a Creed ship. They're going to ... They're going to kill you for that."

"Us. They're going to kill us for that."

"No. I played no part in it. I wasn't even supposed to be mixed up in this down here."

"You *are* a Gracile."

"No, really, I'm just heavily modified."

"Modified? You mean jacked? And you said, 'down here.' You're a Gracile. You're stooping for effect. Admit it."

"No, I'm really not."

"Look, I know you were probably told Robusts are all ignorant cave dwellers, but don't insult my intelligence any further or I may save the Creed the trouble of killing you."

He swallows, panic and indecision written across his face.

"Take off the goggles."

Reluctantly he does, revealing large almond-shaped hazel eyes. They're beautiful. Almost.

"I knew it. No Robust has eyes like that. I bet you've also got perfect skin and hair."

"And teeth, and most everything else." He hangs his head. "Not that it matters."

Are all Graciles useless idiots who talk in riddles?

The Creed gunship creaks as flames engulf it, warping the metal panels. There's no movement inside. My gaze returns to Demitri. He's a Gracile. That means he can jack into this package and tell me what it is—not to mention his sheer size might come in handy.

"Why were you down here, Demitri the rogue Gracile?"

He gives me an awkward look and shakes his head, then glances away and mutters under his breath.

"Hey, I'm talking to you."

Sheepishly he swings his attention back to me. "I needed some DBS."

"Krokodil? Why would a Gracile need krokodil?"

He turns away, ashamed. "I just needed to get more. I was desperate. When you attacked the theoretical physics lab on HAP Seven, my ... connection was injured. I had to come down myself."

"The resistance has never had the ability to carry out an attack on a lillipad. They just resist you when you force our people into the mines to supply your endless energy needs, for ... whatever it is you do up there."

Another confused look on his face. "We use solar energy."

"Look, you're getting off topic. You need some krokodil, and I need something from you—to analyze what's on this data package. I need to know what your Leader is up to."

"What are you talking about?" His eyes search mine.

The creak and crashing of melting metal rings in my ears. A Creed is pulling itself from the wreckage. Clearly the EMP didn't fry everything. I grab the Gracile by the lapel of his jacket and pull him down until his gaze meets mine. "We've got to move. Now. We'll get you your krokodil, and you'll tell me what's on this package. Deal?"

"But the Creed iso'd me. The Leader will know I'm here. I'll be Ax'd."

"Look, I took them out. They're all wrecked. They can't tell anyone anything. You understand?"

He's quiet for a second, but nods. "Okay."

"Good, now let's get out of here and find somewhere to lie low. Follow me."

And follow me he does, right on my heels, with a hurt look in his eyes like a lost little Gracile puppy dog. And in the midst of all the whirling thoughts, the fear, the doubt, and the fact that I'm now marked for death by just about everyone I can think of, there's another feeling in my gut: I've become a part of something much bigger. And it's a great and terrible feeling.

CHAPTER NINETEEN

DEMITRI

"Stop doing that."

The Robust woman is staring at me.

"Doing what?" The spoon squeals on the old metal plate as I hungrily scoop up the last of whatever it was she just fed me. Most Graciles wouldn't have considered touching anything, let alone eating anything, down here—but given the circumstances, it's all a bit late.

"Talking to yourself. It's distracting, and I'm trying to think."

The bolus of food jams between my cheek and teeth. The crowd of people in the crumbling hole-in-the-wall eatery halt their conversations. Every pair of eyes bores into the back of my head. Is it obvious? Can she see when I'm doing it? Can she hear my thoughts? Can everyone?

Of course not, stupid kozel. She's not telepathic.

Maybe she can read lips?

"There you go again." She scowls, her eyes searching for an answer.

"You can hear me?"

She sits back and rests against the wall, one foot up on the chair, her knee supporting her elbow. "Yeah, and it's odd." She shrugs. "A lot of people talk to themselves—down here, probably more than most. But you're different. You look like you're having an *actual conversation.*"

126

Her small dark Robust eyes are judging me. Change the subject. "What's this?" I ask, lifting my bowl.

"Churri churri. Zopat's famous for it."

"Hmmm … ah, we should be okay here for a while—I think."

Her gaze flicks to the people churning through the night market behind me. "Why're you sure we'll be safe here? Frequent the Zopat market much?"

"Safe? I didn't say *safe*."

"You know what I mean."

"The Creed might still find us, but it'll take them time. There are too many genetic signatures around here. They'll have a much harder time isolating us. It *is* only a matter of time, though. They *will* come."

She leans toward me. "Are you going to be able to read what's on this package or not?"

"I guess. I don't actually know. Most of the time I'm not plugged into the neuralweb. I'm not plugged into anything at all. I don't like it—but you probably wouldn't understand."

"Understand what, Gracile?" She sits back and pulls out a short blade, touching the sharp edge.

"I told you, my name is Demitri. You could try using it."

She smirks. "I knew a Demitri once. We used to call him Mity—"

"Just Demitri, thank you."

She shrugs and lowers her voice. "Well, whatever you're called, you're a Gracile. Just a name slapped onto another soulless clone husk. You're no better than the Creed. One Gracile is just like the next. Living in luxury, in your fortress in the sky. While we … well, take a look around you."

Outside, the open marketplace is bustling at this late hour. Bathed in neon light, some people huddle next to burning garbage barrels while hundreds of others jostle and push through the cold, making their way among the stalls peddled by squawking black-market vendors, prostitutes, and all other manner of shady characters. All of it is disgusting. Except her. Her face is bruised and split, and her eyes are full of distrust—yet they hold a glimmer of something else.

"What happened to you? Your face, I mean."

She touches her split lip, a momentary glimpse of pain in her expression—but then it's gone, replaced with resolve and defiance.

"Are you saying something is wrong with my face?"

"No, it's just …"

Her posture relaxes, and she touches her lip gingerly again. "One day I'll learn to mind my own business. This is what I get for sticking my neck out for someone else."

"A friend of yours?"

"Not really." She sniffs and continues to play with the blade in her hand. "It was stupid for me to get involved."

"This person, was he or she grateful?"

The question seems to take her by surprise, and for a moment she doesn't answer. "Yes, he was," she says finally.

"That's good. It would be nice to think if I needed help back home, someone would come, but … I doubt it."

Mila gives me a quizzical stare.

"Where I'm from, empathy is somewhat lacking. Everything is orchestrated, planned. All for the good of the population. But we don't really get involved with each other's lives. Most of us don't venture between lillipads. We know those we work with, or grew up with in the educational clutch. Nikolaj, he used to … well, he used to care. I think I ruined that."

Oh, grow some yaichki. *Your wailing annoys me. Kill her and move on. This one is nothing but trouble—trouble you can't afford.*

"Who's Nikolaj?" She leans forward, studying me.

"My brother. Well, at least my neo-brother. We're from the

same genetic batch. The closest thing to what you might call a family." Why am I telling her this? "You? Brothers, sisters?"

"Everyone's dead."

"I'm sorry."

"Are you really? Because it's your kind's fault I lost my brother. It's your fault he went down into the mines to begin with. Greedily hoarding all the resources so your people can fuel your crystal palace in the sky."

"I'm sorry—but I told you, we don't use fossil fuels. We have solar panels. Very efficient ones. And even if we didn't, Nikolaj has a fusion reactor; he could power us all on his own."

"Do you know how many of my people have gone into the mines and never come out? If they're not digging for fuel, then what are they digging for? Why would you send them down there?"

"I-I don't know. I didn't even know we were asking your people to go into the mines. Nikolaj always said our trade was what kept the Robust people alive. That you were happy to get what you could."

Her already intense gaze flares, and her knuckles turn white as she clamps down on the grip of the combat knife in her hand. But then, almost as quickly as it comes, her anger subsides, and she slumps back to the wall, concealing the blade again in a hidden sheath beneath her clothing.

"Are you planning to kill me?"

As if I'd let that happen, Vedmak says.

She looks up at me, frustrated and weary. "Kill you? Will that bring back Zevry? Will that free my people from hatred and oppression? No, it won't. Killing you wouldn't change a thing for us down here. I can only try to change things for the better according to the will of Yeos."

There it is. Of course a Robust would be clinging to some sort of religion. "You're talking about an omnipotent god?"

"Yes. The Creator. The Lightbringer. His Writ teaches that without His light, we are lost—"

"Yes, I understand it."

Her look hardens, and she focuses back on the package. "I need you to read this. Can you do that or not?" She extends her arm, the data package clasped in her hand.

"I'll try, but your little EMP stunt may have fried it. In any case, I'm new to this. I told you I don't plug in normally."

"Okay, back up and explain this to me so my simple Robust brain can understand." Her eyes are scrunched together, and she's rubbing her temples, one hand still clutching the package. "The first Gracile I ever meet, a genetically perfected superior being—and he's more afraid than an alley cat, talks to himself, and is the only one in history not jacked into the net. Have I missed anything?"

"Yes, you did miss something."

Tell her. Tell her, and then squeeze the life from her. You don't need her. I'll protect you.

"I don't talk to myself. I'm talking to Vedmak."

She sighs in exasperation. "Who's Vedmak? You just said you're not jacked in."

"I'm not. Vedmak is a voice in my head. I'm schizophrenic. Or have dissociative identity disorder, or something." There, I said it. Out loud to someone. To a Robust, but to someone. It feels strangely good.

The woman contemplates this.

"You have a voice, in your head, and it speaks to you?" she says. "And what does this voice say?"

That was not the reaction I was expecting. "Trust me, you don't want to know."

"Trust *me* when I say I wouldn't ask you if I didn't want to know."

And so it pours out—all of it. I don't know why. Vedmak, what he says, how he acts. Gracile life and the need for perfection. How I'll be Ax'd if the Leader finds out. How it's getting worse, and that I need DBS to keep Vedmak quiet—how I need to stop him from acting through me. And even about Evgeniy and how he wanted me to find the package. It's cathartic. But as soon as I'm done, I instantly regret my weakness. The woman stares at me, her face giving away nothing—sympathy, disgust, or otherwise.

Finally, she speaks. "Is he talking to you now?"

I'll do more than talk to this interfering little dog. What are we still doing here?

"Yes."

"And?"

Kill her. And get moving.

"He doesn't like you very much." Not a total lie.

"Sounds like I wouldn't like him, either."

"That makes two of us. I hate that he's a part of me, fighting me at every turn. The darkest side of me. Perhaps I deserve to be Ax'd."

"What if he isn't you? Have you ever considered that?"

"What?"

Scooping up her satchel and holding it to her chest, she studies my eyes. "Have you ever actually listened to the teachings of Yeos?"

"I know of them, yes. But that's just for the wea—" I stop myself. There's no point arguing theology with a woman who has probably clung to her religion as a way of survival.

"Yeos teaches us that our bodies are vessels for the souls we carry. Against the timelessness of the heavens, it's just a brief journey before being released to glory—or damnation. Throughout history, some people have been known to host an eidolon, a shadow. Perhaps you play host to a demon that persecutes you. Or maybe it's a soul bound for damnation that has clung to you."

"You realize *eidolon* is actually just another word for a delusion or the shadowed mind of a mad person."

She shrugs.

"You think Vedmak is an actual demon? Or I'm haunted by the ghost of an evil person? And this is what's making me feel crazy?"

Her eyebrows rise. "Why not? You told me yourself of the vile things this Vedmak says and does, but you don't appear violent yourself. To be honest, you seem afraid of your own shadow most of the time."

"I'm sorry, but we gave up the false comforts of religion long ago. We're practically gods ourselves. We design, create, and take life at will. Perfected life. Isn't that what gods do? Actually, we improved on what your Yeos created in the first place—"

"And yet somehow, *you* are still broken." She lets that sink in, staring into me for what feels like an age. "For what it's worth, we all are." She returns her gaze to the table, flicking a stale crumb away. "Those of us who believe, we clearly aren't perfect. Not in the way you're perfect. But we choose to let Yeos make us stronger at the broken places. It is through the Lightbringer, by our faith alone, any of us are shown the way—a path that is almost always hard for those who choose it. But I guess that's the point." The look on her face suggests the depth of her own words are resonating with her for the first time.

"Well, that's all very nice, and I do hate to disappoint you, but this is a regular medical condition. I know this to be fact, as I can control it with the DBS. Not that it matters. I'll be Ax'd for sure."

"You don't know that. The Creed may not have transmitted anything to the Leader. It's possible—"

"We both know they did. Hell, I'm probably the reason they found that place. Maybe I'm bugged."

"You'd better hope not." Her eyes narrow, then she pushes the data package at me once more. "Please, help me read it. And I promise you, I'll help you get some Easy or krokodil, or whatever you need to make Vedmak go away."

Why don't I look inside? Even Evgeniy told me I needed to see it—that I may be more important to this world than I know.

"Okay."

Brave little dog now, are we?

"What do I have to lose?"

Mila grunts. "Huh?"

"Nothing."

I focus on the package, turning it between my thumb and forefinger. When was the last time I even did this? Ten years ago? Twenty? Have I been hiding that long? What if I'm not ready? What if it kills me? What if it does something to Vedmak?

Nothing can harm me.

Not harm. Enhance. Do something I can't predict.

"You're muttering again," Mila says.

"Oh. Um, I was just saying it's old tech. I don't have the port for this—mine's too new."

"What does that mean?"

"It means I don't have the correct connection for this. I'm going to need a bit of help." My palms are sweating. "Do you have a length of wire, stiff wire, in that satchel of yours?"

"Maybe." She plonks it on the table and begins pulling out the contents, most of it junk—except for one item, a book. Or at least paper pages, written in a shorthand scrawl and tied together with brown string. It can't be more than twenty pages long. Before I can ask about it, she's gathered everything up and stuffed it back into the satchel. "Here, will this do? It's part of the cable I use for my ziplines."

"Ziplines?"

"Forget it."

She hands me a thick piece of metallic wire, twenty centimeters long. It's twisted together with dozens of smaller, thinner wires. I grab both ends and begin turning in two different directions, unraveling the steel twine.

"That's pretty impressive," she says.

"Being genetically enhanced has its advantages." I smile genuinely, then roll up the sleeve of my shirt past the elbow.

"Interesting scar. It looks pretty fresh."

"It is." Though I haven't cut myself today. "I'm used to the next part. I need you to cut me right here. Half-inch deep, one inch across." I point to the inside of my forearm, near the elbow crease. "We all have an emergency port here. I've used so much derma-heal gel that my skin grew over it. The port is slightly too large for your data package. I'll need to wedge it in with the wire to complete the connection."

Mila grabs the blade and hovers over my arm. "This is gonna hurt."

"I know."

She sucks in a breath and pushes the knife in.

The searing pain and hot blood flow are familiar. But they offer no release this time, no moment of clarity from the fog of my schizophrenia. Now, it just hurts.

That doesn't feel good, my sad little Gracile?

"Not now, Vedmak."

"Okay, now what?" she asks.

"The port is just under the surface. You can probably push the data package straight in, but it'll be loose. Put the wire in beside it."

"Okay." Mila nods.

"No, wait a second. I have to switch on the connection."

"What?"

"I have to allow myself to be connected, I won't be able to process the package on my own. I need help from the neuralweb. I was never good at this; I end up opening up to any wireless information web, too. It's another reason I don't do this often. It's just ... scary."

"You're an interesting bird, Demitri the Gracile."

A faint fog creeps over my consciousness as I allow the connection. The signal is weak down here in Lower Etyom, but it's there. My stomach knots.

"Ready?"

"Okay, now."

She pushes in the data stick, followed by the wire, wedged down alongside it.

Nothing. Did it work? I think it's plugged in prop—aargh.

"Demitri. Demitri."

Her voice is muffled and far away. But I can't answer. My lips won't move. The stabbing pain in my mind is overwhelming. Stab. Stab. Stab. It's the agony of sheer volumes of information imprinting into the soft tissues of my brain.

"I can't see." I flail blindly, my hands and feet scraping against the floor and walls.

A hand grabs my wrist and holds it tight. Through my own wails, her voice pushes through. Calm and soothing. "It's okay, Demitri. It's okay. Breathe. Concentrate. Stay with me. You can do it."

My heart slows. The white light fades, and my visual cortex is stimulated with new images, my memory center with new data and knowledge—my synapses crackling and connecting, forming new pathways. But this doesn't make sense.

Kill her. Vedmak's voice shatters my connection with the data package.

"Aargh." I collapse to the floor and yank the package from my arm. A stream of blood jets freely from my left nostril.

"Hey, weirdo. No jacking in my restaurant."

"No, it's fine. We're fine." Mila says to the shop owner.

He glares at us. "No more funny business."

"You got it," Mila says, and turns back to me, helping me back to my seat. "What was it? What did you see?" Her voice strains as she shakes me by the arms. "Demitri."

"I ... I'm not sure. It didn't make a lot of sense. There was an interfering signal. Something close by ... I connected briefly but it managed to break the link. I think maybe, it leak—"

"What was on the stick?"

"Um, the Leader, the Leader is developing something. Some kind of superdevice that will preserve Gracile life the way it is. He wants to be recorded in a state of perfection, forever. But the data suggests total destruction. Tens of thousands will die. All of them Robust ... It's a blur, I can't—"

"Concentrate, Demitri. *How?* How will the Leader do this?"

I close my eyes and search the newly embedded information, fragmented and incoherent in my brain. "Genocide." My eyes snap open. "He'll wipe you out first, then initiate the device. But it's a flawed theory; his calculations don't make sense. This has to be a lie. Why would he do this? He doesn't want war with the Robusts, he just wants peace."

"Are you sure peace is what he wants? I've seen your Leader with my own eyes, down here, manipulating and controlling some real nasty people. Paying them to keep our resistance busy. And this." She motions with the data package. "Sending his Creed to retrieve this package—at the cost of my life. *Your* life. Think about it."

"I can't believe that. I won't believe that. You're mistaken. You don't know him like I do."

Vedmak's evil chuckle fills my head. *Won't you believe it, little puppet?*

Mila grabs my arm. "You better believe it—because we have to stop him."

"We? Stop what?" I cry, leaping to my feet. "Even if it's true, and he has planned this, the calculations are all wrong. He wants to create a *black hole*, a region of space-time with such strong gravitational effects that nothing—not even light—can escape it. Time dilation increases almost infinitely."

"It's a collapsed star. I know what a black hole is," Mila snaps back. "But how would that preserve the Graciles?"

"Look." I drop back down and frantically draw a circle in the dust on the table. "A black hole is bound by a well-defined edge known as the event horizon, within which nothing can be seen and nothing can escape. The necessary velocity to get out would equal or exceed the speed of light—which is impossible. Think of it like the point of no return a boat experiences when approaching a whirlpool and it reaches the location where it can no longer sail against the flow."

"Okay, so?"

"It's generally accepted that information can never be destroyed. What makes you and me, well, *you* and *me*—is information. Anything that falls into a black hole would not be destroyed but stored just outside on the event horizon. As information. Forever. Or at least as long as the black hole existed."

She rubs her face. "All right. You're saying the Leader wants to code you? Onto a black hole?"

"That's what I think the package says. But even if it were possible, the standard model of physics states that spontaneous creation of a black hole is unbelievably difficult. You need enough mass to collapse in on itself. A star, just like you said."

"The Earth isn't enough?"

"No, no, no. There are other theories, exotic physics that

suggests small black holes could be created and exist long enough to grow, but that requires multiple dimensions—and no one has ever proved they exist. At any rate, the data suggests he only wants Graciles coded. That would mean scattering the info of anything else."

"Scatter the info? You mean murder."

"He wouldn't do that. This is all sard."

"I don't care what you think it is, he's going to try to do it." Mila is suddenly frantic. "I have to get this to the resistance, and you have to come with me. I need you to explain all of this stuff."

Her voice is white noise melting into the background. There's something else—a sound nagging at me, and it's not Vedmak.

"Shush, quiet." I grab her arm and pull her to the ground. My heart accelerates.

"Don't you shush me. You don't know me like that—"

"No, listen."

Screams in the marketplace. Screams and the sound of panicked people running.

Mila scrambles along the ground to the wall and peers through the window.

"What is it?"

Don't lose your nerve now, kozel. You were doing so well.

Mila beckons me closer and points to a group of six or seven Robust men with dark skin and strange headgear like wrapped bandages. They charge through the crowd, screaming and furiously attacking anyone in range—hacking at limbs and necks with knives and machetes.

She looks at the men. "This is how your Leader will destroy us. He doesn't have enough Creed to do it. But there are enough Musuls. And once they've done it, he'll take them out himself. He's playing us all."

A little boy stumbles into the middle of the crowd, sobbing

loudly. His chest heaves with each sobbing breath. He can be no more than five.

"Someone has to get him," I say.

Mila grabs my arm. "No, run," she screams. *"Run!"*

She crosses half of the room at a dead sprint before a thunderous boom and a blaze of light send the brickwork in front of me flying in all directions. The high-pitched whistle in my ears is deafening, melding together with the screams of the dying. Smoke and debris burn my lungs as I force myself from the ground. As fast as my metal-laden legs will carry me, I run.

Through the clamor of gunfire and yelling and the smoke, I have no idea which direction I'm supposed to go. People push past and shove me out of the way. Another explosion disintegrates the wall to my right, and I instinctively dive in the opposite direction. Something clangs against my shins, and I tumble headfirst to the ground.

Lying on the ground next to me is the cause of my fall—a little girl, curled up in a ball, sobbing uncontrollably. The world slows. The screams of panicked people echoing in my ears, a spray of brickwork streaking lazily across my path. Instinctively, I grab the girl and hoist her into my arms. My mind catches up—the sounds of war clear again—and I take off through the crumbling streets full of broken bodies and wailing people.

Past the neon lights and deserted stores, I tramp and clang toward the enclave entrance, through the gate and into the freezing wasteland. With the small child clinging to my chest, I run away from the din, away from the screams of war, and away from Mila.

CHAPTER TWENTY

MILA

I touch my ear again. It's not bleeding, but it sure feels like it is. Other than some mild cuts from the flying debris and a little road rash, I'm not injured. The screaming whistle in my ears has now largely subsided into a faint whine. Keep moving, Mila.

Hours must have passed, though I couldn't say how many. I've been walking along this Vapid path since before dawn. At least I escaped. Unlike that poor, terrified boy. A slave, a weapon in a senseless war. It's disgusting.

Many were killed or maimed in the marketplace attack in Zopat. And there's no telling what happened to the rogue Gracile. He's probably dead, which is fine by me ... I think. Why do I care?

I pick up the pace across the barren stretch of road, hardly more than a lane, and sprint across the Vapid toward the only home I've ever known. Ahead, smoke billows.

Logos is burning.

My feet ache with fresh blisters, and the cold has nearly frozen me solid, but I can't stop now. As I stumble toward the front gate of the enclave, which now stands unguarded, the heavy door hangs wide open. Women and children scatter in all directions, screaming. Fire jumps from building to building. Injured men limp back and forth with pails of water in a feeble attempt to put out the flames.

My home has been sacked. The Musuls? The Graciles? Surely

the resistance doesn't have the capacity or desire to do this, no matter how much they want me dead. Who could be responsible?

As I trudge deeper into Logos, the nightmare worsens. Row after row of burning wreckage. Soot-covered women in rags sobbing and cradling the bodies of lifeless children in their arms and crying out to Yeos in desperation.

I arrive at my block. The sight of the wreckage paralyzes me. Not a stick of wood or a fragment of stone or steel still stands. My whole life, blasted into nothing, like those resistance guys who were deconstructed when ... Oh, by the hands of Yeos. The Creed.

None of New Etyom's supports were damaged in the attack. The pristine crystal city above still stands, confirming my worst fears. "You. You and your robot slaves did this to us," I cry out.

The muffled groan of an injured person nearby rises from the rubble, calling something. My name.

"Mila."

"Where are you?"

"Over here," the voice moans.

In the pile of debris is an outstretched hand.

"Hang on, I'll get you out." I dig, tossing chunks of rubble to the side to expose—"Clief."

"Mila, I'm sorry. I just wanted to check on my place. I shouldn't have come back, I know."

"It's all right, Clief, just hang on, let me get you—" A wave of nausea. My stomach seizes. A large piece of rebar protrudes from Clief's chest.

"I don't think I'm going anywhere," he wheezes.

"Oh, Clief. I'm so sorry." I collapse to my knees in the rubble next to him. "This is all my fault. I'm responsible for this."

"Don't say that."

"I am. You don't understand." I shudder, wiping the arm of my jacket across my face.

141

"No, Mila. It's not your fault, but you can be the one to rescue us from it. You're stronger than the rest of us."

You're stronger than me, Mil. You're stronger than all of us.

"I'm not," I whisper.

Clief is calm. He pats my arm. "You'll find a way, my friend." He offers a weak smile before wincing again.

"Clief, I need to find you some help. You're bleeding."

"No. It's too late. Please, Mila, just sit with me for a while."

I cover him with my jacket and hold his head in my arms, and together we watch the snow fall across our ruined home for the last time.

* * *

No second chances. If this plan doesn't work, we're all as good as dead. I run as fast as my shaking legs will carry me across the creaking suspension bridge, my lungs burning from the smoke and exertion. There's a pain in my chest I can't describe, the ache of something lost.

I know what's about to happen, but I can't stop it as the dream shuffles forward, sometimes in slow motion, sometimes skipping and jumping ahead with flashes of light. I know this place. Every sound, every falling snowflake—it's as real as anything I have ever lived, except I haven't …

I have to make it to the launchpad. It's all that matters now.

"I have to go. I have to do this," my companion says to me, his tone resolute.

"No, don't."

"We don't have a choice." He pushes my hand away. "Get in the rocket, Mila. Finish this. Do it for *all* of us."

The explosion, the heat of the fireball—my skin feels like it's on fire. Then for the first time, he's with me. *Demitri.* Everything

142

flashes to white, and the darkness cascades over me again, heralding the arrival of something far worse: the Horseman.

My body surges to consciousness. It's dark and warm, the air tinged with the smell of mountain herbs and incense. My eyes adjust, taking in the arched ceilings with long stone supports covered with elaborate hand-painted murals.

"Where am I? Who—" Hands press me down. "Let me go. I need to see my friend."

"You should rest now." The voice is soothing and motherly, but her hands are unnaturally strong.

"I can't. I have to—hey, get your hands off me."

The pressure releases, and I'm greeted with silence. Then a voice reaches out to me from the darkness. "We found you and your friend alone in the snow. You might have frozen."

"Who are you?"

A round elderly face and long flowing crimson robes emerge from the gloom.

"We are the Vestals of the Word."

The Vestals found me? "Yes, of course. I'm … I'm very sorry, Mother Vestal."

"Do not be sorry, child. A terrible thing has happened in our enclave."

The woman pats at my wounded face with a damp cloth. I can barely find the words. "My friend? You said you found us together? Is he here?"

She nods her head respectfully. "He was. He has since gone."

"Gone … Gone, as in …"

"Worry not for him, my child. We prayed over him and blessed him with the holy remnants before his passing. His troubles are over now."

A weight the likes of which I've never felt presses on my chest, threatening to squeeze out the last gasp of hope. Be with Yeos, my friend. "My friend is dead. Logos is destroyed. Everything I have ever known is in ruins."

"Not everything. Yeos lives. He will give us each the strength we need to carry on."

"Will He? Does Yeos still care for us? Or has He abandoned us to the evil of this world?"

The Vestal stops, her slim shoulders unmoving for what feels like an age before she finally speaks. "He has not abandoned us, dear—nor will He ever. His love reaches out to us, even in the midst of this."

"But He still allows so much suffering, so many of our people to die. How can a god like that be good?"

"You want to trust in Yeos, but you are afraid to place your trust in the unseen?"

"Oh … I didn't …"

"It's okay, child." She smiles softly, patting my thigh, then drapes a weathered hand across the edge of my collection of writings, now sitting exposed outside my bag. "This tells me more about you than your words ever could." Bound together with a bit of dusty string, an old photo of my parents, my brother, and me is wrapped tightly against pages and pages of my scribbling. Rewritten words of faith I've heard many times from the people I loved, friends, and mentors. I've never showed this to anyone.

"Oh, you found that?"

"I did, while looking for some way to determine who you were, Mila Solokoff."

She knows me?

"I remember your father. He, and later, your mother, used to bring you here when I was a much younger woman and you were just a child. You all were a handsome family—and he was a good man, your father."

"You knew my father?"

144

"He came here to pray for you often when you were sick with the plague as a child. To hear the purity of a father's prayer—for Yeos to spare his daughter's life in exchange for his—was something special to witness. Not long after, he took ill himself from the sickness of his child and passed away, but his daughter recovered. Yeos heard the prayer of the father, and we knew the girl had been spared for a reason. *You* were spared for a reason."

My throat is dry. "I ... I never heard that story."

"It is just the perspective of an old woman." She hands me a clay mug of ice-cold water.

It's beyond delicious.

The old woman's hand hovers back over my writings. "You have a sharp mind. This collection of teachings is excellent, Mila. It appears to be faithful to the words of the original Holy Writ. Unfortunately, copies of the true Word disappeared during the years of the purge that followed World War III. The Musuls were intent on seeing our holy teachings wiped from the face of the earth." Placing my writings safely back into my satchel, she turns to me. "And yet here, in the most unlikely place, the Word of Yeos lives on—with you."

I take another drink of the nearly frozen water, listening as the senior Vestal continues in gentle tones.

"It warms my heart to see this."

"Why is that, Mother Vestal?"

"Our days are numbered, no matter how we choose to live them, dear girl. What's most important is for each of us to strive to know the truth and to understand how we are to best live the days we have. You are choosing to live with purpose."

"It's not that simple."

She winks and nudges me gently with two bony fingers. "Ahh, but it is that simple." Pulling a basin of cool clear water over, she continues tending to me, washing the grime from my blistered feet.

145

"You were fashioned with love by your creator to do one thing. You have a destiny even you do not yet fully understand. Yeos has placed this fire within you, and in doing so set you aside for this purpose—to endure the path of the Lightbringer. It is a great honor."

Every fiber of my being comes alive with her words. She speaks to me in a voice that feels like love. Her simple, tender prose flows over me, washing away my fear.

"We were never guaranteed peace or safety. But we *were* guaranteed an opportunity to change our world."

"But how am I supposed to do that?"

"With love, dear. We change the world with love—and sometimes, just sometimes, standing in the name of love also means fighting for it."

"It does?"

"Indeed. But remember this: if you must fight, you fight for love. You must never allow the infection of hate to dim your light—for that is not the way."

"Forgive my unbelief. I'm just …" I suppress my tears. "I'm nobody. I don't know how this became my life."

The gentle woman wipes her hands and embraces me, then holds my face and lifts my chin to see her wizened eyes. "You are *somebody*. Do not ever let your fear stop you from attempting the greatest things, Mila Solokoff. No matter how dark the path, you are destined to carry the message of the light." She winks at me. "For the ways of Yeos are mysterious and wonderful, dear girl; and from the dawn of time until the end of it, they will remain so. You would do well to remember this."

I want to stay in this place—a place where the true spirit of my faith feels close. But I can't. To do so would be to concede to the enemy, and defeat is not in my nature. I pull on my boots and clothes and say a reluctant farewell to the good Mother Vestal of the Word. A brief amble through the catacombs and up the stairs leads me to the heavy oak and steel-banded doors at the entrance.

At the mercy offering, I drop the rest of my bills and a few nuggets of raw silver into the ancient chest. Supporting their cause is worth it. The Vestals are one of the oldest organized remnants of my faith. Their convent, nestled safely at the foot of Zhokov Mountain, has remained hidden, sheltered through many terrible storms of fate. These resilient women have long been known for their faith, kindness, and wisdom. I have benefitted from all three this day.

Standing shin deep amid the snowdrifts outside the entrance to the convent, I follow the plumes of smoke still rising into the air. It's slowing now, the blaze controlled as men carry buckets of water from the river to the edge of the dying fire.

Inside my sling bag, the data package is still there. But I need to get some elevation to try to get a grip on what happened here. I need a plan. Another breath of the cold mountain air. It's intoxicating. Okay, Mila. There's work to be done.

* * *

The trip across my enclave takes more effort than usual, as I now have to navigate the wreckage and debris of my old neighborhood. I stop only briefly at Bilgi's place to confirm that it—along with the things I stored with him—are gone. I can't help but wish my mentor were here with me now. He would know what to do.

Climbing the support pillar takes effort but feels good, a distraction from the endless spinning of my mind. Climbing hard and fast, I'm buffeted by an icy wind that snaps against me as I reach the upper ledge. Wiping the ice from my gloves, only now do I notice the bloodstains on them. The knot in my gut tightens.

Don't you worry, Clief. I'm going to get to the bottom of this. I fire a quick e-message to Gil from my PED. He might know something.

At this elevation, the full scope of Logos's devastation can truly be understood. It's all my fault. There was no need for the Gracile forces to try to kill all the workers who faithfully mine their precious deep-earth resources for them. This was a tactical strike aimed at killing me and the people closest to me. The Leader ordered this— and he's going to pay for this evil with his perfect life.

What happened to Demitri? Was all of this really chance? Was he actually rogue? Maybe a double agent planted to interact and gain information from me? What if he went straightaway to tell the Leader all about me, the data package, and where I was from. That would explain the precision attack on Logos. That's the only thing that makes sense—he betrayed my trust. But, if that were true, why didn't he kill me and take the package when he had the chance? He would have been more than capable of doing it if he were actually some tough-guy double agent. What if he wasn't lying? What if he was just a scared scientist running for his life and trying to understand his condition—a condition they'd kill him for having? And why, of all things, is he in my dream? Damnation, I have no time for this.

Still no response from Gil. He's either dead or too high to care. There's no more time to waste. I have to get this data to the Opor faction in Fiori. The trip won't be difficult going straight from Logos. Even though I've now violated the terms of the deal a second time, I don't have much choice. The resistance is the only hope for me now. They'll know what to do with the information I carry.

The zipline whines as I make my descent, hitting the bumpers correctly and slowing enough to drag my feet and come to a stop. Fixed the stupid thing after all. Detaching my T-bar and pulley from the line, I stow them in my bag and make for the enclave's main entrance.

The guards have returned, but they're now arguing with a man outside.

"Let you in? You can't be serious. Do you see what happened here? It was probably the doing of your people." The guard jabs a spear at the man.

"No. It was not me—my people, I mean."

"How should we know, when you send people in here to kill us all the time? You're a towl'ed spy."

"I say we kill him." One of the guards grabs the man, who squirms like a trapped animal.

"Please, I saw what happened. Let me go, I just need to see—" The man sees me approaching and shouts, "Logosian. Oh, uh … Mila. Help. Tell them."

It's Faruq.

"What are you doing here?"

"I'm looking for Husniya, my sister."

"Okay, okay, let him go."

"No. He could be involved in this. We kill this towl'ed now."

I step between the guard and Faruq. "Hey, hey, enough with the slurs, all right? Haven't we all seen enough hate for one day? This man didn't do anything to us, and he's *not involved*. Trust me. Let him go, and I'll speak to him." Reluctantly the guard releases Faruq with a shove.

"Faruq. I'm sorry. They're on edge. Let's walk."

Faruq nods and walks with me through the gate of the enclave and out into no-man's-land.

"Thank you," he says.

"It's been a long day, Faruq. Tell me you know something."

"I do," he says, straightening his jacket. "And it's all much worse than you think."

CHAPTER TWENTY-ONE

DEMITRI

The burning enclave lights up the lillipad stem. Orange flames lick at the walls, and thick black smoke chokes the cold night air. The VTV is close, but the faint screams and loud pop-pop-popping of ancient firearms still linger in the distance. Those Robusts attacked everyone. There was no strategy other than total destruction. They didn't target the resistance, or those who may have fought back. They hit anyone in reach. Women. Men. Children. Oh, for the love of the Leader, they used that boy to carry the bomb. Why would they use a child?

My stomach convulses, and I crash into the snow, heaving up my last meal with Mila. It spatters the white-gray slush and my pants, somehow missing the little girl who still sticks to me. I want these images to be erased from my brain. But his little face is branded into my gray matter. And then, there were the other Robusts in the market; nothing could prepare them for watching a child die that way. Instead they ran, shrieking in terror. Just like me.

The snow is cold in my hands as I force myself to my feet. I readjust the small child on my chest, holding her cold skinny frame close to me, and trudge toward the VTV. The bodies of the first Robusts—the Rippers, Yuri called them—have either been scavenged or are concealed under fresh snow. The geminoid is nowhere to be seen, either.

I disarm the security system and tap the door. It swings up and open. Without hesitation, I shuffle inside and close it behind me, sealing out the frigid air.

Are we going somewhere, boy? You didn't even get your DBS, but somehow picked up a new pet.

Vedmak. I almost forgot he was there—almost. But he has a point: What the hell am I doing? Going home, no DBS, and with a Robust child in tow. But if I tell the Leader the truth, tell him I'm unwell, maybe he'll have a cure. Maybe he'll let me live.

Let you live? You'll be Ax'd, and you know it. You saw the data package. Don't be a naive child. You're as good as dead. And I can't let that happen.

"Shut up, Vedmak, just shut up. I need to think. Let me think."

You don't need to think—I do. You're a weak little puppet. You need someone to pull your strings. His horrible, mocking tone slithers around inside my head.

The little girl still hangs on to my chest for dear life. She's so light, she's barely noticeable. A pair of wet dark eyes stares back at me from under a mess of matted black hair. Tears have glued strands of it to her cheeks. She sniffs repeatedly, but says nothing. She can be no more than ten.

Vedmak snarls again. *Kill it. Throw it from the hatch.*

"No, she's a child. Look at her."

Yes, look at this little dark-skinned rodent. Throw it out. Do it or I will.

"Please don't do that. Don't kill me," sobs the girl. She lets go and slides down my torso to the floor, then shuffles back against the bulkhead.

"It's okay. No one is going to kill you. Are you from that enclave, Zopat? Was your family there?"

"I'm from Baqir," the girl says with a sniffle. "I ran away from

Kapka's men. My brother told me to run. I hid in a trader's cart, and it took me all the way to Zopat. But those bad men were attacking, so I ran."

"That was very brave of you."

Ugh, you've got to be joking.

The girl's face drains of color. "There it is again."

"There's what again?"

"The other man. He wants to kill me," she replies.

"Who wants to kill you?"

"That bad man. The one you're talking to."

"You can hear … the bad man?"

"Yes." She bursts into a fresh bout of crying. "He speaks with strange words, like he's far away. Please don't let him hurt me."

Slit its throat. Vedmak's voice is but a hiss.

The girl clasps frantically at her neck and shoves herself as far into the corner as she can. "Please, don't."

She heard Vedmak. How is that possible? "Do you know the name of the other man? The one I'm talking to?"

Vedmak gives an evil chuckle. *The dead need not know my name.*

"No." She shakes her head slowly. "He said I don't need to know it if I'm to die anyway."

The floor comes up fast as I slump on my ass. What the hell is going on? She can hear Vedmak? Who is this girl? "What's your name?"

"Husniya."

"Okay, Husniya. I'm Demitri."

"Are you a Gracile?" She sniffs again.

"Yes. I am." I shuffle forward on my backside to get a little closer. "Husniya, I need you to be a brave girl, okay?"

She just stares at me, her eyes glassy.

"When I talk to the man, to Vedmak, you can hear him—

right?"

She nods once. "Kind of. It's crackly. I can't hear everything. Just some words."

This makes no sense. Why would she be able to hear him at all? "Husniya, have you always been able to hear voices?"

"Yes," she replies. "Margarida. She sings to me sometimes."

"Margarida?"

"Yes, she's nice to me when Faruq goes to find food and I'm alone. Margarida sings to me. I don't know the words; they're funny. I like it." Husniya wipes the tears from her cheeks with her forearm.

"An imaginary friend?"

"No," she replies. "She's real."

A faint noise crackles in the recesses of my mind, like an interfering radio signal. A voice overlapping with Husniya's.

... *no es ... imaginary ... señor.*

"Did you say something?"

"I said: no, she's a real person," she replies.

"Yes, I heard that. But, did you not say something about *imaginary?*"

"That wasn't me." She giggles. "That was Margarida. My friend."

¡Sí. says the voice again. It's difficult to make out, far away and broken.

"For the love of the Leader. What's going on? Husniya, how long have you had this voice, I mean, Margarida, in your head?"

"Always." The girl shrugs. "She's nice to me."

"Husniya, I think I can hear her, too."

"You can?" the little girl squeals.

"This is incredible."

She can hear Vedmak. I can hear her voice, Margarida. That would mean I'm not schizophrenic. That Husniya and I are in contact with something, someone, somewhere else. I should have asked this long ago. "Vedmak ... where are you?"

There's a long silence. Then he speaks, his tone bitter and angry.

Clever little kozel. Finally understanding, are we? I live in the darkest place. A place of pain, of separation. It feeds me. Nourishes me. Prepares me for my rebirth. For my second chance—through you.

... demon, spits the faint, old voice, Husniya nodding frantically in agreement. *... monster.*

"You're in another place. You're not me. I can just hear you, wherever you are. You said rebirth. You died? But somehow still linger?"

Vedmak cackles maniacally. *We all die, Gracile. I died for my comrades. For Mother Russia. Fighting pigs like you who believed they were better. Nothing has changed. Your kind, oppressing the common man, polluting Russia's land. And you will die, too, leaving me your body.*

He died? He died, and somehow, his brain pattern survived. And we can hear it. And Margarida's. "Margarida. Margarida, where are you?" I scrunch my eyes closed and try to concentrate on the distant voice.

... home, says the voice. *... warm ... I'm free.*

"She's with Ilāh," Husniya explains, her face full of pride. "She's my guardian angel."

"Heaven?" Is it possible? Brain patterns, or quantum information, are retained and kept intact? Held somewhere in space-time? Maybe another dimension? Maybe multiple dimensions? Vedmak and Margarida describe a different existence. Quantum entanglement, maybe? My subatomic particles entangled with those of Vedmak's—trapped elsewhere. "Quantum entanglement. And multiple dimensions. Of course, that would mean—"

"What?" Husniya asks.

I might be living proof of exotic physics, of multiple dimensions. And so could she. But if that's the case, then the Leader might well be able to create a black hole from small mass, one that would grow. Is this what he's waiting for? Does he know what's wrong with me? Did he already think of this theory, and that's why I've not been Ax'd? I leap to my feet, pacing like a caged animal inside the VTV.

"If he knew, then he's been watching me. He wanted to weaponize my condition. If he could figure it out, then he could open a door to a dimension where black holes could exist on a small scale—using a supercollider."

The pieces fall into place, clicking and clacking into the gaps in my understanding of his plan. He knows humans can be coded—an information soul—because I am in contact with exactly that. Vedmak.

"Is that bad?" the little girl asks.

"There must be something specific," I blurt. "A protein in the brain or something that's entangled at the quantum level, like a bird."

Vedmak groans. *What are you going on and on about?*

"Birds, when we had many more on Earth, would migrate relative to magnetic lines between seasons. The field is far too weak to detect using ferric-based molecules, but they had a protein in the brain that comprised atomic particles that were entangled with others, and this relationship was affected by magnetic fields. Husniya, you'd have it, too. We need to get to the med lab and look for it."

"Why?" she asks.

"Because if I can isolate the protein, then maybe I can suppress it. Vedmak will be gone."

She starts to cry again. "I don't want Margarida to go. She's my angel."

"Look, Husniya, we don't have to make Margarida go away. But it might be easier to find the protein if we look for it together. It's something we both have in our DNA. I need your help. Will you help me?"

"Will you help me find my brother?" she asks hopefully.

"Sure. You come to the med lab, and then we'll go find your brother."

"Okay." Excited, she throws her arms around my legs. I can't remember the last time someone hugged me so tightly. In fact, I can't remember the last time I was hugged at all.

Oh, boo hoo, lonely little Gracile. Soon you will be gone, and none of this will matter.

"Oh no, Vedmak. Soon *you* will be gone." For the first time, I feel strong. For the first time, I feel like maybe I'm a good person. Vedmak isn't me. And I can beat him.

CHAPTER TWENTY-TWO

MILA

We march along the well-worn trade route between Logos and Fiori, one of the few paths in the Vapid left alone by the Rippers—at least most of the time. It took a bit of time to convince Faruq to come with me and make contact with the resistance. His reservations were understandable, but the resistance may be the only way to find his sister—and besides, Fiori is one of the few enclaves where Musuls seem to be free of Baqir and Kapka, not to mention the criminal warlords in Kahanga.

Without warning, Faruq stops and surveys the horizon. He pulls a small prayer mat from I don't know where, lays it out, and kneels on it, facing east.

"What are you doing?"

He glances at me. "It is time for me to pray."

"It most certainly is not. Get up, we have to keep moving."

"No. This is my duty."

Faruq touches his forehead to the mat, offering prayers to Ilāh.

"You're going to do this right now, in the middle of the Vapid, while we stand exposed?"

Faruq does not answer.

No point arguing. Just let him get it over with. Who am I to judge him for being true to his ways? His faith is valuable to him. It's all he's ever known. Just like the rest of us, he is trying to make sense of the madness in his life.

Mere minutes later, he stands and collects his mat.

"We ready?"

"Of course."

One tired foot in front of the other and without speaking, we move at a painfully fast pace down the snow-covered Vapid road. Every step brings us closer to Fiori and our destination: the Forgotten Jewel.

The silence is too loud, even for me. "When we get to the Forgotten Jewel, you'll need to tell them everything you know about Kapka and your sister, so they can help find her. Think of it as a trade. When was the last time you saw her?"

"We got separated after I came back to Kapka's palace for you. She was hiding, but when I returned, she was gone. One of the street merchants told me he thought he saw her hide in a trader's cart. If this is true, she could be anywhere."

"And you figured she may have come to Logos?" I keep walking, head down, chin tucked into the rat stink of my furry collar.

"Partly, though when I saw Logos destroyed, I knew she would have fled already. She's resourceful."

"Why all the effort to get past the guards?"

"I was looking for you."

"Oh?"

"I know it seems strange, but I felt I knew too much. I had to come and tell you, and ..."

"Yeah?"

"I thought you might help me find my sister in return. You know how to get around better than I do."

"You said you knew something. That it was bad. Are you going to tell me before we get to Fiori? Probably best if I'm aware, so we're singing from the same hymn sheet."

"Hymn sheet?"

"Forget it."

Faruq shrugs and sinks his hands deep into his pockets, his breath steaming from his lips. "I saw it. The Creed ships dropping from the clouds. Logos burning. I came to find you and instead, I watched it all. Your home, destroyed. I'm sorry for your loss."

"Yeah. I appreciate that. Sorry won't bring them back, though. It won't bring Clief back."

"Your friend?" he asks.

"He was."

"That's not the worst of it, Mila."

"Go on."

"While looking for my sister, I overheard a few of Kapka's guards talking. He's planning on blowing up the lillipad supports over all but the Musul enclaves, wiping out the non-Musuls above and below all at once. He has the men and the resources to do it. With nearly all who might oppose him out of the picture, his rise to the top of the ash heap would be swift. There would be no one who could effectively oppose his rule."

"He's insane. Or he already believes the Leader will double-cross him. Maybe both."

"The Leader?"

"Of the Graciles."

"Double-crossing? I don't understand."

"They're in league with each other, or at least they were. Joined forces to keep Robusts at bay. I saw it with my own eyes. Though I think the Leader is deceiving him."

"That's a terrifying thought."

"Tell me about it. Hang on a second, Faruq." I stop along the path, watching a trader's small convoy with a security contingent approaching us along the frozen road. "Help me understand something."

Faruq turns expectantly.

"You believe your god is the one true god, just as I do. Correct?"

Faruq nods and raises his hands. "Yes. Ilah is great and merciful."

"What I experienced as a child was not great or merciful."

He studies me intently.

"Okay, answer me this: Why are you against Kapka if he is promoting your god, your people, and their ways?"

Faruq sucks in a breath. "When I was young, Kapka murdered my father out of jealousy and took my mother as a wife."

"What's that got to do with—"

"Let me finish. The story of my father is for another day— what's important is I lived in Kapka's fortress with my mother for years. He tolerated me at best, treating me with indifference. I hated him. I knew what he had done. When my mother became ill, I was old enough to know things were changing for the worst. Kapka offered me a place in his ranks, but I had seen the things those men do. I refused. I was beaten and, along with my sick mother and half sister, cast into the frozen streets. We were told we should be grateful for our lives. The cold was too much. My mother died in my arms."

"We all have a story, Faruq. But does that mean you disagree with his religious beliefs and his agenda?"

"My god's message is one of peace and unity. Do you think what Kapka did to my family, his own people, reflects that message?"

"I guess not, no."

"He has manipulated my people through fear, bribery, and the worst types of deception. Many stay silent for fear of retaliation against their families if they speak out. Others are confused, brainwashed into believing that the murder of unbelievers in the

160

name of our god is honorable."

"I see."

"Okay, now it is my turn," Faruq says.

"Oh."

"Yes. My turn to ask you something."

I don't like this reversal, but it's only fair. "Okay, Faruq. What do you want to know?"

The trader's cart approaches, and we step off the path to let them pass.

"Why do you hate us so?"

"Isn't it obvious?"

"For most Logosians, yes. But for you, it's personal. You said what you experienced wasn't great or merciful. Explain it to me."

I don't want to talk about this. "Some other time, okay?"

"No. I answered your question. You should do the same for me." Faruq stares expectantly.

A moment passes, the bitter wind biting through my clothes. "You want to know why? Here it is. It was evening, and I was on my way to meet my mother in the markets of Zopat." My chest is tight, and I'm unable to hold his gaze. "Mother always said to stick to the crowded streets. I decided to take a shortcut through an alleyway. It was a game. I was racing my brother. It was stupid, but I ... I was just a girl—like your sister."

Faruq shifts uncomfortably.

"I was surrounded by a group of savag—uh ... men. They were Musuls." I've never said this to anyone. Why this man? Why now? I can't stop my hands from shaking. "They cut my face." I motion to my scar. "And um ... they, uh ... they ..."

"It's okay. That's enough." Faruq holds up his hand.

"No, it's not okay. I need to say it. They dragged me into an abandoned building and raped me. They took advantage of a child who couldn't fight back." The words stick in my throat. "After that, I guess ... I wasn't sure how I could ever be a whole person again."

Faruq stands in silence, head bowed, eyes closed. The traveler's cart with its piles of silks and wares passes us and continues on its way.

"The teachings of Yeos say I should forgive them ..." Zevry would tell me to forgive them.

"But you can't. I understand."

"I'm trying, okay?" I let out a loaded sigh and flick the hair from my face. "This is a part of me."

Faruq nods and graciously says nothing, turning back toward the path.

The awkward silence doesn't last. Ragged sounds like wounded animals trapped in the metal teeth of a snare pierce the air. A mass of Rippers rises from behind a rocky outcropping and descends upon the nearby trader's caravan.

Faruq shoves me from the path and drags me to the ground. "Be silent," he whispers.

We watch as the maddened Rippers surround the caravan, flooding the road, howling and yelping and swinging their primitive weapons fashioned from scrap and junk. The security contingent is paralyzed with fear, and one by one they're viciously murdered. An antique single-shot rifle pops and echoes across the frozen landscape, sending one Ripper to the ground. The trigger man, the last surviving member of the security contingent, tries to fight them off with his now-empty rifle. He has no time to reload. In moments, he's overwhelmed and speared through the chest. Another Ripper cleaves the man's head from his body with what I can describe only as an old pirate cutlass. Pulling it free, the Ripper hoots and parades the gore-covered head for the others to see.

For a while, they scavenge—stealing everything they can lay hands on from the cart—fighting over every little perceived valuable. Then they start to eat, pulling on the uncooked flesh of their victims with their bare teeth. Above, on the rocky outcropping, a large Ripper stands watching over the group. He howls, and all movement stops. The chieftain grunts and motions with a heavy spear, prompting the Rippers one by one to come forward and leave something at his feet—a portion of their spoils, a trinket, a hunk of meat. When they're finished, he screams again and thrusts his spear into the air. The rest of the Rippers erupt into a squall of screaming and yelping and jumping.

They were people like us once, criminals maybe, but people nonetheless. Before they were cast out into the Vapid. Forced to live like animals, to kill or be killed. My eyes widen at the unbridled carnage. The horror stories about them are real.

Faruq nudges me sharply in the ribs, and I follow his lead, slinking away from the road. They won't be preoccupied forever, and if we're seen, we'll undoubtedly share the same fate as those unfortunate travelers. Easing back down the slope, Faruq and I exchange worried glances as we slip out of sight. I'd like to keep my head on my shoulders for just a while longer.

CHAPTER TWENTY-THREE

DEMITRI

The VTV clangs onto the self-made platform. I grab Husniya and fling the door open. The bright light of day is caustic, and a cold, high-altitude wind whips by. I'm not wearing my hazmat suit, and Husniya doesn't have one. A slap of the lever and the door quickly shunts closed.

"I need to change. And how are we going to get you up there?"

She just smiles and shrugs.

"Maybe I don't have to." I just need her DNA. "Can I have some of your hair?"

"My hair?"

"Yes, I want you to stay here. You'll be safe. I'll go to the med lab and run the tests. Then I'll come back with food and water and some warm clothing for you. And maybe something to sleep on."

"Like a fort."

I crouch down to her height and move the straggle of hair from her face. With a quick jerk, I pull out a few strands—enough for a good sample. The child winces, but a quick kiss on the forehead makes her giggle. "Absolutely. We'll build you a fort. But for now, don't touch anything, okay? Just stay warm in here. I'll be a couple of hours, but I'll be back."

"Okay, Margarida will keep me company."

"Good girl."

Minutes later, I'm back in slacks and a polo-necked pullover,

164

enveloped in the hazmat suit. It's claustrophobic. Old Norilsk felt free. No time for this, Demitri. I climb the rope ladder to the top of the platform. The same frigid wind lashes out, but nothing is going to stop me. Won't be Ax'd if I'm cured. And the Leader won't initiate any plan if he doesn't have the ability to use me to figure out multiple dimensions. Evgeniy was right. I can fix everything.

* * *

It's the middle of the day, and thankfully everyone who will commute has done so. I scurry from lillipad to lillipad, hopping on and off the cable cars unseen. Our isolation works to my advantage here. No one bothers me.

Lillipad Two. Almost home. I quicken my step and pound across the tarmac to the apartment Pistil. A quick read of my retina using the internal scanner embedded in the hazmat helmet, and I'm inside airlock one. A quick pressurization cycle, then the light flicks to green and the inner door pops open.

It doesn't take long to make it to the apartment. More scanning, more identification. More locks and rules and barriers. But finally, I'm home—though it's just a collection of rooms, like any other apartment here in New Etyom. No individuality. No personality. No … life. Would I rather be down there in the dirt, living hand to mouth? Fighting for my life every day? No, of course not. And yet, as I run my fingers along the vacuum-formed plastic chair in the open-space apartment, it feels decidedly cold and inhuman. Enough of this. What am I here for? Food. Food and clothes and blankets for Husniya.

I sweep through the kitchen and pull as much as possible from the refrigeration unit—a few pieces of fruit, some rice and barley, and some protein and carbohydrate packs for food printing. It's not tasty, but it'll do. I stuff these, along with some bed sheets and a random assortment of clothes, into the duffel bag at the foot of my bed. I sling it over my shoulder and spin on my heel to march out the door. But then, my beloved books catch my eye. Bound in old leather, hues of red, brown, and blue, they offer the only warmth in the room.

Gold lettering, broken and peeling, spells out my favorite titles: *The War of the Worlds, Twenty Thousand Leagues Under the Sea, Children of the Fifth Sun, Into the Dark of the Day, Looking Backward*—and then, this one. I slide it out and rub the cover. Forgot I had this one. A smile spreads across my lips, and I slip it into the bag.

Vedmak's consciousness scratches at my brain again. *Shouldn't you be running, stupid kozel? You're going to get us both Ax'd.*

He's right. Need to get out of here. I grab the last few items, cram them into the bag, and run to the door, pulling on my helmet. Two pressure doors later, and once again I'm storming across the lillipad toward the cable car. Got to get to the med lab on Eight.

The cable car swings in the wind, which has now picked up a bit. The steel groans and squeals as the car sways. The inside of my helmet feels more claustrophobic than ever, the air thick and the inner lining too close to my skin. I yearn to yank it off and just suck in the crisp air up here, but there is little to breathe, and I'd die pretty quickly—and for once in my life, I don't want to die. For once, there is hope I can be free.

Vedmak cackles. *Free like your new dirty Robust friend?*

"Mila?"

Yes, that ugly little goblin who almost got us killed.

Mila. Is she okay? Did she escape? Where would she have gone? She said something about another enclave. Logos? Was that it? Maybe that's where she's from? I left her. Abandoned her, after she saved me from the Creed.

Because you're a coward.

"Oh, now you want me to have gone with her? You contradict yourself, Vedmak. You just like insulting me. But you'll soon be gone. I'll soon know how I'm talking to you. And then, I can shut you up."

The cable car clangs into its dock, and the doors slide open. Standing on the platform is another person. Identical in height and build, he or she is concealed behind an ink-black visor, causing my fishbowl reflection to stare back at me. My heart stops, and my larynx grows tight. Nikolaj?

Push him off. Vedmak shrieks.

"Good day," a male voice says over my headset. It's not Nikolaj.

"Uh, good morning."

"Getting off?"

"Yes."

"Okay ..."

What's he waiting for? Oh, sard, I need to get off. I shuffle off and even more awkwardly gesture for him to get on. He must be frowning inside his helmet.

Well done, idiot.

"You could have helped me."

To teach a fool is the same as teaching a dead man. And unless you get us out of here, we will both be dead.

"I don't have time to bother with your riddles. We need to get to the lab, and then back to Husniya."

And what will you do with the rodent, hmm? You haven't thought that far ahead, have you? Help her find her filthy family? You think you can be away that long and no one will notice? You think no one has noticed already? Kozel.

"I haven't got time to think. I'll explain everything to the

Leader once I have proof. He'll have to see sense. There has to be another way. If we're coded after death anyway, he doesn't need to create a black hole or wipe out the Robusts."

I storm into the airlock to leave and head for Pistil Eight.

* * *

It's much busier in here in Pistil Eight. People hustle and bustle, shuffling through the great expanse of the foyer, chattering away about who knows what. I step inside and cautiously make my way through the crowd, my bag over one shoulder and helmet wedged under one arm.

Everyone else is already out of their hazmat suits, the morning commute over for most people hours ago. I enter the elevator with two other Graciles, a man and a woman. They offer a brief acknowledgment.

"Floor?" the woman asks.

"Oh, um, med lab, please."

"Med lab," the elevator's computer replies.

"Hydroponics," the man says.

The elevator lifts smoothly upward and then slides effortlessly to a halt—my floor. I offer another fake smile and squeeze between the other passengers out into the corridor. They give me a quizzical stare as the doors close, and then they're gone.

I shuffle through the darkened embryo library, fixing my eyes to the floor, watching my feet take long strides: left, right, left, right. Don't look up. Don't look at the fetuses. The pink haze of light reflecting their tiny little bodies colors the floor, lighting my way through to the lab at the opposite end. The EYE whirs above me, making another round. I quicken my step and duck into the archway. Another press of my thumb and I'm granted entry.

In contrast to the embryo room, the lab is stark white. With no need for staff most of the time, it's small, less than fifteen square meters, with a cluster of four monitors and a deep DNA bioscanner at its center.

I grab a chair and slide up to a monitor. "Request biomedical comparison."

"State nature of the comparison," replies the computer voice in its usual female tone.

"Search for similar genes coding for protein structures in the brain, using two samples. Then compare against genetic database. Isolate proteins shared by both samples, but unique from ninety-five percent of subjects in database."

"Confirmed. Insert samples into bioscanner tray."

A small white plastic drawer slides out from under the monitor. I pull off my gloves to retrieve Husniya's hair. The large *Z* carved into the back of my right hand catches me off guard. The gnarled skin is already pink; even without nanobots, my enhanced genetics repair the damage faster than a Robust's. It still looks a mess. I fumble around in my outer pocket. The few strands of hair are still there. Delicately I place them in the tray, then pull a few eyelashes from my right eye and sprinkle them in with Husniya's hair.

"Begin analysis."

The tray whirs closed, and the computer silently begins its work. I tap on the table nervously. My foot won't stop jiggling.

"Fourteen genes unique to samples have been identified," the computer says.

"Display."

Husniya's and my DNA codes are laid out side by side, with specific genes highlighted as similar to each other and unique from the database. The little girl's genome is imperceptibly different from my own. Despite all of our honing and tweaking at the molecular level, our DNA is almost indistinguishable.

How poetic. Not feeling so superior, pathetic whelp?

"I never felt superior in the first place."

Using the touch screen, I zoom in on each group of bases—a gene coding for a unique protein. Most seem benign, identified as a co-transporter or enzyme of relative unimportance. But then there's this one. A protein in the right parahippocampal gyrus. The computer doesn't know what it does. Husniya and I both have it. The signature is homozygous recessive; two nondominant genes are required. I can understand Husniya, but how did I end up with this? Perhaps the fact it has no known function, detrimental or otherwise, means the EYE missed it. I lived because a single protein went unnoticed by a machine designed to notice it. Mila might call that a miracle.

CHAPTER TWENTY-FOUR

MILA

The enclave guard in the poufy colorful uniform and floppy hat checks my hand. "Logosian," he says, then pats me down for weapons. "What is your purpose in Fiori?"

"Business."

"Three-day pass. Keep it with you at all times."

"Thank you."

I step through the enormous gate decorated with colorful banners, then wait as the guard interacts with Faruq.

"Baqirian." The guard looks long and hard at Faruq, whose face remains expressionless. "Where did you come from?"

"Baqir."

"Why?"

Faruq raises his eyebrows. "That's where I was born."

"What brings you to Fiori?"

"Business."

The guard levels a suspicious gaze at him. "What sort of business?"

"A delivery."

"What sort of delivery?"

Faruq, still calm, flicks a glance at me.

I've had about enough of this.

"Where are you taking it?" presses the guard. "How long do you plan to stay here?"

"Look, he's with me, okay? Can we get going, please?"

The guard gawks at me with his mouth open, then looks back to Faruq. "This is true?"

Faruq nods. "Yes."

"You and the Logosian are traveling … *together?*"

I roll my eyes. *"Yes."*

His mouth hangs open as he spins and yells to another guard in Fiorian. *"Superio Succicci. Avemu una minaccia. Veni più di ccà e di succorsu."*

Another guard, a supervisor with gold bars sewn onto the shoulder of his tunic, approaches with a brisk step, chattering away to our guard. *"Cosa hè u prublema?"*

"St'omu, iddu veni'n viaggiu cu idda," our guard stammers, pointing first at Faruq and then me.

Now it's the supervisor's turn to look dumbfounded. He turns back and forth, dramatically yammering in Fiorian before locking on me. "It is true? This man is … *yours?*"

My cheeks are burning. "No, I … Yes, he's with me but we're not …" Sard. "It's not like that. He's my friend." What am I, twelve?

The guards laugh out loud. Faruq has a small but amused smile on his face.

My embarrassment quickly turns to irritation. "Are you two finished? He's not a threat, and he's with me. Any other stupid questions?"

The guards just laugh. *"Unu momentu, Madama."* They give Faruq a thorough pat down.

Breathe through it, Mila. I need to know where the Forgotten Jewel is, but I'm not asking these jackbags. Arms folded, I wait, restlessly tapping my foot until they release him into Fiori with a three-day pass like mine.

Faruq gives me a sly grin as he approaches. He's not upset in the least.

"Is it always like this for you? I'm not sure I could put up with it."

"You almost didn't." Faruq stifles a chuckle.

"I know." It's hard not to smile back.

"The guards are doing their job. It can be frustrating, but I understand the reason for it. If one spider bites you, you assume the next one has teeth, correct?"

Faruq's common sense causes the tension to bleed from my shoulders. "Yeah, you do."

"Hey." He bumps my arm. "At least they let us both in. You would not be allowed in my enclave."

"Nor you in mine." I give a laugh. This man is full of surprises.

Fiori is like another world. I've been here several times, and it never ceases to impress. Yes, it's still freezing cold, and yes, it's still in the shadow of the lillipads, but there's something about it, something intoxicating. All around us buildings crafted of carved stone and mortar stand like fortresses. The music of stringed instruments hovers in the air. Rippling colored silk awnings and tents line the heart of a great marketplace that's filled with the din of a bustling crowd. A woman begs from a street corner. Dingy miners pass on their way back to work, grumbling about another grueling double shift. Children with worn but colorful clothes run this way and that between the stalls. Vendors call out for us to sample their wares. It reminds me of Logos—only more vibrant. This is what the great cities of the old world must have felt like, before the war.

Faruq walks unnoticed and unchallenged. There are other Musuls here in the market, buying or selling their goods—able to live and raise their families in this place, free from Kapka's oppression.

"I'm going to ask them about Husniya," Faruq says.

"Sure."

He shuffles off into the crowd.

I approach a bread vendor and muster my best, broken Fiorian. *"Ve sete scurdat de* Jewel*?"*

The woman wordlessly shakes her head and motions me out of her way. Not sure if I said that right or if she simply doesn't know. Moving farther into the marketplace, I stop a short, thin man peddling krig. *"Ve sete scurdat de* Jewel*?"*

His face lights up. *"Iè. You desideri di u* Jewel*? Hè induve tutti i minatori andà. Attenti à sè per ghjè—"*

I understand *yes* and *Jewel*.

He smiles, broad yellowed teeth jutting in all directions, and points toward the mines. Gil said the Forgotten Jewel was a sloop dive. Of course it would be close to the mines.

I mumble a thank you in Fiorian and push on through the crowd.

The little vendor jumps up and down, waving his arms and shouting, *"Stai attentu. Un hè micca un postu sicuru unni doppu scura."*

A warning?

Faruq approaches from a throng of Musul vendors.

"Nothing?"

He shakes his head. "I have to find her. She's resourceful, but we've never been apart this long before. Besides, she's … special."

"How so?"

"She speaks to herself. Says she can hear a voice. She can be fragile."

A voice? Demitri—he had a voice in his head, too. I pat Faruq on the shoulder. "Get your head up. We'll find her."

As we make our way out of the heavy crowds of the market and toward the mines, the landscape changes. Simpler dwellings, crafted from stone or brick, line the roads, now just a slurry of mud and ice. The bulk of these people don't live differently than Logosians. Fiori is just as poor as the rest of us—they just hide it a little better with silks and music.

The sun moves low in the sky, occasionally peering through the clouds to give our gray world a hint of orange. The stone dwellings turn to shacks, and the roads fade into muddy fields. The entrance to one of the largest mines in Etyom is ahead. The tunnels below are supposed to run deep and even connect with mines in other enclaves—if you know the way.

Faruq bumps my arm. The Forgotten Jewel stands in a lonely corner of the mucky field. Its ramshackle exterior is filthy. Rough, mud-covered men move in and out in a constant stream, trailed by an awful grinding music that spills out every time the door swings open. We're going to stand out.

We slog our way through the field toward the old saloon and are about to climb the two or three steps to the door when a shadowy figure steps into our path.

"Ecco bella I pò interessu vo a signura?"

Faruq and I glance at each other and shrug.

"Oh, eh … something can I have to interest you? Yes?" The scruffy man opens his jacket to reveal several stim cocktails in syringes. "Make very nice for love." He winks.

"Sard off, or I'll force-feed you that garbage and watch you embarrass yourself further."

Grumbling, the man curses me and slinks back to the shadows.

At the entrance to the Forgotten Jewel, a large, dark-skinned Kahangan doorman stands ready for us, arms folded across his chest. There's no doubt he's on Swole or some other muscle-enhancing stim.

"You two look lost." He laughs.

"I'm here to see Lemmy."

The doorman sobers. "There's no Lemmy here. Best be on your way, kids."

I'm in no mood for this. "I'm glad you think you're cute. I'm here to meet with Lemmy. You're going to pretend there's no Lemmy because that's what you've been told to do, and you're scared you're too stupid to do anything but play it straight. Sound about right so far? Let's skip the games and get on with it. I'm expected, and I don't want to have to hurt your feelings, big boy."

The doorman steps closer, his fists already balled. A chuckle from within the doorway stops the Kahangan. From behind the stout bouncer comes a little man with wire-framed spectacles and a devilish grin on his face. "I think she just called you stupid, Mos."

The Kahangan is furious. "I'll pull her arms off."

"Not just yet," he says with a smirk.

"Yuri?"

"The one and only. You're late ... again."

"You're alive."

"In that way, I'm a bit like a cockroach—just one not so easily stamped on. But you, Mila, you have broken our deal twice and now arrive here with a Musul in tow. What are we to think?"

"Fine. I broke the deal. But you saw what happened at the meet. The Creed destroyed my home—I've been running for my life."

"I'm sorry for your home. But you seem to have a lot of excuses, I'm afraid. You broke the agreement. You could have accessed or sold the information a hundred times by now. It was a mistake doing business with you. You were supposed to be a professional."

"Hold on a second, Yuri. Now you're just insulting me. Between the Creed vaporizing everyone, Kapka's thugs detonating themselves everywhere, and now your people, I can't take a step without someone trying to kill me. This isn't what I'm used to."

"Not my problem."

My skin prickles hot. "Yeah, I can see that. And what about you, Yuri? You had me pick up a package to deliver here because it was too dangerous for you to do yourself—and yet here you are. Why not just deliver it yourself? This doesn't add up."

"So many questions, Mila. But questions do not always have easy answers," Yuri says, clearly relishing his secrets.

"Okay. Thanks for the non-answer."

"Where is it, Mila?" He cocks his head.

"In my sling bag."

"Did you access it, Mila?" Yuri locks me down with a steely gaze.

Lying here could be bad for me, but telling the truth—that I allowed a Gracile, of all people, to access it—will get me skinned alive and hung on the outer wall. "Of course not. What happens now?"

Yuri sighs and puts his hands on his hips. "You brought the data. Better late than never—but you really shouldn't have involved him." He flicks his head at Faruq.

"What are you trying to say, Yuri?"

"I'm saying you will not like what happens next."

Before I can think of anything witty, someone yanks a bag over my head. The doorman's gut punch knocks the wind out of me, my legs buckle, and I slump to the ground. I'm pulled back up and slung over the doorman's broad shoulders. My legs lash out, striking nothing. In the distance, I hear Faruq's muffled groans as men drag him away. Why do I always have to learn the hard way?

* * *

After a short walk and a long descent down an echoing stairwell, I'm unceremoniously plonked down in a freezing metal chair. The

Kahangan moves behind me and secures my arms to the chair with his bare hands, meaty fingers clamping down above my wrists. I'm not going anywhere for now. The bag is snatched from my head. I flick my hair from my face. That's too many bags over my head in the last forty-eight hours.

The air hangs thick and musty, dripping with moisture like the inside of a cave. No, not a cave—a mine. A single candle hangs in a lantern above, casting a funnel of light over my head. The rest of the room and the figures in it lie in shadow, only the tips of a few muddy boots or the outline of a person's face peering out of the dark.

"What's the holdup? I came all this way to try to find someone reasonable, and this is how I'm treated? You're going to bring me down in this mine and do what? Let me talk to Lemmy already."

"There is no Lemmy," a man says from the shadows.

"Then why did I waste my time coming here to talk to—"

"Foolish girl. *I need to speak to Lemmy* is just a phrase used to tell us why you're here."

"Oh … right." Good job, dummy.

"The data stick is fried," the voice says.

"No. You're just too stupid to activate it. The stick is fine."

"The stick. Is. Fried." From the shadows the data package, now outside its lead capsule, lands in front of me. It's attached to my PED, the plugged-in holo-screen fizzing in a wash of static. "There's no accessing this information anymore. What did you do to it?"

A tingle of fear slides across my skin. This really could get me killed. "I didn't do anything."

"You didn't access the package?"

"Look, it was functional, okay?"

"Did you activate an EMP around it?"

"Yes, when we fled the Creed, but the packet was encased in

lead, and it was working afterward when—"

"How do you know it was working if you didn't access it?"

"We—"

"Who's we?"

My mouth is sticky and dry. "I had to know what was so important—why the Creed wanted me dead for it. Let me talk to Yuri."

"Yuri is busy. I'm in charge of this group. You deal with me now."

"Okay?" The doorman's hands squeeze tighter around me.

"Who else knows what was in the data package?"

"Nobod—"

"*Who else.*" The room echoes with the words.

The truth will get me killed. There's no good way to spin the fact that I got a Gracile to access secret information. If Demitri is against us, then the Leader's plans have likely been accelerated. If he is somehow with us and still alive, then I have to find him. He's now the only one who knows exactly what was in the packet. Gotta stall for time.

"I'm going to ask you one more time," the voice whispers menacingly.

A short man with thin eyes steps into the light, brandishing a kukri blade.

The voice continues. "If we don't like the answer, then my friend here is going to cut you into chunks and throw your parts down a shaft, like we did with that Musul you stupidly brought with you. He cried like a woman when we cut his throat—"

With a practiced twist of my shoulders, I slip the doorman's grip. Spinning to his outside, my boot catches him across the chin. He stumbles, falling into the shadows. The others come for me.

"You … murderers." I punch one across the jaw, following the strike with a low kick that buckles his legs. Then I take the fight to the next one, and the next, working my way through them. "You killed my friend. *For what?*" Thick arms encircle my neck and lock down. I cough, sputtering and slapping at the muscly chokehold. "He came here to help and you … you … gahhhh." The pressure releases, but the arm around my neck continues to hold firm.

"Very good," the voice says into my ear.

That voice. I know it.

"You have done well to get this far, young *krogulec*. This is why we need you. Let her up."

The arms relent, and from the dark, a familiar face appears.

"Bil?"

He extends his hand.

I swipe it away. "Are you trying to kill me? You scared me to death." I rise on shaking legs and crash into him, squeezing with all I have. "Bilgi. I can't believe it. I thought you were dead. You were in Logos when … I'm so confused."

"I heard of what the Creed did in Logos. It's shameful. They were after you."

"I *know*. Why do you think I came here?"

"I'm sorry to have scared you like this, girl. You've been through a lot." He squeezes me quickly, then pulls from my embrace and grabs my shoulders. "We're alive and undiminished; that's what matters now."

"Faruq?"

"Your friend is okay. We didn't harm him."

I shake my head, pulling away. "But I don't understand. You're with the resistance?"

"I am."

"Why all this deception?"

The large Kahangan doorman shuffles up, rubbing his jaw. Bilgi glances at him then back to me.

"We had to know you were serious. We had to know the data

wasn't in the wrong hands. This mission is that important, Mila."

"Oh, the data has been in the wrong hands all right—mine. Yuri had it, and he's here now. Why involve me? The last forty-eight hours have been a trip through hell."

"I'm afraid it's not over yet. Yuri's cover was burned. The Creed were tracking him when they hit the drop point. He never would have made it here. We had to hand the information off to someone who could get it to this location, despite being tracked by Creed. I hated to involve you, but I knew there was no one better."

"Well, it's obvious the Creed want this information, and they want us dead for having it. But how do you know how serious this is if you haven't seen the information yet?"

"I trust my source inside the Gracile network. All he could tell us was the data outlined some sort of existential threat, one we had to see to believe. But now it's destroyed. That's why we need you. You've seen it."

"Well—"

"How bad is it, Mila? Tell us."

"I don't fully understand it—something about creating a black hole with a doomsday device. The Graciles want to live forever, and they're willing to kill everyone else to try. To make it worse, the Leader has employed Kapka and his goons to keep you from finding out. That's why I came."

Bilgi's expression is a mask of stone. "Join us. The Gracile oppressor and his plan must be stopped."

"You know what this means, right? This will mean war with the Creed and a large segment of fanatical Musuls. Are you sure that's what you want?"

My mentor lowers his head and levels a hard gaze at me. "So sure of it we will sacrifice every life we have to stop them."

CHAPTER TWENTY-FIVE

DEMITRI

"Hi, Mitya."

"Oksana?" I didn't even hear her enter. "Where did you come from? And don't call me that, I do hate it."

She's taken aback, but she smooths down her beautiful hair and smiles. "Demitri, where have you been? Everyone's so worried."

"They are? Everyone who?"

"Me. Nikolaj. The Leader," she replies.

"The Leader? I doubt that. But I do need to speak with him."

"Talk to me, Demitri." She takes a step closer and offers an even softer look. "Tell me what's going on with you."

"For the first time, good things, 'Sana. Good things. I—" Something doesn't add up. "How did you know I was in here?"

"I ... I uh ...," she stutters.

I stand and use my full height to seem as imposing as possible. "What's going on, 'Sana?"

The door hisses open and four men step in. Two Creed, my brother, Nikolaj, and the Leader. The Creed stand there, as the Creed do, expressionless and unemotional, clutching their energy rifles. Nikolaj says nothing, glowering at me from behind our Leader, his stare a mixture of frustration and concern.

"Well, we have been busy, haven't we, Demitri?" the Leader says. Strangely, he's wearing his nasal rebreather. He holds an awkward stance, his limbs stiff—coiled as if ready to launch if provoked.

"I have, that is true. But for good reason."

"What reason could be good enough you would soil yourself by going down into that Robust cesspool, then coming back and risking infecting us all?"

"We're immune to the plague, we know this. But our obsession with it clouds our judgment. You wear your rebreather even up here in the clouds."

The Leader holds my gaze. I haven't answered his question.

"Sir, my Leader, I thought I was sick, and I needed medicine that I could only get from Lower Etyom. I was afraid of being Ax'd. But I'm not sick."

We're going to die, stupid kozel—and for what?

"Not now, Vedmak."

"You see, he's doing it again." Nikolaj shakes his head. "I can't babysit you forever, Mitya."

"Demitri. My *name* is Demitri, dammit."

The Leader raises his hands, his face still calm. "Demitri, who is this Vedmak?"

"A voice. A man long since dead, but his quantum information was kept intact. He's somewhere … else. But you, you know this, don't you? You've known for years. Is that why you kept me close? Why you took me and Nikolaj under your wing? Were you just going to use me?"

"What is he talking about?" Nikolaj looks to the Leader.

The Leader narrows his eyes. "Demitri, I don't know what you mean. Why would I have been using you? Are you so special?"

"You know why. You let me think I was schizophrenic, or had some kind of split personality. You let him torture me for years. But you knew."

"You're schizophrenic?" my brother whispers.

"No, I'm not. I can talk to people in other dimensions."

Oh, now you don't look like a crazy idiot. Are you happy? Are you trying to get us Ax'd?

"Shut up, Vedmak." I pace back and forth, staring at the floor. "You want to preserve our kind, on the event horizon of a black hole. You've been using Nikolaj and me to research the possibilities of creating it—but you knew the standard model of physics wouldn't allow it. You had to prove exotic physics. You had to prove multiple dimensions. You *knew* I was talking to someone who had died and was coded somehow in another dimension. You wanted to know how it happened—*I* was the key."

Nikolaj and Oksana just gawk.

"You believe you can talk to someone in another dimension?" The Leader's gaze is locked on me.

"I don't *believe* it. It's true. I found it, a protein in my brain, something that would allow quantum entanglement." I wave my hand at the monitor, the DNA code displayed on it, the genes highlighted. "I can hear a specific voice. But I met someone else who can hear a voice, too. I'm not crazy."

The Leader is silent for a long beat, but eventually he clears his throat. "Demitri, my boy, I believe you are unwell. We need to get you to the infirmary and see what can be done."

"Like you did with Evgeniy?"

Get ready to fight, little puppet. This isn't going to end well.

"Evgeniy's wounds weren't bad, but you Ax'd him anyway. I don't need to be Ax'd. I'm not sick."

"Mitya." Nikolaj holds up his hands. "You think the Leader wants to code us all onto an anomaly in space-time. You gotta admit—"

"I don't think—I've seen the plan. On a data stick. That's why *he* had Evgeniy killed. Evgeniy knew." I turn to face the Leader. "*You* blew up the lillipad, to make us think it was the Robusts. To keep us occupied. But Evgeniy sent me to look for it, before you killed him."

The Leader's eyes flare. "I think we have all had enough of this theater, young Demitri." He nods to the Creed, who step forward.

With one hand, I grab Oksana by the throat, spin her to face them, and trap her in a choke hold. She gags and squirms under my grip.

Vedmak sneers. *You're learning well.*

"Let her go, Demitri." The Leader's tone is soft and condescending, as if he's talking to a child.

"Why? So you can Ax me? I'm not sick. Why won't you listen to me?"

"Mitya, do you hear yourself? You're not making sense," Nikolaj pleads.

I ignore him, focusing on the Leader. "Mila was right. You don't want peace. You only want the future you've decided for us. And for them. Wiping everyone out so only we are coded. You're a monster."

"I'm afraid the only monster here is you. Well, you and perhaps the one you brought with you—and I'm not talking about your imaginary friend." The Leader nods once more, and the doors behind him slide open. Another Creed soldier rushes into the room gripping a squirming Husniya, dirty and half dressed, her dark hair strewn about her face.

The Leader glances sideways at the child and touches the rebreather under his nose before shifting back to me. "Your return to New Etyom was quite clumsy, young Demitri. You showed up on radar easily. Did you not think we would find the VTV, or your little Robust pet?"

Husniya sobs and tries to wriggle free from the grip of the Creed. The geminoid drags her to the front, between me and the Leader. My own grip on Oksana tightens, and her struggling grows

185

more urgent.

"She's just a little girl. She hasn't done anything to you. Let her go."

"And what? Let her live up here with us?" The Leader flares his nostrils, feigning the detection of an awful stench coming from the girl. "I think not." He presses the rebreather firmly into place.

"I'll take her back myself. Just leave her alone."

The Leader shakes his head. "No, you won't. She'll receive an honorable death, which is more than she deserves. And you will be confined to the infirmary."

Husniya will be Ax'd. I'll be Ax'd. Everyone will die. The Leader isn't listening. He's made up his mind. No one will believe me. I stare into the eyes of my neo-brother, willing him to feel my pain, hoping against hope somewhere deep inside he remembers the bond we once shared.

Perhaps he heard me. Perhaps Mila's god heard me. Whatever the reason, Nikolaj nods an acknowledgement of my silent plea and tightens his lips: *be ready.* He lunges forward and yanks down on two of the Creed's ballistic helmets. While the geminoids don't budge, they are temporarily blinded.

I shove a gasping Oksana free and into the arms of the Leader. Then, using her body as a shield, I snatch up my bag. Grabbing Husniya by the hand, I deliver a pressing kick to the chest of the Creed by her side. It flies backward, crashing into one of the other geminoids and narrowly missing Nikolaj. We slam through the sliding door, my sheer force bending it inward. The collision spins us a little, enough to catch a glimpse of the Leader, who seems unconcerned with my attempt at escape. He paws at the glowing image of my DNA code on the screen.

I scoop Husniya up onto my shoulder and tear across the gangway. There's no time to wait for the elevator. Over the railings we go, slamming into the outer wall of the elevator shaft. It's smooth, so we slide uncontrollably toward the ground.

Friction burns the skin on my hands, and my blood leaves a crimson streak down the otherwise impeccably white wall. We crash to the floor below, and I cover Husniya's head with my chest and arms. The slap of my back hitting the ground reverberates around the foyer, stopping everyone in their tracks.

Run, you coward. Run!

Wheezing, I'm already on my feet. Husniya clings to my chest, her tiny legs and arms wrapped around my body. I look around, frantic. "Where do we go? We're eight kilometers up."

"What about that?" Husniya squeaks.

It's just the airlock. "What about what?"

"The big ship, outside," she says.

Through the frosted glass of the Pistil is the mottled image of a Creed gunship sitting on the lillipad. Probably the one they were going to take me away in. I pull her tight to me and hold her head close to my neck. "Hold your breath, little one, okay? For as long as you can."

She readjusts herself on my chest and holds on even tighter.

A Creed soldier crashes feet-first right in front of us. But before it can grab either of us, I'm gone. Mila taught me this trick. Screaming long and loud, I charge with my head down at the window, and at the last second, use my free shoulder as a ram. The window squeals, cracks, and finally shatters. We slam into the tarmac of the lillipad, glass splinters puncturing my back. Mercifully Husniya appears to have only minor scratches.

Through the gaping hole in the Pistil, the Creed stomps toward us.

With Husniya stuck to my chest, I scramble to my feet and streak across the tarmac. The icy wind burns my cheeks; tears stream from the corners of my eyes and across my temples. The atmosphere is thin. Can't take a breath or it will all be over.

We careen into the side of the gunship, and I pound on the outer door-release button. It sounds an acknowledgement, and the door begins to open. At a creep, it folds downward to form a ramp. My lungs burn, and I clamber inside before the door fully opens. My skull clangs into the bulkhead. Sarding bastard. I thump the "Close" lever, and the ramp starts to lift again. A Creed careens into the side of the vehicle and shoves one robotic arm through the gap.

Damn lifeless creatures.

It's unclear if Vedmak makes me do it, or if I think of it myself, but my right foot stamps down on the geminoid's arm—it easily comes free at the elbow. The door squeals shut and locks with a clunk.

Oxygen-rich air whooshes into the cab. Placing a gasping Husniya on the floor of the cargo hold, I rush to the cockpit and leap into the pilot's seat. The dash is full of switches, panels, and screens with displays, none of it familiar except one button: autopilot. I slam my fist down on it, and the ships engines whine to life. We begin to lift from the platform.

Through the tinted panoramic glass of the cockpit, I spy the Leader marching Nikolaj across the lillipad. Both are wearing a nasal rebreather, but Nikolaj's gait isn't confident. In fact, he's limping.

The gunship begins to turn slowly away, but Nikolaj locks his gaze with mine and offers a brotherly smile, like he did when I was in trouble but he took the rap.

In the Leader's hand is an energy weapon. His face devoid of emotion, he lifts the small metallic plasma pistol, aims it at the back of Nikolaj's head, and pulls the trigger. There's an electric-blue flash, and my brother's body slumps lifelessly to the tarmac.

I know I'm screaming. I can feel my vocal cords straining and the veins in my neck bulging. Tears stream down my face. But no sound comes.

The Leader has murdered my brother.

I smash the autopilot key again, switching it off so I can take control. The vessel immediately drops. I grab at the control yoke and pull on it—saving the craft from crashing into the lillipad. A blue light on the dash flashes next to a message: *Iso-weapon charged.* Without a second thought, I initiate it, place my index finger over the trigger on the yoke, and squeeze.

The energy weapon buzzes for a split second, then *crack.* A bolt of lightning releases from somewhere under the gunship. It snaps across the lillipad, blackening the tarmac, but the Leader remains unscathed. The gunship sways from left to right as I struggle to fire the weapon and control the roll and pitch. Each time a bolt releases, it strikes the HAP, but the Leader stands defiantly still. The readout on the dash flashes red: *No DNA lock. Weapon recharging.*

I yell through the glass, once more cursing the Leader. Husniya cowers in a cubicle, her hands clamped over her ears, her eyes screwed shut. On the lillipad below, Creed pour out of the hole in the Pistil and target our ship with their energy rifles. Hyperventilating, I yank on the yoke, pulling the ship awkwardly away, then press forward as hard as I can in a nosedive toward the cloud line.

CHAPTER TWENTY-SIX

MILA

The warmth encapsulates me. It feels like home.

"Not yet, Mila. We're not there yet."

"Zev, I have a terrible feeling."

Zevry touches my cheek, dabbing away a tear with his scarf, his eyes twinkling. "Yeos will be with you, my sister. There is nothing for you to fear."

"I'll try to be strong like you, Zev. I'll keep trying."

"You're already stronger than me, Mil. You're stronger than all of us."

Suddenly I'm there, in the midst of a raging battle. I flinch as everything flashes to white. Then, as the darkness advances, the presence of evil, true and terrible, creeps over my skin. I cry out for Yeos to be my shield, but the fear is oppressive, sinking into the pit of my soul. The figure strides forward, his hand outstretched, accusing me without a single word. For the first time, I hear his voice, ancient words spoken through the fire and the flames: *"Menya zovut smert', i ad prikhodit so mnoy."*

With a gasp, I pull from the dream, the wooden bed below me quaking with each shudder of my body. I lie shaking on a tiny cot, my eyes fixed on the ceiling of the dilapidated underground mining station. Breathe, Mila. You're in the resistance headquarters. You're safe. Bilgi must have let me sleep. He knows I've been through the wringer already. But now he'll want to make a plan to

190

stop the Leader, and only Demitri has seen the Leader's plans. I have to tell Bilgi the truth. He needs to know what Demitri knows. That means finding Demitri and hoping he's not the enemy.

Someone knocks on the door.

"Come in."

"You are decent?" Faruq asks from behind the door.

"I'm not sure that's what you'd call me, but sure, I'm decent."

Faruq eases the door open, holding the handle tightly, but doesn't peer around. Such old-world chivalry.

"Come on in, Faruq. I'm dressed."

Cautiously, he steps into the room and quickly surveys the space. He's dressed in old miner's clothes like any regular joe. There's a quiet strength in his demeanor and unwavering conviction. I'm grateful to have him with me.

He brings his hands together and smiles. "How are you feeling?"

"Much better, thank you." I slide to the edge of the cot, finding the cold boots with my toes and slipping them on.

"These friends of yours are interesting," Faruq says.

"They're not my friends, except their head guy, Bilgi. He and I go way back. I guess they're the only people we can trust right now. That's why we're here. Have you been treated fairly?"

"Oh yes. I was given food and a place to rest. They have treated me well, except for that business at first. They questioned me and told me they'd killed you. It was, um …" He looks away.

"Distressing. Yeah, I had a similar experience. I guess it was necessary to make sure we were who we said we were."

"Yes. Well, I'm glad to see you are not dead."

"Thank you, Faruq. I appreciate that." We stare at each other. Okay, that just got awkward fast. "So, uh, how about we check with Bilgi and see how we can get this mess figured out—or if he knows anything about your sister?"

191

"Yes, let's do that," Faruq says, clearly eager to break the uncomfortable silence.

No time for nonsense.

We chitchat as we make our way through the ancient mining complex, occasionally passing a resistance member scurrying off somewhere. The old halogen lamps lighting the hallway flicker, no doubt running on some antiquated generator that could go down at any minute. A murmur of voices greets us as we approach a set of heavy iron doors.

Pushing through, we find ourselves in a bustling room filled with people listening to an old shortwave radio system, making notes and relaying messages. Some of these people appear to be heavily jacked, with implants protruding from their heads and arms or wearing parts of scavenged Creed exo-suits. Bilgi leans over a table, examining a hand-drawn map and talking with a female Robust. He looks up as we approach.

"Mila, Faruq. Good of you to join us. Feeling better after some food and a few hours of sleep?"

"Yes, better." I shrug.

"But there's a lot going on here, and you don't even know where you are." Bilgi flashes a creased smile.

"Right."

"Follow me," Bilgi says, pushing through the heavy doors and out into the flickering light of the musty hallway. We follow as he continues, "Where you just found me was in our intelligence center. All incoming tips and outgoing messages pass through there. Our favorite tool is the old radio system. We have a limited number of portable radios we can use, but the main hub is our crown jewel. Using single sideband frequencies, we have intercepted Creed transmissions. Did you know they still use old-fashioned radio waves to communicate long distance?"

Faruq and I shake our heads.

"Neither did we." He laughs. "We have limited tech and resources, but we make do."

"But you did have the ability to access the data stick I brought?" I ask.

"It's scrambled, but yes, off an enhanced PED we hacked into. It's a little newer than that old junk you carry around."

"It works fine for me." I fold my arms, unable to ignore his jab.

"Right now we're in an abandoned mining station below Fiori. We have a fossil-fuel generator that keeps our power on, access to fresh water from a spring on the north end of the complex, and plenty of space to conduct our operations unnoticed. Mostly we have to steal or scavenge food and medical supplies from Gracile outposts or transports—but we make it a point to not take from our own kind." Bilgi pushes into another room and snaps a heavy switch on the wall. Bright lights flicker and fizz before holding steady. "This is the headquarters of Opor and where I spend most of my time these days." He motions to a table with a few chairs. "Have a seat."

I sit with Faruq. A few others follow us into the room, including Yuri, the broad, dark-skinned Kahangan, a short Zopatian, and a female of unknown origin.

"You don't have a son, do you, Bil?"

"No, I do not, dear Mila. I'm sorry I had to lie about that to maintain my cover. Rest assured everything else you know about me is true." He lets that sink in for a moment before turning his attention to the others in the room. "Let me introduce my captains. I believe you've become acquainted with Mos?" He motions to the Kahangan. "He's my head of security."

"I figured you were Kahangan. I didn't think anyone ever made it out of that enclave alive," I say.

The barrel-chested man nods and crosses his arms. "Most

don't—but then again, I'm not most Kahangans."

"By the looks of you, you must have *eaten* your way out." I open my eyes wide.

The Kahangan glances at Bilgi, who tries unsuccessfully to stifle a laugh. Mos's face softens. "Sorry about the gut punch—sort of." He grins with big white teeth.

"Sorry about your face. Though, hitting it that hard didn't rearrange your looks enough to help, I'm afraid."

Mos gives a good-natured guffaw.

Bilgi smiles. "I think you two will get along just fine. You've met my second, as well. Yuri is as loyal as the best hound, as you will soon see. He's a good fellow, too, once you get past all the secrets."

Yuri bobs his head. "Glad to have you with us, Mila."

"The quiet fellow in the back with the kukri blade is Ghofaun. He runs our reconnaissance missions and trains our people to fight. And the lovely lady next to him is Denni. She handles operations here and balances our tech."

"Nice to meet you both," Denni says.

Faruq nods and gives a small wave of his hand.

"I know you, Mila, but tell us about your friend." Bilgi looks to Faruq.

Faruq beats me to it. "I owe Mila a debt. While passing through Baqir, she saved me and my sister from Kapka's guards."

"And then he returned the favor," I reply. "When I was captured by Kapka's men, he broke me out of Kapka's dungeon."

"I see." Bilgi nods. "But you still owe her a debt?"

"Yes, for the life of my sister. I have become separated from her. She means the world to me."

"Do you know where she is?" Bilgi asks.

"No. The last I heard, she got into a trader's cart to escape Baqir. That is all I know. I came to Fiori to help Mila, but also to ask the locals about my sister."

Bilgi rubs his chin. "Give us her description and I'll send out a message and put my people on the lookout for her. With any luck, we'll scoop her up."

"Oh, thank you, thank you. You don't know what that means to me," Faruq says excitedly. "I am here to help Mila, but if she is with you, then I am at your service."

"How generous of you, Faruq. We will certainly take you up on that."

"You need to know about Kapka," I interrupt.

"Yes." Bilgi nods. "You mentioned they're working together?"

"When I was captured, I saw him meet with the Gracile Leader. They're in league with each other."

"We did receive reports," says Denni, "indicating a Creed ship was sighted arriving and leaving from Baqir during that time."

"It's not good. The Leader made it clear to Kapka he wanted the data package. He was desperate to have it. But he also indicated he was paying Kapka to keep Opor busy. I heard it all while captive."

"All of it makes sense," Bilgi says. "Several hideouts were hit in Zopat just the other day—like they were targeted. We were confused as to how the Musuls—" Bilgi raises his hand toward Faruq. "Apologies. Kapka's men knew to attack there. It was like they had inside information."

"Information only Creed intelligence would likely know," Denni interjects. "Kapka's guys aren't that savvy."

"It's bad if they're working together, or at the very least, we have to fight them both at the same time," I add.

"We'll just have to cross that bridge when we come to it," Bilgi says with a sigh. "It's all right. We're headed in the right direction. Yuri has been overseeing the development of several plans of attack for us." He gives the bespectacled man a nod. "They all involve ways for us to climb or fly above the pillars in order to breach the Gracile stronghold and destroy their Leader. They are all theoretical and full of holes, though, without precise information." He turns to me. "That's where you come in, Mila. I've already issued orders that you are now a part of our command staff. Any call you make, especially in my absence, will be treated by my people as if it came directly from me."

"Hold on, Bil. I didn't ask for this—"

"No. But it is asked of you." His gaze is stern. "You'll not have any problems from my people. Having you in this position is what is best for all of us. We need you, Mila."

Sard. That's disquieting. He's putting so much trust in me. I swallow away a guilty lump. "Bilgi, I have to tell you something first. I lied to you earlier."

Bilgi's eyebrows shoot up. "Oh?"

Everyone in the room grows still. My face is hot, my heart beating faster. "I thought you were going to kill me. I was afraid to tell the truth."

"Out with it, girl."

"I wasn't the only one to access the information. I didn't have the ability to do it on my own. I only know what he told me."

Yuri's face lights up in revelation. "Evgeniy's replacement. You found out about him."

"The informant?" Bilgi looks to Yuri.

"The informant was dead, but he sent us another. One who was sympathetic to our cause. His name was Demitri."

Bilgi half rises from his chair. "Why did I not know about this?"

Yuri bows his head. "I'm sorry, Bilgi. A lot was happening. We didn't have time. Evgeniy set him up for us. He was vetted properly. Considered a loner, questioning the Gracile way of life."

The Gracile seemed helpless and scared. Was it just an act? Or

196

was that really who he was? And why is he a fixture in my dreams?

"Mila, what happened?" Bilgi sits back down.

"I needed his help to access the information. He was on the run with me from the attack on Zopat. The Creed tried to kill him along with the rest of us. They referred to him as a rogue Gracile."

"He saw the information? He knows the whole packet?"

"He told me about it, but I never saw it for myself."

Denni moves to the door. "I'll put out an alert over the radio to our people. If he's on the ground, we'll find him."

Bilgi takes a deep breath and holds it for a moment before letting out a hiss. "This could've been bad for us."

"I know. I was scared. I had to know what it was."

"This is most unfortunate, Mila."

"You've still got the element of surprise. The Leader doesn't know."

Bilgi shakes his head. "There was a data leak onto the neuralweb. And it occurred exactly when Zopat got hit. We didn't know what the leak contained, but the increase in attacks by the Musuls, together with your intel, suggests it was the Leader's plan, or at least part of it. I'd surmise Kapka intercepted it, and finding out the Leader is only using him to kill us off has sent him over the edge."

Kapka's been double crossed. The Leader only wants to preserve Graciles.

Bilgi sighs. "It's a fair bet the Leader knows his plan was leaked, and if he's lost Kapka's support, he'll need to accelerate his timetable. This is a disaster. We can't stop him if we don't know how he's going to do it."

"I don't know what to say." This is my fault.

My mentor leans across the table, his steely gaze probing. "Say you know where to find this rogue Gracile."

197

CHAPTER TWENTY-SEVEN

DEMITRI

The gunship plummets through the cloud line toward the frozen ground below. I press hard on the yoke, feeling the metal column bend under the strain.

Despite the meteoric speed, the scene below opens up beneath the clouds in slow motion. All seven enclaves come into view, spread out below the stalks of the lillipads. The walled cities are huge, several kilometers across—yet decidedly pathetic when seen against the vast, bleak backdrop of gray countryside outside the city walls. At least two of the enclaves are burning. Huge red tongues of fire snap and lick against the old high-rise buildings and ramshackle abodes.

Several slashes of light streak across the sky, followed by a deafening crack and a high-pitched screech. In the distance, a lillipad support buckles—the metal squeals as if in pain. The safety balloons will hold the platforms for a while, but not forever. Chunks of concrete the size of old-world cars crumble away from the platform and slam into the ruined city below. Far in the distance, to the east, sits some kind of platform, separate from the enclaves. What is that?

Who cares? You're going to kill us, you fool.

Indeed. What does it matter? If the Leader didn't have the evidence to create black holes before, he does now. I practically handed it to him, with a full scan of my DNA and thus the

198

protein—and the link—to other dimensions.

I force the yoke to its absolute limit. The engines whine, the wind whistles past, and the windows to the cockpit vibrate to near-resonant frequency.

A small delicate hand slips over mine and begins to pull the yoke back gently. It's Husniya. She's as calm as can be, balancing herself in the near-vertical orientation of the gunship. Her eyes bore into me.

"Don't do it," she says. "You only hurt those you leave behind. Killing yourself is a selfish act that passes your burdens to those around you."

Those can't possibly be her words. Perhaps Margarida is speaking through her.

Vedmak claws at my consciousness, desperate for control.

The ground is less than fifty meters from the nose of the ship. My jaw clenches and my biceps strain as I pull on the yoke, attempting to lift the weight of the massive vehicle and prevent us from smashing into a million pieces.

Husniya begins to float, then sails to the back of the hold, bumping into the bulkhead and storage units until she's pinned to the rear. The engines choke, splutter, and finally burst into flame. The bow of the vehicle strikes the ground with a thud, sending a painful shudder through my spine. Powdered snow puffs up around us, obscuring any kind of view. I pull and twist the control, but it's useless. Like a stone skipping across the surface of a pond, we bounce two, three, four times.

Giving up hope of controlling the ship any longer, I hold on tight and wait for the final impact. The ship collides into something, and my whole world quakes with the violence of the crash. The nose of the vessel rips open, exposing us to the sleet and frigid wind. Eventually we stop.

I uncurl my aching body, then touch my forehead and check

my limbs. All okay. Husniya throws her arms around my neck and hugs me tight. It hurts like hell but is totally worth it.

"Thank you," she whispers.

I wish this moment could last forever.

She doesn't care about you, kozel. No one does.

Vedmak's voice is drowned out by a louder noise; a mob of Robusts, like the ones who attacked the Zopat market, swarms the ship.

Three men grab at me, dragging me from the wreckage. A fourth grabs Husniya and throws her over his shoulder. I kick, squirm, and bite. By the time we've cleared the hole in the wreckage, they've all but lost their grip.

Now. Let me save us. Give me control.

"No. I won't let you butcher anyone else."

The men stare at each other, confused at my outburst.

I shove the heel of my boot into the nose of the man nearest my feet. His face bursts into a spray of red, and he tumbles backward. The other two men, unable to hold my weight any longer, drop me in the snow.

"Let the little girl go." I scramble to my feet, grab a thin, three-meter piece of the hull weighing at least sixty kilos, and swing it about my head like a sword. Who knows where this strength is coming from, but my muscles tingle and my head swims.

Vedmak enjoys my anger. *Do it.*

A deafening snap, followed by a pained cry, breaks the stalemate. The man carrying Husniya slumps to the ground, a geyser of blood spouting from his side. The girl runs to me and clings to my legs. Two armed Robusts, dressed differently than my current attackers, trudge up the bank. They carry old mechanized weapons—revolvers and shotguns.

More shots are fired, and the remaining Robusts scurry off

like frightened hyenas, whooping and yelping. The gunmen talk among themselves as they approach me.

"Damn Musuls," says the taller of the two men, slipping another round into the cylinder of his revolver.

"They're attacking anything and everything now," says the shorter man with orange hair and a bristly beard. "Seems the Gracile Leader wants to wipe everyone out. Including them. And now they're pissed."

"How did they find that out?" the taller man asks.

"Who knows, but now Kapka's given a blood order. They're killing anyone who isn't a Musul."

"Even some who are." The tall man nods at the cowering girl between my legs.

"Well, well, well. Look at the size of this one," the tall man says, waving his handgun at me.

"Fall off your cloud, your majesty?" mocks the other.

"Look, I—I don't want trouble. Just leave us alone." My heart pounds against the inside of my chest, and my grip tightens on the steel piece of hull.

Kill them both. They are in our way. Stupid dogs.

"I don't want to kill anyone."

Your hands are already stained, you pathetic kozel.

The resistance fighters take another step closer.

"Did you hear that BOLO transmission?"

"The one about the Gracile Bilgi wants?" the orange-haired man says.

"Yeah. That's the one."

A gust of wind ladened with sleet and soot bites at my face, contrasting with the heat from the burning buildings. I squint, struggling to keep focus on the advancing men.

"I think Yuri might be interested in this one."

Wait. Yuri? Did he say Yuri?

201

A crunch in the snow. I swing around but am only met with a blast of pain to my temple. Husniya's muffled screams meld with the gloom that closes in. I wish, just once, I could do something right.

CHAPTER TWENTY-EIGHT

MILA

"Nice one." I touch the corner of my mouth where Ghofaun just struck me and glance at my fingertips. No blood. He smirks and continues to step to my left, his hands raised in a defensive position. I shove forward and our forearms make contact. He folds his elbow over mine and drives it toward my face. I deflect the impact with my free hand and counter with a knife-hand strike toward his neck—a movement he anticipates, trapping me with his free hand. Now we're all tied up.

He raises his right leg to kick me, but instinctively my leg rises at the same time. Our shins collide. Okay, that hurt. He shoves into me, but his style is familiar. Using his momentum to my advantage, my hips pivot to swing his body around to where I just stood. Our shins clack again. Damnation. If it hurts the tough little man, he doesn't show it.

In an endless exchange of strike and counterstrike, we shuffle back and forth. I trap his strong side, torque my arm free, and punch him squarely on the chin. His teeth click as his head jerks back from the impact. He freezes, daggers in his narrow eyes. I hold his gaze steady, maintaining gentle pressure with a closed fist against his chin. With a burst of hidden movement, my feet are knocked out from under me, and I slam flat on my back, the air forced from my lungs.

Ghofaun unleashes a broad smile, clasps my forearm, and helps me up. "You are every bit as good as your teacher said, Mila. He called you the Sparrow Hawk. I can see why." He puts a hand on my shoulder and squeezes in admiration. "Bilgi was right to make you an officer of Opor so soon. There aren't many with your skill and determination."

Still struggling for breath, I give a short bow. "You got me. Thank you, Master Ghofaun. Your defense is impenetrable."

"Nearly impenetrable." He rubs his chin.

"Thank you, again, for sparring with me."

"It was my great pleasure, Mila. I will sharpen my steel against yours any time you wish."

As Ghofaun turns to leave, he slips a set of traditional Lawkshan beads back onto his left wrist. "What is it?" he asks.

I must have been staring. "Oh, it's nothing. I just recognize those." I motion to his beads.

"Remnants of an old life." He nods, his gaze suggesting he is half lost in the grip of a memory. "I was a Lawkshan monk once. But that seems like a long time ago, now."

"Oh, I didn't know. That's a great honor. May I ask why you left?" The question leaves my lips before my brain can stop it. Too personal.

His face darkens. "It was not by choice. I lived at the Lawkshan Temple in Zopat practically my whole life. Did you know Bilgi and I trained there together?" He allows a fleeting smile, but the pain in his expression returns.

"Oh, no, I mean ... yes, I knew he'd trained there at one point. I didn't know it was with you."

"I was a boy then. I lived there, but Bilgi, because of his different beliefs, did not take the oath of the monks. He did, however, show up every day without fail to learn our ways and our fighting art, chum lawk. He was much my senior, a middle-aged man in those days, and yet the masters let him come and watch at first. After a long spell, he was allowed to help set up or fetch things, or bring us food, never saying a thing or offering any complaint."

"Sounds like Bil."

"After a while longer, they saw his devotion and took him on as a student. I was only sixteen or so, but they assigned me to work with him. We trained together for a long time and became good friends. Those were good years."

The short man before me is seasoned but much younger than I'd expect a master to be. His disposition is calm and worn, with an air of old-world simplicity. "What happened, Master Ghofaun? Please continue."

He takes a deep breath, his gaze drifting. "We had a visitor one day. The man asked for a demonstration. It was something we did all the time. I invited him in. The grand masters gathered everyone together for the demonstration, and when we had all circled up inside the temple, the stranger detonated his bomb vest. He was a Musul terrorist."

"That's terrible."

"The temple was ruined. Only Bilgi and I and a few others survived. In the ruins we found the remains of the stranger's bag. Inside was a New Etyom credit tag. 'Why would a Musul be carrying a credit tag? We use cash. No one uses a credit tag,' Bilgi kept saying. No one except …"

"Graciles."

"Exactly." He nods. "It was enough to convince him the Graciles had paid the Musuls to attack us. He became consumed with the thought of some grand conspiracy, eventually leaving the order in an attempt to discern the truth." He shrugs. "It turns out he was right, and that's how the resistance was born."

"I never knew. If that's true, why would the Graciles pay

terrorists to attack the peaceful Lawkshan monks?"

"We were peaceful. But we were also a fighting force to be reckoned with. Maybe the Graciles feared us."

"And you? What did you do then, Master Ghofaun?"

"Our temple was never the same. The guilt I felt was overwhelming. I had to find a way to make amends for my lack of vigilance." He looks away momentarily, a flutter of shame in his face.

"So you ended up here?"

"I did the only logical thing I could think of: I joined my friend and helped him to build the resistance into what it is today."

"You are a remarkable person, Master Ghofaun. Thank you for taking the time to share your story with me."

He bows again. "Ah, I am glad to share it with you, Mila. Especially if it helps to keep you true to your path."

"My path?"

"Each of us has a part to play in the ever-changing winds of destiny. Know your path and you shall know yourself." He winks.

We're interrupted by a sudden shuffling of resistance fighters as they pass the training room. "One of the scouting parties came back," a soldier calls to us. "They captured a Gracile."

* * *

As we enter the largest cavern in the Opor hideout, I survey the ancient mining equipment lying half-sunken and rusting in the reddish clay, dormant for hundreds of years in this condemned section of the mine. Everyone is cheering and clapping their hands.

Faruq enters from the command center and approaches me. "What's happening? Is something going on?"

"It appears so. Someone said they captured a Gracile."

Faruq's face holds many questions, but he remains silent.

The group floods into the chamber dragging a tall, muscular figure alongside another much smaller one. They both have sacks over their heads. I step forward and onto the tips of my toes to see better. The sacks are yanked from the captives' heads.

Faruq cries out. "Husniya."

"Faruq. Faruq, help," the young girl wails.

The growing crowd of resistance fighters taunts the Gracile with slurs, throwing trash at him. He hangs his head, unresponsive. The scouting party whoops and yelps, clearly proud of their catch.

"We found these two together," a scout shouts. "Two for the price of one."

I shove my way to the front and immediately sock the Gracile hard in the jaw. The crowd roars in approval.

"Who did you tell?" I shout, grabbing his shirt. "Who did you tell about the data? Tell me."

Demitri casts his gaze toward the floor. "I didn't tell anyone, Mila."

Something in his voice steals my anger—the sound of pain, of total loss. I know that sound. I've heard it in my own voice.

Faruq rushes up to embrace Husniya. She lays her head on him, her arms tied behind her back. Faruq turns to me, his eyes full of desperation. "Can we …?" He motions to her bonds.

"How about we untie the *little girl*?" I stare at the nearest scout.

"But she's a Musul from Baqir," calls out one woman from the crowd.

"And?" I snap, motioning at Faruq. "So is he. That makes them what? Naturally evil?" I grab the nearest resistance fighter by his jacket. "Untie her. *Now.*"

The scouts fumble with the ropes, untying Husniya, who leaps into the arms of her brother. Faruq doesn't even try to hide his tears.

I step back to Demitri and turn his face to me. "Demitri. The Creed destroyed my enclave. Murdered my people. How did they find out where I lived?"

He just looks at the floor. Another fighter calmly walks up beside me and throws the hardest stomach punch he can into the Gracile's solar plexus. Demitri doubles over and drops to his knees, coughing and spluttering. But he still does not speak. I press the stocky man back, and he swipes my hand away. We lock eyes for a long, tense moment as the crowd looks on.

"Enough, Giahi," Bilgi says from the back of the group.

The Robust soldier turns with a look of disgust. "She gets special privileges to strike the cloud prince, but it's off limits for me?"

"I said, that's enough."

Giahi storms from the room, flicking another angry glance at Demitri, then at me. "Sure, it's enough. For now."

Husniya pushes between us and throws her arms around our prisoner. "Don't hurt him. Please, Faruq, don't let them hurt him. He didn't do anything but help. He's my friend."

"Figures they'd be friends," someone snickers in the crowd.

"Everyone, listen up." I shout. "Gracile or not, he's not to be treated like an animal." I turn to the fallen Gracile and drop to my haunches. "Demitri. How did the Creed find out where I lived?"

Husniya covers him with her arms.

"It's okay. We're not going to hurt him anymore, but I need to talk to him. Okay? Go to your brother now."

Husniya reluctantly releases him and moves back to Faruq's side.

"Demitri." Has he been crying?

The Gracile raises his head to reveal two weary, bloodshot eyes. "I told you before: you were iso'd. They could track you by DNA. Your apartment would have been full of it. They just followed the trail. Not that it matters. Everything will end now, anyway."

The crowd roars again, this time in disapproval. "Not if we kill you first," someone screams.

I've got to get him on his own or this is never going to work.

I flick my head toward the scouts. "I'm going to question him further in private. Search him and bring everything he has on him to me. Then confine him to a room and post two guards." I take note of the Gracile's oversize chest and biceps. "Make that three guards."

"Get moving, cloud prince." the scout says, kicking Demitri and narrowly missing Husniya.

I whirl on the scout. "And that's quite enough, you understand?" If a look could kill, he'd be six feet under.

"Yes. I ... understand," he stammers.

"That goes for everybody here. Hate him all you want, but anyone who further mistreats this Gracile will have problems with *me*. Secure him, allow him to rest, and give him food and water." I jab a finger in the scout's chest. "I want you personally overseeing the humane treatment of our *cloud prince*."

Humiliated, the man looks to Bilgi, who has been silently observing in the back of the room.

"Don't look at me. Do what the lady says."

Grumbling, the scout pulls on Demitri's arm. Demitri stands and shuffles out into the mineshaft. Husniya steps toward him, watching him leave, then runs back to the arms of her brother. Faruq simply nods to me, holding his sister tight.

The crowd disperses, unhappy I've ruined their fun. Bilgi

leans against the far wall, watching me. He may not say it, but by the look on his face, he approves.

* * *

There's nothing ceremonial about this. Standing at the simple wooden desk, I dump the contents of the duffel onto its marred surface. These are all of the material possessions Demitri brought with him.

Rice, barley, and some protein and carbohydrate goo packs. But there's too much for him alone. He must have packed food for Husniya as well. Why does he care about a little Musul stowaway? A few more items. It all looks like junk. Wait, what's this? What would a Gracile need with a book? The tome is dense, with a heavy leather cover and flaky gold lettering, too disfigured to read, that falls away at the touch. The smell of old parchment and the feel of thin, uneven pages makes my skin prickle.

This volume is clearly ancient. But more than that, it feels like I'm on the brink of some great discovery. I cautiously leaf through the first few blank pages—and then my breath catches in my throat. There on the page are five incredible words: *The Holy Writ of Yeos*. It's not possible. This precious book shouldn't exist, and yet here it is, safeguarded among the belongings of a Gracile. None of this makes sense.

Forgetting its fragility, I clutch the book close and storm from the room, heading straight for the holding cell, the book tucked under my arm as I approach the guards outside Demitri's room.

Faruq strides out of the cell. I almost collide with him.

"Hey, what were you doing in there?"

"Talking," replies Faruq, his voice calm. "Bilgi gave me permission."

"About?"

"About Husniya," he answers. "I had to thank Demitri for saving her. From the Gracile Leader. And Vedmak." He gives me a knowing look before sauntering off. "It seems I do not have enough lives to give to repay my debts," he calls over his shoulder before disappearing into the dark.

Diverting my attention back to the guards, I toss my head toward the hallway. "It's okay. You can go." We lock eyes. Eventually they get the message and amble off.

Pushing into Demitri's room, I pull the door shut and stand waiting for him to look up. He doesn't. I clear my throat. Still nothing. I drop the heavy volume against the wooden table next to me with a thunk. "You know what this is?"

He glances at the book, and nods.

"It's an original volume of the Holy Writ. Handwritten from memory by the last scribes of my people and compiled from the burned fragments of a previous age. Where did you get it, thief?"

"Does it matter?" Demitri resumes staring at the floor.

"Yes. It matters."

He sighs and sits up, his swollen eyes registering me for the first time. He has a small red blemish on his jaw where my fist made its mark. "You can call me a thief, but I've had that since I was a youngling. Because we're Graciles, we can't enjoy things from the old world?"

"Why this book, Gracile? You don't believe in this."

"No, but you do." He offers the weakest of smiles.

He brought it for me, a Robust, just as if we were old friends. For the first time, I actually see the big Gracile for what he is: broken. He was right; the Graciles wouldn't abide someone like him in their culture. He's too ... human. I lower myself into a chair across from him, my voice softer now. "What happened? After the kid ... I mean, after the bomb in the marketplace. Where did you go?"

"I had to get away. I didn't know where to go, so I went back up." He motions with his head.

"And the little girl?"

"She was scared. I couldn't leave her there in the middle of the chaos. You won't believe it, but she has a voice in her head, too. She can talk to it. And for the first time, I realized I wasn't crazy—but I had to know why."

"Dare I ask?"

Demitri gives a snort. "I doubt you could understand it any better than I do, but suffice it to say, you were right."

Ignoring his obnoxious tone, I sit forward. "About?"

"My voice, Vedmak, about him being tangled with me, or attached to me somehow. He's not me. He's somewhere else."

"Where exactly? Hell?"

Demitri shakes his head. "I don't believe in that, and yet, he's not here. It's like our signals got intertwined. I think he died, a long time ago, and his information was encoded somewhere."

I can't help but smirk at his description of a soul.

"The girl has it, too," he continues. "Except her voice is good to her. I don't know why I'm telling you all this. There's no point anymore."

"I need to know what you know, Demitri. There are people in this base who would kill you if I let them. Tell me why I should vouch for you."

"Vouch for me? We're all going to die, and it's my fault. I wouldn't vouch for me."

"What are you talking about?"

"I leaked the data onto the net down here. I tried to tell you. The Leader's plan, I was the key. Or at least I am now. I didn't mean for it to be like this."

"We know Kapka knows. His radicals are blowing themselves up all over Etyom. They've even succeeded in crashing a few lillipads."

"I saw them falling, on my way down." His face drops.

I hadn't even considered his people would suffer in this—just as mine have. "Look, it's my fault as much as yours. I forced you to access the info."

"I've killed us all because I'm the key."

"To creating the black hole?" I ask.

He nods sheepishly.

"Explain to me, Demitri."

He huffs out a breath. "Look, normally I'd tell you it's impossible to create a black hole. It would be so tiny it would disappear before it could gain enough mass. Pop in and out of existence."

"Okay."

"That's based on the standard model of physics. Exotic physics states you can create and sustain a black hole, but for the equation to work, you need to assume multiple dimensions exist. That's never been proven before. Until now."

I search his eyes. He's willing me to find the answer myself. "Vedmak?"

He nods. "He's proof of other dimensions—purgatory, Hell, whatever you want to call it. I did the scan on Husniya's and my DNA. I found the protein responsible for our connection, for the entanglement. The Leader only needs to recreate the protein and generate enough to study the interaction of the subatomic particles. He'll figure out how to manipulate another dimension. Now he just needs a powerful enough supercollider. I thought he already knew, but he didn't. I gave it to him on a plate—shut up, Vedmak, it's not my fault."

Half of that went over my head. All I heard was: black hole, possible, and everyone will die. "Can we stop him?"

"With what? Against the Creed? The Musuls?" He shakes his

head. "We're dead. You, me, everyone here. My brother ..." He breaks down again, fighting back tears between arguments with Vedmak.

"Demitri, focus on me."

He taps his forehead with two fingers.

"What about your brother?"

"The Leader ... That monster executed Nikolaj just to hurt me." Demitri scrunches his eyes closed and buries his face in his hands.

I don't know what to say.

He stares at the floor, waging some internal battle, alone. He's an outcast, without a home or a family. Just like me. And in the midst of all that has happened, he thought to bring me something priceless he knew I would take comfort in. I don't want to care. The Graciles are cold and cruel, with no love for anything but themselves—but this one is different. I cast a glance at the old book. What would Zevry do? What would Yeos want from me? *Judge a man not by what he is but by what he is to become, as he searches for the path of the Lightbringer.*

"Demitri." I lean in, touching the outside of his knee. "I'm sorry about what happened to your brother."

"Are you?" His large hazel eyes are full of sadness.

I give an earnest nod. "Yeah. I am."

There's a long silence before I continue, my tone steady, my words more confident than my heart. "Listen to me. The people we love shouldn't have to die for nothing. Tell me what we need to do to stop this, Demitri. I need your help. We *all* need your help. You're the only one who understands this well enough to stop it. Do it for the little girl you saved. Do it for Nikolaj, for yourself. Your life is more valuable than you know."

My words seem to strike a chord. Demitri sits up and makes firm eye contact with me. "Okay, Mila. I'll try. We're going to die anyway, but I'll try. Are you going to bring your people into my prison cell so I can explain everything to them?"

"I can do one better." I stand and place my hand on his shoulder. "We'll walk out of here and go tell them together."

"Together," Demetri says, as if only to himself.

CHAPTER TWENTY-NINE

DEMITRI

I've never had so many people's gazes fixed on me before. Each pair of eyes searching and studying. Each holding a different expectation. Most expect me to die. Probably slowly and in pain. Especially the one called Giahi, who now stands in the back, alternating between staring coldly and laughing with his friends. Their hatred for my kind is palpable. Others hold the hope I will be the answer to their problems—to the war between the Graciles and Robusts, even between Robusts and other Robusts. Musuls, Rippers, whatever. They'll get an end to their war, just not the one they want.

The brother of Husniya holds my gaze; his demeanor is warm and almost comforting. He stands among them but not with them. He, of all of them, understands my predicament. Other than Graciles, his people are who these Robusts seem to hate most of all. Musuls. At least that's what he told me in my cell. For reasons I can't fathom, he came to thank me for saving Husniya—even telling me he owed me a life debt. He doesn't owe me anything.

And then there's Mila. She's now basically in control of this militia, at least in as much as their leader, Bilgi, has given her command of those who can fight. Right now she's addressing the whole group, telling them a bit about herself and how they should give me a chance.

These people have come to hear what we're up against. Those

with nowhere to go amid the chaos have now come to cling to this group for protection—hiding in the mines for safety. Mila has her arms folded across her chest, all her weight shifted onto one leg, her eyes wide. It's her stare that holds the greatest expectation of all, that I'm a friend to the Robusts, that her faith in me is well placed. It isn't. I'm a failure. Just ask Nikolaj. I can't save anyone.

You couldn't get laid in a brothel. Vedmak guffaws. *Let alone formulate a battle plan to save anyone. But I could. Look at this pathetic band of misfits. They'll just get in my way. Let me kill them, and then I'll go after your elitist, inbred dogs.*

Your answer to everything, Vedmak. Murder. Violence.

It's nature's answer to everything. Even for these stupid kozels. Look at the hate in the eyes of that Giahi. The need to kill. He and the rest of these wretches are no different than me.

"Some of them are, Vedmak."

"Demitri?"

Sard. Did I say that out loud? How long have they been waiting?

"Demitri, you wanna speak up? We can't hear you." Mila's lips are tight, and she's studying me. *Don't let them know about Vedmak.* That's what she said. *You need to seem credible.*

"Sorry, yes. Well, I, um, where do I start?" I pace back and forth, tapping on my forehead with two fingers.

"How about the beginning," says a firm but warm voice from the rear. It's Bilgi.

"Yes, okay, the beginning." How to explain to these Robusts in a way they'll understand? "Okay, look. The Gracile Leader believes we—Graciles, I mean—are now as perfect as we're going to get. Does that make sense? Without considering upgrades and hacks, biologically we are where our ancestors wanted us to be."

There's an uproar from the crowd, cussing and shouting. They did not like that. "I said he *believes*. I didn't say it was true."

"Continue, Demitri," Mila presses, waving her hand. "We don't have much time."

"He wants to preserve us this way for as long as the universe will allow. The best way to do this is to make us part of the universe, turning us into a packet of information that can be held in that state for many, many millennia."

"Are you talking about a soul?" a man calls out from the crowd. "Existing for eternity, with Yeos?"

Simpletons, but I guess if it works. "Sure. Imagine the Leader's found a way to ensure your soul is kept intact forever. The way he wants to do it is to create a black hole—it's a point in space where the gravity of something huge is squished down to the size of a pinprick. Everything nearby gets sucked in and crushed into nothingness. That said, on the edge of a black hole—the point of no return, the event horizon—information, or souls, can be stored. Anything that falls into the black hole isn't actually destroyed; it's converted to information and sits on the event horizon."

They have the brains of goats. They don't understand a word.

Shut up, Vedmak. Keeping him at bay is so exhausting.

"He wants to create a black hole," Mila repeats, trying both to support me and to move the explanation along.

"Right, a black hole. There's a lot of complicated physics involved I won't bore you with." Or reveal it's my fault he even knows how to do this. "But he has something called a particle accelerator. When he fires it, it could eventually create a small black hole that will grow and swallow everything. You, me, Etyom—the Earth."

A short, stocky man, not too far from Faruq, grunts, "Why hasn't he fired it?"

"He had two problems," I reply, holding up two fingers, which again end up nervously tapping on my forehead. "One is *you all* exist. Robusts. Musuls, Rippers, all of you. You muddy the perfection. He wants you all dead first. Your information—your souls—scattered."

"Right," Mila interrupts. "He's been using Kapka and his terrorists to keep us in line long enough to finish his project. Now that he's near the end, he'd intended to use Kapka and the Creed to wipe out every other enclave and the Rippers, and then clean up what was left with his remaining Creed soldiers. Except Kapka found out he was being double-crossed."

"Yeah, he's gone crazy. Killing everyone in sight," a woman calls from within the gathering. "What are we gonna do?"

"It doesn't matter now," I interrupt. "The Leader's hand has been forced. He has to fire it with some of you still alive."

"You said there were two problems." A small man with thin eyes and a calm manner studies me. I think his name is Ghofaun.

"Yes." I nod and start talking faster. "Disregarding I have no idea where he's put a collider powerful enough to generate a black hole, he'd need an escape plan in case it went wrong."

"Went ... wrong?" Mila squints at me.

"Strangelets."

"What?" she snaps.

"Strangelets. Look, there's a distinct possibility he could get the experiment wrong. If he doesn't set up the accelerator correctly, he runs the risk of creating strange matter, strangelets. If that happens, he won't create a black hole, he'll instantaneously transform all normal matter—the whole Earth—into strange matter. When strange matter touches normal matter, the latter is instantly converted. There's no stopping it, save the vacuum of space." Their faces are blank again. "A blob. The Earth and everything on it will become a giant amorphous blob."

A gasp ripples through the troop.

"What can he do about that, Demitri?" Mila presses. "He must have figured out a backup plan. If he's so adamant he wants to preserve you, then he would have a plan to try again if it went wrong—correct?"

How am I supposed to know? "He'd need to trigger the accelerator from a safe place. Somewhere the strange matter, if he created it, couldn't get at him. Somewhere ... well, it would have to be off world. Put a vacuum between him and it."

"Off world?" Bilgi repeats.

"Yes, as in not on Earth—but I have no idea how. I mean, he'd need a—" I saw it on the way down.

"He'd need a *what*?" Mila demands.

"A rocket. He'd need a rocket. And a rocket needs a—"

"Launchpad," Mila says, finishing my sentence.

"Right."

"There's nowhere to launch a rocket from within Etyom," Bilgi says. "On a lillipad?"

"No, no. The lillipads are too flimsy to take the thrust required. And you're right; there's no launchpad in Etyom. But there is one outside the walls. I saw it on my way down, way out east."

Most of the audience appears as confused as when I started. Faruq isn't even paying attention. I follow his stare to Mila, who stands, eyes wide, the blood drained from her face.

"Mila, you okay?" Bilgi asks.

She doesn't speak for a long moment, but then composes herself and nods. "Yeah, I'm okay. Look, we've got explosives, right? We get to that rocket before it takes off and blow it wide open with the Leader inside."

This woman is crazy. "How do you expect to do that, Mila? How do you think you're going to get there? Through the enclaves, with Robusts, I mean Musuls, and the Creed running around—not to mention the Rippers out there in the no-man's-land."

"Demitri, can you for once—" Mila begins.

220

"He has a point, Mila,'" Bilgi interrupts. "If we move as a group up there, we're a big target."

"What do you suggest?" She taps her foot expectantly.

"We use the mines," a Robust woman says, working her way through the crowd.

"You gotta plan, Denni?" Bilgi asks.

The woman drops to the floor in front of the crowd and sets down a small holo-projector. She flicks it on. Streams of green light spider out from the center to form a skeletal map of the mines.

"Not a plan so much as a decent idea. We haven't mapped everything yet, but there's one tunnel that's been bugging me. It's pretty much a straight line from here way out to the east, where our Gracile friend here says he saw the launchpad." She points to the tunnel she's referring to, following its length to a dead end. "Problem is, it just stops. One recon team said they thought it was blocked up manually. Like it was filled in. Could be this is our way there undetected."

Bilgi nods. "I like it. The element of surprise."

"And if it's not?" Mila says. "Then we've lost our chance, and the Leader escapes to kill us all. No, we go over the top."

"We do both," Ghofaun interjects. "You're both right. We need to double our chances. I'll take a small team to the surface. As a stealth unit, we'll move in the shadows unseen."

Mila glances at Bilgi and then at the little thin-eyed man. "Okay, Master Ghofaun. We do it your way. Double our chances for success."

Slow, deliberate clapping from the rear of the group draws everyone's attention. "Let's give our fearless leaders a hand." Giahi continues to clap. "Can anyone else believe what they're hearing? Not only is this plan the most far-fetched, ridiculous nonsense I've ever heard, but they want us to do it according to the counsel of a Gracile? Then there's the towl'ed over here." He motions to Faruq.

"We're just supposed to be okay working alongside him, too?"

Mila bristles, and Bilgi takes a step toward the gruff Robust.

Vedmak chokes on his own laughter. *Ohhh, this is good. I like this one. If we're lucky, maybe he and the old man will kill each other.*

"Giahi, your opinions are well known to us," Bilgi snaps. "You don't have to like the plan, and you can choose to leave—but if you are going to work with us, you can start by shutting your fool mouth and actually doing something useful. Am I clear?"

Giahi says nothing for a moment, his crew looking on. "Of course, Bilgi, of course. You're crystal clear, as always." He flashes a disturbing grin. "Hey, I'm always a team player."

"Well, does anyone else have any other xenophobic remarks? No? Please, speak up if so." Bilgi scans the crowd. No one moves. Even Giahi has settled into the back of the room. "This is not a popularity contest. This is about the survival of our species. Can everyone understand where we're going with this? What we're doing here is the last resort. I promise you we would not take such risks unless we had no other choice." Bilgi takes a deep breath and steps back, glancing at Mila and Faruq. "Please continue, Master Ghofaun."

Ghofaun nods. "I'll take three men over the surface. Any more and we risk detection. No heavy weaponry or gear. We will be as the night chasing the dawn."

How poetic. All of these fools will still die. Sad little sheep blindly following the only one with a sense of direction—even if it's off the edge of a cliff.

"Okay, Demitri?"

What? Oh no, what have I been asked? "Umm, I'm sorry?"

Mila looks at me expectantly. "I said, you come with us down into the mines, okay? We don't know if you'll come in handy. You're the only Gracile we have on our side. We might come up against some tech we don't know how to deal with. We need you."

Now I know she's insane.

* * *

The Robust resistance fighters scurry around like worker ants, busying themselves with who knows what. Ghofaun has already taken his three men and left. Making his way through the enclaves and the Vapid will be time consuming. If he makes it at all.

Husniya clings to my leg, watching me watch Mila. What is it that drives this woman? She's seen the depths of desperation and suffered more horrors than most would care to imagine. Yet here, in the face of certain death and against a force she cannot hope to beat, she shines like a beacon for these people. She doesn't even know she's doing it. They follow her and hang on every word, every order, taking each instruction as if it were the word of Yeos Himself.

Crouching down on my haunches, I pick up Husniya and sit her skinny frame on my knee. She perches there, a vague smile on her face, staring at the side of my head.

"Margarida likes you," she whispers.

"She does?"

"Yes." Husniya nods. "Listen, she's telling you."

"I don't hear her."

"Close your eyes. Concentrate." She slides her fingers down my face and over my eyelids, stroking them closed.

In the darkness, beyond the chatter between Mila and her team, is a faint voice—one that might once have belonged to a loving mother. It's soothing and kind.

"Hey."

My eyes snap open and I nearly topple to the ground, taking Husniya with me.

"C'mon, big guy, we gotta show you some tactical basics,"

223

Mila says, almost laughing.

I hate guns.

I don't, Vedmak whispers menacingly.

"Let's go." Mila grabs me at the elbow and gives it a tug. There's no way she can lift me, but I rise anyway and allow the little girl to slide safely to the ground.

At the table in the middle of the room stand two members of the resistance. One is Denni. The other is a large man with skin like night. He doesn't look friendly.

"You know Denni. And this is Mos," Mila says, waving her hand at her companions.

For a Robust, Denni is beautiful. Her shoulder-length blond hair is tied back, but strands fall about her face and into her round blue eyes. Her frame is short but voluptuous. Our eyes meet, and she blushes.

Female urges, Vedmak says, his tone heavy with disgust.

Mila squints at us both but says nothing.

"So, Miss Solokoff, since you insist on nonlethal weapons, I've put this little doozy together that you might like." Denni plonks a tubular weapon onto the table. It's bolted and bound together with all manner of screws, tape, and wire. Something between a rifle and a bazooka. "It fires forty-millimeter lead beanbags. May not sound like much, but it'll hurt like crazy. Think of it as a flying knockout punch."

Mila nods approvingly and inspects her weapon.

"You're not even using a lethal weapon? You'll get butchered." She's crazy.

"The only person who needs to die is the Leader. His sacrifice will be enough to stop this war. If I can prevent more deaths, isn't that my responsibility?"

"I guess …"

"Doesn't mean I won't knock a few teeth out, though. They

can live without teeth." Mila winks at Mos, who chuckles.

And what does the big one get? A slingshot?

Vedmak has a point.

"This one's for you, big boy." Denni heaves a huge piece of equipment onto the table with a thud. Mos picks it up. It's an enormous, long, cylindrical barrel, cut off into an angle at the end, with a convex lens inside, bolted to the body of an old machine gun. There's a crude breaker switch made from an old screwdriver jammed into the side. Two large handles have been welded onto it—one near the front, the other, with a trigger, at the rear. Four energy packs are embedded into the butt. A large woven strap hangs from two climbing clips attached to the top.

"What on earth is *that*?" Mila asks.

Denni grins. "*This* fires a laser beam."

"A laser beam?" That's not going to do anything to the Creed.

Ignoring me, Denni continues. "I used four blue diodes from a fallen Creed gunship. When they're focused together, this thing can pack a wallop. You might wanna cover your eyes." Denni picks up the hefty device, turns, and cranks the exposure lever halfway back. We all squint and shield our eyes as a brilliant, blinding light streams forth, blackening a patch on the stone wall about the size of a dinner plate. She cranks the lever forward and sets the laser back on the table.

"It only causes mild burns if it hits skin for a few seconds. But with a direct hit to the eyes, it's thirty-three million times more intense than looking at the sun. It'll fry the eyeballs of Musuls, Rippers, even Creed. It's pretty damn effective—just watch the exposure. If you crank it wide open, it gets more powerful but also unstable."

"But in case that doesn't work, I always have Svetlana." Mos grins, showing a row of surprisingly white teeth, as he pulls a heavy chrome Magnum from the back of his pants. "Svetlana doesn't have a problem with killing people."

Was that a threat? That could have been a threat.

"And for you, Demitri, something a little less violent. A sick stick. No one should be getting anywhere near you anyway, but one poke with this thing and they won't be bothering you anymore. Difficult to attack anyone when you're vomiting uncontrollably." Denni giggles and hands me the stick. "It's not on yet. Don't poke yourself."

"Thanks. Can I use it on that Giahi guy?"

The whole group glares at me in horror.

"Uh, I'm … that was … I was just joking …"

Everyone bursts into laughter.

"Relax, Demitri." Denni pats my arm. "You don't always have to take everything so seriously."

They were joking? "Oh … yeah."

Mos laughs. "I might borrow that from you just to see Giahi embarrass himself in front of everyone."

"Seriously, though." Mila sets her weapon down. "What's that guy's problem?"

"Giahi?" Denni says. "He's always been difficult, but since you showed up, he's been intolerable."

"He thought he was in line to be a part of the command of Opor," Mos chips in, "an aspiration that was dashed when he realized how close Bilgi was with you."

"Why keep him around if he's such a problem?" Mila asks.

Denni shrugs. "He's a great fighter. Aggressive and resourceful."

Mila places her hands on the table. "Well, we can use good fighters, as long as he can mind his own business and I don't have to shut his mouth for him."

This elicits another round of laughing.

"What else have we got?" Mila asks.

Denni coughs nervously. "We all pack standard melee gear—knives, axes, etc. Most of us have a revolver or some kind of handgun from the old days. The bigger guys have shotguns and a couple of Kalashnikovs. Not much ammo, though. There are also a few bits that I've cooked up. But all our explosives have been packed into two satchels. One is with Ghofaun's team, and the other's with me. That's pretty much it."

We're all gonna die.

CHAPTER THIRTY

MILA

"We're all gonna die."

"Enough of that. What is it?" Bilgi strolls over to the diminutive woman stationed at the radio.

The room falls silent. Faruq raises his head, and Demitri stands from his chair. I take a step closer, shadowing my mentor.

"Go on." Bilgi leans closer. "What is it?"

"The ..." She swallows and wets her lips, her hands shaking. Bilgi waits patiently, encouraging her to continue with a nod of his head.

"I picked up some chatter on the radio. The Creed are *en route* to intercept *the target*. I'm pretty sure they just gave our coordinates."

Bilgi snaps his head around, his gaze fixed on me. I know what he's thinking: the target is me. I've been iso'd. That doesn't just go away.

Bilgi turns back to the radio operator. "How many are there?"

"One strike ship and a single squad of Creed, maybe five or six soldiers."

"Enough to wipe us out if they trap us in here. How long do we have?"

"Six minutes. That was about a minute ago."

Bilgi jerks into action. "Mos!"

"Defensive positions," the Kahangan bellows. "Yuri, I need

the doors at the front entrance welded shut. Giahi, I need bunkers erected in the main cavern. Everyone else, arm yourselves and assist where necessary. Make sure you have good fields of fire for when they breach the cavern. They're machines, so we'll have to shred their neural processors to stop them."

"Where's that?" I say, trying to catch up.

Mos taps the side of his skull. "Just like us. Aim for the head. They'll be armored, and it won't be easy." He spins, clapping his hands. "Let's go. Everybody find work to do."

The room bursts into a frenzy of activity. Suddenly I've got wads of cotton in my mouth. "Bilgi, where do you need me?"

"With me, girl. Arm yourself and do your part to motivate everyone else."

I grab my single-shot beanbag launcher from the desk. Breaking the tube open, I pull a heavy lead-shot-filled bag from my pocket and thrust it into the chamber, then snap the breach closed.

Demitri is standing by the wall, stiff as a statue.

"Demitri, you're with me," I call out.

"I don't want to fight," he says with a whimper.

"You don't have to fight. Just do what you can to help."

He nods, clearly terrified, and falls in step behind me as I exit the command center and move into the main chamber.

Yuri already has two men welding shut the steel doors to the cavern with blue-flamed torches and blinders. People run back and forth, piling sandbags or turning over furniture. Faruq helps to mount a long, fabricated weapon with a lengthy coiled hose leading to a metal cylinder. The fighter behind it lights a small burner at the nozzle and squeezes the lever on the handle, launching a stream of fire toward the door.

"Demitri, help them at the door."

The Gracile nods and moves. The men at the door mutter among themselves as he arrives, but they quickly shut up when

Demitri rolls a massive boulder against the door to brace it.

Mos continues rallying everyone as new fighters rush in. "Two lines of bunkers," Mos yells. "We need positions to fall back to." Desperate to seem important, Giahi shouts to the others building bunkers, instructing or scolding the fighters about their fortifications, a fixed look of anger on his face.

Denni trudges up, lugging the sunbeam weapon that dwarfs her. My mouth hangs open.

"What?" She flashes a defiant smile and shrugs. "I wanna test this baby out."

A shuddering hum vibrates in the earth above us, followed by multiple concussive impacts. Screams echo down from the Forgotten Jewel above.

The Creed have arrived.

Bilgi struts into the main cavern, larger than life, wearing a faded leather duster that extends below his waist and toting a long rifle with shiny brass parts, like the kind I saw once in an old book about American cowboys.

The screams above grow louder, accompanied by the sickening thud of plasma rifles. Bilgi scans the room's defensive setup. The hush is deafening as we all wait for him to speak.

But he doesn't. He just looks to the welded and barricaded door. As if on cue, a pounding begins, rapid and violent. Screams accompany the banging. People are out there. Our people.

I take a step forward, but Bilgi stops me with a severe glance. He looks back to the reverberating door. "Yuri, Demitri, the rest of you, back away from that door."

They cast questioning looks at each other.

"Back away from the door now. There's nothing we can do for them."

A series of thudding impacts cascades across the door, and the screams are silenced. Yuri, Demitri, and the others back away.

Bilgi straightens, working the brass lever on his rifle. "Honor our brothers and sisters with your ferocity." The door shudders from an inhuman force slamming against it, dust swirling from the frame. "Our enemy is not human. They do not deserve our lives." Another rippling concussion rattles the door as the weld separates and the bolts come loose. "We are free people. The elites do not control us!"

Our general's words echo across the cold stone walls. Then the steel doors explode from their hinges, and the cavern screams to life with the sounds of war. I pinch my eyes and duck with my hands to my face. Open your eyes, Mila. Fight.

Through the smoking opening the Creed march. Their faces are expressionless behind the visors of their armored helmets, their bodies protected by bulky avalanche-patterned exoskeletons. Blue streaks like twisting bolts of lightning rocket from their plasma rifles, vaporizing resistance fighters with deadly precision. Before I can yell to the fighter manning the flamethrower, a plasma bolt strikes him in the chest, and he explodes in a puff of dust.

Sard.

"Fire!" Bilgi shouts.

The room bursts to life with a roar of deafening gunfire. The Creed armor is impervious to our small arms, and they stomp forward, death dealers only interested in our destruction. There are only five of them, but they're going to kill us if we don't outthink them.

I lock eyes with Denni, who's crouched with her heavy weapon. "Denni, do it."

Resolute, she cranks the throttle forward. A blinding ray streaks from the device like a bolt cast from the hands of Yeos Himself. The magnificent beam hits the face of the first Creed soldier, and its mouth pops open. The geminoid soldier spins, firing against a nearby wall. Mos collides with the disoriented

Creed, draws Svetlana from his waistband, and presses the muzzle beneath the geminoid's chin. There's a resounding crack, and the Creed slumps to the ground. Denni shouts in triumph. One down.

"Denni, hit them again," I scream.

Denni cranks the throttle open and sweeps another Creed with it. The soldier takes the laser directly in the eyes and fumbles blindly against the wall. Denni moves to hit another, but the beam flickers and goes out. Panicked, she yanks on the lever and fiddles with the switches and knobs. It's no use.

"Denni, look out," Demitri yells.

She drops the weapon and dives for cover, a plasma bolt slamming into the stone behind her.

"Bilgi." I point to the blinded Creed, still stomping about uselessly. "Get ready." The old man tracks my meaning and readies his rifle. Taking a knee, I set the beanbag launcher into my shoulder. *Phoot.* The bag sails lazily through the air, flying harmlessly over the Creed's shoulder. Bilgi snaps a look at me.

Hold on, damnation. The tube breaks open, my fingers dropping another bag into the breach. Snapping the weapon closed, I shoulder it and fire again. The bag slams the Creed in the side of the helmet, jarring it loose. Bilgi is ready. With a precision shot, he fires his cowboy rifle, striking the lifeless soldier just below the ear. It crumples to the floor like a sack of stones.

Demitri whoops a victory cry, but it's drowned out by Bilgi's scream. His rifle clatters to the floor as he falls, clutching at the ashen stump where his left arm used to be.

Time slows. The Creed march forward, firing pulse after pulse. The resistance fighters stare in horror at the broken form of their felled leader. I spin, searching frantically for Mos or Yuri. Among the smoke and flashes of plasma rifles, the only one I can make out is Giahi—crouched down behind a rock, frozen in terror.

"Giahi," I call out over the din.

"I ... I can't ...," he mumbles.

I'm not going to wait here to die. "Somebody cover me."

In one swift move, I sling my launcher over my shoulder, vault the barricade, and grab Bilgi beneath the armpits. Plasma bolts streak past, narrowly missing us, as I struggle to drag my mentor out of danger. He's too damn heavy. I trip over my own heels, and we crash to the rocky ground. Through a break in the smoke, Mos, Yuri, and Denni valiantly fire their small arms at the relentless Creed. Yeos save us.

Powerful hands clasp my shoulder.

"I've got him."

I crane my neck to see the rogue Gracile behind us. "Demitri?"

He nods. "I can do this. Let me help."

Demitri hoists Bilgi's limp body over his shoulder with ease and makes for the back of the cavern.

"Fall back!" I scream, reloading my beanbag gun. "Everyone fall back now." But we have nowhere left to go. This is our last stand.

The flamethrower turret squeals as someone turns the heavy weapon toward the Creed. What in the name of—

"Faruq."

He stares at me, wide eyed, no idea what he's doing.

"Do it, Faruq." He pivots the flame cannon and squeezes the lever clamp on the handle. A jet of flame streams from the nozzle, dousing all three of the Creed in a liquid fire that clings to them, melting the rubbery flesh off their faces.

"Keep it on them," I shout, slinging my rifle behind me and jumping for the scaffolding above. I swing up to the elevated platform, stretching my legs to reach the scaffold. A blast from a plasma rifle slams into the section behind me, but I'm already in midair, on my way to the next platform. I barely make it, pulling myself up and onto the metal plate.

"Destroy the target," the Creed chant, their endoskeletons poking through melted rubber.

Below, Faruq hits them again. The Creed return fire, blasting apart the cannon just as Faruq dives from the fortified nest. The fuel canister erupts in a ball of fire that engulfs the screaming resistance fighters around it.

"Faruq!"

I fire a beanbag from my elevated position and strike one of the Creed, knocking it to the floor. The closest resistance fighters swarm it, knocking the rifle from its hands and removing its head with a few vigorous downward swipes of their blades.

"Hit them with everything you've got," I shout at the top of my lungs, my ears ringing with the chaos of battle. The cavern roars to life once again. Rounds fly, and the last two Creed are staggered by the sheer volume of firepower poured out upon them. The breast armor of one comes loose, and it takes a barrage of bullets to its chest cavity. More resistance fighters swarm the downed robot.

I drop from the platform, ditch the beanbag gun, and break into a sprint. Launching from the top of a nearby set of storage crates, I sail through the air and kick the rifle from the hands of the final Creed. It assumes a defensive stance, its close-quarter combat protocols engaged.

"Come on then."

The machine is clumsy, but extremely powerful. I slam my body against its lower axis, using my momentum to force the geminoid to the ground. Its ballistic helmet clangs against the floor and bounces free. Rolling forward, I draw a short combat knife and spear the lifeless abomination through the eye, but it intercepts my strike, crushing my hand in its viselike grip.

Bang.

My shoulders seize and my eyes pinch shut at the sound of the gunfire so close. The grip of the Creed soldier relaxes, and its arms flop to the ground. Over me, the long barrel of Bilgi's cowboy rifle smokes. The old man groans and falters, dropping to one knee, driving the barrel of the rifle into the dirt for support.

The cavern is now silent, the smoke clearing, leaving only the stink of burning geminoid. We won. But there are no cheers for our victory. The Creed assault has left its mark. Our force is half of what it was. Friends are now nothing more than ashen heaps.

"Bilgi, your arm …"

"I'm okay, Mila." He winces. "I'll live." He looks over the smoldering husks of the defeated Creed soldiers and the scorch marks where his comrades died. The burden of leadership is heavy in his eyes. "We're all alive because of you and your friends. We owe you our lives, Mila."

My cheeks burn. "I can't take credit for …" Everyone is staring at me.

Faruq steps forward to stand alongside Demitri. They're both blackened like coal miners, but otherwise unharmed. I can only give a grateful nod. My two most unlikely of friends.

Bilgi grunts in discomfort. "What's next, my girl? You call it."

Taking a deep breath, I try to slow the hammering of my heart. "We're down some good people. We need treatment for the wounded—including you. They're going to come again if we stay here."

Bilgi raises his eyebrows. "Maybe. Maybe not. I think they expected you. I'm not sure they expected the fight we gave them. The Leader doesn't have unlimited resources."

"Even so, they could have transmitted intelligence to him, and the fact still remains if he activates that supercollider, we're all doomed anyway. Stopping it is still priority number one."

Bilgi nods. "Are you okay if Yuri takes a team and relocates the wounded to one of our safe houses?"

"On one condition: you go with them."

"Not going to happen," Bilgi says. "I'll be going with you."

"Support. You're going with me as support."

Bilgi inclines his head, acknowledging my stern look. "Very well, my dear."

"Denni, that thing was effective against them." I motion to her sunbeam weapon. "Can you get it up and running again?"

"Yep. Just a few kinks to sort out."

"Make it happen. Everyone else, re-arm, grab some basic rations, and meet up at the mouth of the tunnel. We leave as soon as possible." I wipe my brow, take a deep breath, and help Bilgi to his feet. "Go get yourself taken care of, old man."

"Leave without me and I'll shoot you myself."

"I was afraid you'd say that."

Yuri and Mos help him away. People scatter in all directions to initiate the directives I've given. Still not used to this leadership thing. I reholster my knife and sling my beanbag gun over my shoulder. Faruq and Demitri are staring at me.

"What?"

"Nothing." Faruq shakes his head, innocently.

"No ... nothing," Demitri repeats.

They glance at each other in amusement.

"Come on, you two, get going. We hit the tunnels in ten minutes."

CHAPTER THIRTY-ONE

DEMITRI

The tunnel is dark. Only the flames of the Robusts' torches illuminate our way, casting foreboding shadows on the reddish-brown walls. It's not damp in the tunnels as I expected; the air is actually arid.

I trudge along the dark, rocky corridor, protected on all sides by a motley crew of warriors who have apparently gone from wanting my head on a pike to accepting I'm a part of this mess. Husniya walks beside me, quietly keeping me company. She should have gone with Yuri, but she and her brother both happen to be persistent.

Mila, as always, takes point, moving ahead as far as she can without losing us—Mos, Faruq, and a few others at her side. She's either incredibly brave or absolutely insane. Maybe a little of both. It's hard not to admire her. In her bag she carries the Writ—my gift to her. This simple tome seems to have renewed her strength. Bilgi told me she's not bold because she believes her Yeos will save her; she's bold because in her heart she knows He has a plan for her.

The notion of a god is for younglings or people too afraid to admit the universe just *is*, and that we are meaningless. Yeos, Ilāh, whatever, is just a way to make people, Robusts, feel safe. Even now, the concept of a soul—something that has long eluded science—may be explained by my entanglement with Vedmak.

But maybe there isn't anything wrong in such beliefs. The burden of knowledge is lonely, and the prospect of death terrifying. Mila and those who share her faith never seem to be alone or afraid to die.

Such a nice story. Go and tell it to your Leader, you simple idiot. He thinks you elitist scum are worth preserving for as long as the universe will allow. But why? You exist, but you do not live. It disgusts me.

Maybe Vedmak is right. I'm worthless, anyway. I haven't had a hit of DBS in a long time. Yuri said he had no more. I'm slipping away, the control over my own limbs waning.

"Margarida says you shouldn't think that way." Husniya tramps alongside, clutching at my little finger and swinging my arm back and forth. "It'll be okay."

Younglings. If only we were all so innocent.

* * *

There seems to be no passage of time down here. Only my aching feet inform me of how long we've been walking. No one says much, all concentration focused on what may spring out of the dark. Every so often, Mila stops the troops by holding her hand up. A few men run off ahead into the gloom, leaving everyone holding their breath in anticipation. So far, they have always come back. Dull thuds and pops tell us of the battle raging aboveground. Musuls, Robusts, and maybe even a few Creed slug it out in an endless exchange of munitions. Is Ghofaun still alive? I doubt it.

"You know, it's probably better not to focus on what's going on up there." Denni's soft voice doesn't attract the attention of the others.

This little Robust woman is really pretty. The orange torchlight makes her blue eyes sparkle. Her face is warm, her lips full, and her smile bright. She gazes at me in a way I once desired from Oksana.

I wouldn't get too attached, little peacock. You're all feathers and not much else. She'll figure that out quickly enough. Would you even know what to do with the little sooka *if she lay in the dirt and offered herself to you?*

"Don't talk about her that way, Vedmak. She's done nothing to you. Leave her alone."

"Who are you talking to?" Denni asks.

Dammit. I must have been mumbling. "Oh, just myself."

"Uh-huh. Try telling me the truth." Her eyes are wide, expectant.

"You wouldn't believe me if I told you."

"He has a voice in his head like mine," Husniya pipes up.

Oh, sard.

"His name is Vedmak. My voice is called Margarida. They died a long time ago, but we can hear their souls." The little girl beams at me and Denni, who looks surprised.

"Is that true?" Denni asks.

The air huffs from my lungs. "Kind of. Husniya is right. I hear a voice. I named him Vedmak. I don't think he's a soul, I think he's proof of another dimension. I think when we die, our information isn't lost. It's encoded somehow. His information was kept more intact. As was Margarida's. Perhaps it somehow transferred to another dimension."

"Or heaven," Husniya interrupts, again.

"Can't it be both?" Denni asks.

"Can't what be both?" I ask.

She shrugs. "Heaven, Hell, other dimensions …"

What is she talking about? "The idea of Heaven or Hell is predicated on an individual's behavior and where the soul is sent after the person dies. People are judged by an omnipotent being or beings. When in fact, the universe doesn't judge anything. It just is."

Denni shakes her head. "I don't necessarily agree. I'm a Fiorian, and I believe in Yeos, but I don't necessarily get too wrapped up in organized religion." She smiles. "Taking Yeos out of the equation, if you'll pardon the pun, what if *how* we live our lives, the choices we make, changes our information. And thus when we die, how that information is handled means it ends up in one place or another."

I had never thought about it that way, but it's entirely possible. Are Heaven and Hell merely representations of a universal sorting system for different information types? Can our information, our souls, be inherently good or bad?

"Demitri?" Denni presses.

"Denni, we need you up here," Bilgi calls. "We got a fork— which way?"

The young woman touches my arm and runs off to the front of the group. The rest of us bunch up behind and come to a stop, confronted by two rocky corridors splitting off in different directions.

Denni pulls out the holoprojector and fires it up, bathing the passage in an eerie luminescent green. "Here, to the right, the blockage is actually only thirty meters ahead. We're real close."

"Mos, Faruq, come with me." Mila takes off into the right tunnel, her companions close behind. We all follow suit, shuffling along in the dark.

By the time I get there, they are already feebly pulling at the large rocks. At the pace they're going, it'll take forever.

Giahi barges past me. "Stay right here, your majesty. Wouldn't want you to callous your perfect fingers with a little manual labor."

Mila scowls at him.

He laughs, calling me delicate, and steps forward to move rocks with the others.

They're not very efficient, these Robusts. The boulders are arranged in a pyramid-like structure, the larger ones at the bottom supporting everything at the top. If I pull just the right one, the whole load should topple. "Would it be okay, if I, um, asked everyone to back away for a second?"

Giahi bows mockingly and waves his hand at the blockage. "Be my guest, cloud prince."

"My name is Demitri."

Which stone to pull on? There—a keystone in the structure. That's the one. I rub my hands together, then clasp the stone with my palms and forearms. A few deep breaths, and then I pull with all my might. There's a slight scraping sound, the grit of rock on rock. My biceps bulge and strain through the thin material of my top—the veins in my neck swelling with blood. I screw my eyes together and clench my jaw.

The rock pops out, and I fling it to the ground with a loud thud. As predicted, the rest tumble around our feet, dust billowing up in plumes.

"Good job, Demitri. You just bought us a few hours." Mila pats me on the shoulder, then gives Giahi a sharp glance before clambering through the hole—careful not to catch her weapon on jagged rocks. Giahi says nothing, his face a picture of loathing.

"Pretty impressive." Denni beams as she slides past me.

Little Husniya is smiling as she beckons me to lean down. "She likes you," the child whispers.

"Just get your little self through that hole, miss." I clamber over the rocks, catching my shins and elbows on everything.

Denni gasps. "Whoa."

"What is that?" Bilgi asks.

The tunnel doesn't need torchlight anymore. Halogens hang

from the rocky ceiling and bathe a huge metallic cylinder, more than three meters across, in an orange light. The machine in front of us is familiar—a supercollider. A replica of the one Nikolaj used, but many times larger. Thin tubes cover the surface like ivy. Some of them run along the roof of the passage and disappear into the dark. A deep hum vibrates in the surrounding walls.

"Demitri, what is it?" Denni asks.

"A supercollider. I didn't know where he'd build one powerful enough. Now we know."

"It's huge. What are all the pipes, and why is it humming, and—"

Denni quiets as I place a hand on her shoulder. "Judging by the diameter of the containment unit, I'd guess it's a sixty-kilometer ring buried in the earth around us." There are no mines down here. He was building this machine. "Usually, two beams of particles are fired at nearly the speed of light in opposite directions. When they collide, you can examine what other particles are released. But this one probably has ten beams inside—the Leader doesn't care what things come out other than a black hole. He's upping his chances. Anyway, the beams are guided around the accelerator ring by strong superconducting electromagnets that need to be cooled to minus 271.3 degrees Celsius—colder than outer space. The pipes you're looking at are full of liquid helium, which cools them."

"And this is what he'll use to destroy us?" Mos asks.

"Yes."

"Then we can stop it from here," a man calls from the back, his arm stretching outward to grab a nearby pipe.

"No," we yell in unison. But it's too late.

A cobalt flash and the smell of burned flesh fills the tunnel as an energy shield vaporizes the impulsive Robust. He shrieks, but it's only momentary, his horrible demise cutting it short. It

242

happens so quickly most only gasp in confusion. My stomach, on the other hand, comprehends exactly what has just happened—and I immediately lean against the rocky wall and brace myself to vomit.

"What the hell?" Bilgi shouts, staring at me as if it were my fault.

"It has a protective energy shield," I reply between fits of coughing. "There's no way the Leader would risk this being damaged from down here. I don't know where the power source is for the shield. You'll still have to head to the rocket."

"Sard. No one else go anywhere near that thing," Bilgi orders. "Mila, we need to keep moving. Ghofaun is probably close to the site by now. Mila?"

But Mila isn't with the rest of the group. She's in a darker corner of the tunnel, staring at a hole in the ground.

CHAPTER THIRTY-TWO

MILA

Standing at one of the thermal vents, I look straight down a seemingly bottomless hole. Next to it, a dust-covered bag lies against the wall. I approach apprehensively, noting the blackened scars that streak down the wall toward the opening of the vent.

I stoop, pinch the edge of the small crumpled satchel, and give it a little shake to clear the dust. *I know this bag. I've seen it before.*

"What is it?" Bilgi asks from over my shoulder.

"I, uh ... I don't know yet. I ... I've seen this bag before."

"You don't remember where?"

"Give me a second." I wave him off.

The others gather around.

"What is it?" says one.

"What did she find?" asks another.

"Just wait. Hold on. Give us some space," Bilgi says. "Have another look. See if there's anything inside."

Crouched close to the floor, I lift back the flap to expose an interior pocket. And there it is, scrawled onto the underside of the fold: *Zevry Solokoff.*

"Zev," I whisper, drawing the bag closer. He was carrying it when he left for the mines.

"Who?"

"Her brother," Bilgi answers. "Give her a moment."

Faruq stands close but says nothing. Demitri is close as well, his large shadow looming over me. Pulling the bag open, I look inside. The satchel is completely empty.

"Nothing?" Bilgi asks.

"I don't understand. Why is his satchel here?"

"Mila," Demitri says, his voice soft. "Those are plasma burns." He points to scorch marks along the thermal vent.

"That's what I was thinking—from a Creed's energy rifle?"

"Yes. From the look of the bag against the wall, it was dropped, or thrown there," Demitri continues.

"Are you saying the Creed were shooting at my brother?"

"If I had to guess? Yes."

The Gracile looks nervous.

"But why would he be running toward the vent?" I say.

"Mila, check the bag one more time," Bilgi says. "Are you absolutely sure there's nothing in it? Why would he throw it down?"

Turning the bag upside down, I give it a shake. "I don't know. I can't—"

A piece of paper flutters to the ground. My breath held, I scoop up the faded sliver of paper and unfold it. The writing is rough, scratched out with a piece of sharpened coal. I can barely make out the words, but I read them aloud.

They almost caught me trying to sabotage the device this time. The Graciles' robot slaves are relentless. Day and night they force us to work without sleep and with just enough rations to keep us alive. I can feel my strength failing. I don't know much about what we're building for them, but I know in my heart it's a work of evil. The Graciles will never let us escape this prison. Just as our ancestors died in the gulags—so shall I. I must use what energy I have left to stop it. If I can steal a critical part and destroy it somehow, I must. This device cannot be activated. For all we know it could open the door to the pit of Hell itself and release unspeakable damnations. I will try again tonight. May Yeos guide my hand. ~ Zevry Solokoff

I'm holding the final words of my brother. He died trying to stop the madness of the Leader. He died trying to do something that mattered. That's why he never came home. I clutch the letter close to my chest. Speak to me, brother. Tell me what I must do.

"He must have stolen some piece of the machine and then flung himself into the vent," Faruq says.

"While the Creed were trying to shoot him down for it," adds Bilgi. "Your brother was a hero, Mila. He did what he knew was right—he risked his own life to stop this madness."

My brother was enslaved by the Graciles and forced to work on their doomsday device. He would have come home to me if he could have. After all this time, this small bit of knowledge is more than I could have ever hoped for.

"Mila, are you okay?" Faruq asks.

"Yes." I swallow the stone in my throat, drop the old bag on the ground, and stuff my brother's note into one of my pockets. "I am. I'm better than I've been in a long time. It's time for us to confront our oppressor. It's time for the Leader to hear our cries—every single one of us."

Gathering together, we press farther into the tunnels. The scouts tell me we're going in the right direction, but there's no way for me to know for sure. We shuffle along, unsure of each step in the darkness. The tunnel gently slopes upward. Perhaps we're headed out of this forsaken graveyard.

Faruq steps up alongside me, Husniya tucked beneath his arm. "Do you think we are close to this launch site?" he asks.

"I think we're closer, yes. Hopefully this tunnel will take us there."

My friend eyes me.

"What? Don't look at me like that."

246

He just smiles. "I wish you could see yourself the way others see you." He turns and motions to the throngs of resistance fighters walking the tunnels behind us. "The way all of them look at you."

"Stop it. That's not funny."

"I'm not being funny," Faruq says. "You've come a long way, my friend. And these people have chosen this fight because they believe in the cause and they believe in their leaders."

Time to change the subject. "You don't have to come with us. You have your sister now. You can always go home."

"Home? To what? Continue living in oppression under the heavy boot of a madman like Kapka? No, I can't. I won't subject my sister to that."

"Then, go live somewhere else."

"With this?" Faruq holds up his hand to reveal the large *B* scarred into the flesh. "No, Mila. I made you a promise."

"I relieve you of your obligation." Don't look him in the eyes.

"It's not just the obligation. It's a commitment to a friend. I will stand with you in this. That is my final word."

Highly unusual, and yet as predictable as the rising of the sun, this man. I shake my head and offer a small smile. "Very well, Faruq."

"Then it is settled." Faruq grins.

"What will I do, Faruq?" Husniya says from under his arm.

"My dear sister, I will not put you in danger again. You will stay with Bilgi this time. They will protect you until we return."

"But I want to go with you."

"No, no, that is not possible. It is far too dangerous."

"But what about you? You could get hurt." The little girl clings to the side of her big brother.

"Mila will protect me." He winks at me.

My fingertips gently touch my brother's note in my pocket. I understand what little Husniya is feeling all too well. I pat her on the back and stoop just a little. "I'll try to look after this dummy for you."

Husniya gives a sheepish smile.

A squall of static erupts from Denni's heavy backpack radio system. "We're picking something up. We must be closer to the surface than we think."

Everyone halts and waits with labored breathing as she fiddles with various knobs. The noise begins to resolve into voices.

"What is it, Denni?" I ask.

"I'm not sure. Give me a second." She pulls off the backpack and sets it on the ground. Immediately the radio goes silent.

"What happened?"

"I lost it."

"Get it back up. Get it back up. Mos, can you get that pack in the air?"

"I got it." Mos grabs the pack and heaves it into the air. Voices gush forth in the darkness.

"*The primary asset is go. All systems nominal. En route to designation X-Ray. What is your status? Over.*"

"*Copy primary asset is en route. Be advised, X-Ray is under siege from multiple Robust factions. Perimeter is intact. Asset will be secure upon arrival, but expect heavy engagement, over.*"

"*Copy X-Ray is under siege. Asset advises we continue the extraction as planned. Over.*"

"*Copy. X-Ray command over and out.*"

The transmission stops abruptly. Mos lowers the pack with a bewildered look on his face.

"What was all that?" Faruq asks.

"Creed transmission. It's all coded. They've been programmed to use old military terminology to conceal their messages," Denni says.

"What do you think of the message?" I ask.

"Well," starts Denni. "It seems pretty straightforward. The primary asset is the Leader. *X-Ray* has got to be the launchpad. The Leader is already headed there now."

"Yes." Bilgi nods. "That's right. We've heard references to the primary asset in previous transmissions we picked up back in headquarters. It's definitely the Leader."

"That means we've got to get moving, right?" I ask.

"This mission is supposed to be a surprise attempt to destroy this rocket?" Demitri asks from the back.

"Yeah, why?" What's his point?

He shuffles on the spot, tapping his forehead again. "The last part of their transmission, they said X-Ray was under siege."

My skin crawls. "Rippers?"

Demitri nods. "They must have kept the rocket concealed below in the mines. I saw a launchpad, not a rocket. The raising of it must have drawn a lot of attention."

"Radicals as well." Faruq nods. "Kapka is in a frenzy. If he got word the Graciles are raising a rocket to the surface, he likely thinks it's a weapon. He'd try to possess it. If he couldn't, he would try to destroy it."

"Shouldn't we just let him do that?" a scout says.

"Yeah, why should we risk our lives if that maniac will destroy it for us?" another man calls out.

"No. Hold on." I wave my hands for everyone to calm down. "We can't do that. We can't risk Kapka gaining the rocket intact. Who knows what he'd try to do with it. No, the mission stands. We've just got a few more hurdles to leap now."

An ethereal shriek echoes through the tunnel ahead.

"Everyone quiet. Douse the torches," I call out.

We stand in silence, waiting.

Then we hear it again, a low groan farther up the tunnel in the direction we're headed.

Bilgi makes his way to me. "Speaking of hurdles, what was that?"

"Sounded like there's someone up ahead."

"It didn't sound much like a person," Bilgi replies. "Take a small group. No torches. The more noise you make, the more of them you'll attract."

"Faruq, Mos. You two come with me."

As slowly as possible, we make our way up the tunnel. As the slope gradually grows steeper, a faint light gets stronger. The air is colder here. In the dark, a wall and an unstable wooden ledge jut upward. I can hear him now—incoherent groans and mutterings reaching out to us in the gloom.

The smell of death hits me. The odor is overpowering, a putrid stench of funk, feces, and old bloodstained garments. I tap Mos on the shoulder and draw him in close. "It's a Ripper. There may be more. Watch my back."

"I got ya," Mos replies.

Crawling my way slowly up over the rim of the ledge, the Ripper comes into view. Backlit by the exit to the tunnels, the feral man sits alone, grunting and stripping raw meat from a broken bone with his black teeth. His eating is both disgusting and mesmerizing. He looks up at me, and I freeze.

The fiend snarls. I lunge forward and strike him hard across the face. I sink into an unrelenting chokehold. Struggling in the dimness, we fall against the tunnel wall. The struggle draws another Ripper into the tunnel. Damnation. I can't let this one go. The other one comes at me screaming, his primitive weapon raised.

I clamp down on the one in my arms. Go to sleep already.

A shadow streaks down the far wall.

Mos crashes into the incoming Ripper, the force so strong the Ripper's head snaps back and his legs fly out from under him. Mos grabs the Ripper in midair and jams him violently against the ceiling of the tunnel, then slams him headfirst against the floor, rendering him unconscious.

The Ripper still in my arms grows weak, slapping at my elbow. He gurgles a final time, then drops unconscious. I let him slump to the ground.

"Mos, you okay?" I rub my jacket over and over. I can't get this stink off me.

"I'm okay. The way they smell, I didn't want to get too up close and personal," Mos says. "Faruq, can you come and tie up the one Mila had?"

"I'm coming up now."

Desperate to distance myself from the stench, I trudge toward the inviting cold draft coming from the mouth of the tunnel. Between us and the frozen outside world, a heavy steel door hangs off its hinges. Concussions pop and thud in the distance, followed by screams of pain and terror. What in all of creation is going on?

As I make my way to the wind-blasted opening, waves of sick anticipation pulse with the sounds of war beyond. I pray to Yeos it won't be the nightmare I've dreamed over and over—but it is. I recognize every rock, every snowflake, and every body lying in the blood-spattered snow.

"Guys." My tongue's heavy like a shank of lead. "Get everyone up here. You're going to want to see this."

* * *

Stretching from the mouth of the tunnel is a vast mining complex, ancient and abandoned. Inside are tiers of sleek, sterile fortifications of Gracile design. A thirty-foot-high plasma shield encircles the entire site. And there in the center, deep within the mining pit, sits a rocket of some kind, its nose peeking over the edge of the rock. A deep rumble, perhaps its engines, can be heard even from here. A suspension bridge connects the rim of the pit to a loading platform level with the fore section of the rocket.

Outside the walls, an army of Rippers scream, challenging and testing the force field. One of them grows overzealous, runs screaming into the barrier, and flashes into a fine gray powder, sending the others into further frenzy.

Toward the other side of the complex, another force gathers. Kapka's fanatics, hell-bent on gaining access to the launchpad and the rocket itself, launch a barrage of antique munitions. Bullets fly. Grenades cross over the top of the shield and explode inside the fortifications.

Strange music plays over a loudspeaker, and a voice repeats the same words over and over: *"This is the will of Ilāh. We will strike at the dark hearts of the infidel, and we will restore the Musul people to their rightful place. You will be shown no mercy, for Hell awaits the foes of the chosen. We are destined for paradise."*

Along the perimeter the two armies mix in isolated skirmishes. A swarmed Musul detonates himself amid a pile of Rippers. A lone Ripper charges into the ranks of the Musuls, cutting and killing before being struck down. Though the two groups seem to be more focused on finding a way inside the barrier than on killing each other.

Inside the shield, ranks of emotionless Creed soldiers stand ready to defend the rocket, their sterile, avalanche-pattern exoskeletons poised with plasma rifles raised. If that shield were impenetrable, why would the Creed be standing ready? They wouldn't be. That means they're worried about the shield coming down—but how?

"Ghofaun, do you copy?" Denni says over her radio.

The sound of static greets us.

"How far of a range do you have?" I ask, motioning to the radio.

252

Denni grimaces. "Not far with this old equipment. A few kilometers at best—and that's with perfect line of sight."

"Yeos save us," Bilgi mutters, making his way through the enthralled resistance fighters.

"We're trying to raise Ghofaun to see if he's got anything different."

Bilgi nods but says nothing.

Next to Faruq, little Husniya cowers and tells her brother she's scared. He responds with silence, his hand stroking her back.

"Ghofaun, come in. Ghofaun, do you copy?" Denni repeats.

"*I copy,*" a voice replies, distorted through the static wash. "*We can see the top of the rocket rising into view. It looks like—*" There's a prolonged wash of static. "*This isn't good. Can you see what's going on?*"

I take the receiver from Denni and key it up. "We see it, Master Ghofaun. Listen, the only reason they would stage so many Creed here is if they were afraid we might disable the barrier. We need a way inside. What do you think?"

The group around me grows restless. Bilgi and Mos work to control their fear, reassuring them we can still do what we came to do.

After a long pause, Ghofaun comes back over the old radio, his voice faint and fuzzy. "*I can do it. See the antenna jutting from the main building?*"

"Yes."

"*I say we destroy that building. I don't know if it controls the shields, but either way, we'll at least cause some chaos, disrupt their control, and maybe take out their communications.*"

"Okay, but if those shields go down completely, there's nothing to keep the Musuls or the Rippers out. It'll be a total free-for-all in there."

"*That's true,*" Ghofaun says.

Bilgi looks at me and shrugs. "Make a beeline for the rocket," he says, pointing to the enormous ship, "and hope everyone else is too busy to worry about us. It's all we've got."

I key the radio back up. "Ghofaun, your idea may be the best thing we have going right now. Let's do it. How will you get in there to plant the explosives?"

"Leave that to me. I'll need a few minutes, and I'll have to go radio silent. When the building goes, that's your signal."

"I got it. You get us in, and we'll take care of the rocket. Copy?"

"Copy. My team will meet you on the launchpad to cover you as you plant the explosives."

"Copy. Just get us in there."

"You can count on me. Stand by."

The radio clicks off.

I hand the receiver back to Denni. "Everyone get low and wait for Ghofaun's signal. When it's time to go, we push hard for the rocket, and we don't stop for anything. You guys hear me?"

Everyone murmurs and nods.

"Until we go, everyone stay ready. Make sure your weapons are accessible. Make sure your minds are right. Once we move from here, there's no turning back." I check the less-than-lethal weapon in my hands one last time. Please, Yeos, let it be different this time.

With a whoosh, a Gracile ship drops through the clouds and circles above the madness. The Leader. The Musuls fire their rocket-propelled grenades at the vessel, their rounds screaming over the shield and dropping out of sight. They can't reach the ship. Swooping low, it nears the landing area, a stone's throw from the rocket.

The silver-haired man briskly exits the ship, flanked by his personal guard. He pivots and moves with purpose toward the rocket. His Creed are carrying something.

"Demitri, what is that?" I point to the case in their hands.

Denni offers the Gracile her binoculars, but he dismisses them.

"It's Nikolaj's portable fusion reactor." He taps his forehead again. "I'm so sorry, it's all my fault—"

"Come on, Demitri. Stay focused."

"But if it weren't for me—"

"Let it go." I soften my tone to reassure him. "That's not helpful right now, Demitri. Ghofaun is going to get us in. When he does, you stay with me, understand?"

Demitri nods. "Okay. Yes, I can do that."

"Got your sick stick?" Denni asks Demitri.

"Uh-huh." His eyes are wide.

"Here, take these, too. It's a modded firecracker and a small torch. If you get lost, light it up and it'll pop, make a high-pitched sound, and let off red smoke. We'll find you." She pats him on his massive shoulder.

"If I get … lost?"

"Don't worry, Demitri. Just stay close."

As I stare into his scared eyes, knowing what's to come, I can't help but take the opportunity to ask my selfish question. He may be the only one who can tell me. "Do you speak Russian?"

Demitri looks utterly lost. "Russian?"

"Old Russian, before us. Before this."

"Why does that matter?"

"Just tell me."

He shrugs. "Some, but I don't have tons of formal instruction. I learned by reading—"

"What does this mean: *Menya zovut smert', i ad prikhodit so mnoy.*"

The Gracile wets his lips. "Umm, if you're saying it correctly, it means: my name is Death, and Hell follows with me."

"Great. That's just great."

"Why? What is it?"

"It's nothing. Just something I heard. Don't worry about it." Demitri taps his head.

Way to offer comfort, Mila. Get your mind back to the task at hand. "Faruq, Mos, and Denni, you stay with me as well. We'll focus on going straight for the rocket." They nod. "Denni, you have the nitro?"

"I have it." Denni pats the bag of high explosives slung across her shoulders.

"Good. Drop the radio pack here. I need you light and fast."

"Okay." Denni leans the radio pack against a nearby wall. She secures the nitro and grabs her old-fashioned bolt-action hunting rifle.

"Mila." Faruq nudges my arm.

"Yes?"

"I, um, just wanted to say …"

"What is it, Faruq?" His eyes are as deep and dark as krig, but somehow they comfort me. My cheeks are burning again. Do I have feelings for this man? I most certainly should *not* have feelings for this man.

He holds my gaze in a way that stops my breath short. "Mila," he nearly whispers, taking my hand in his. "Whatever happens, I am glad to have known you."

He gently squeezes my fingers. I squeeze back. However wrong everything else in the world is, at least one thing feels right.

"Hey," Mos calls, catching me off guard, "take this." He presses an auto-injector with a strange yellow liquid into my hand. A single handwritten word is scrawled on the side—"Hyper."

"Thanks, Mos, but I don't do this stuff." I try to push it back, but he won't take it.

"It's not extreme. Mostly just synthetic adrenaline, some

256

stimulants, and endorphins. Just keep it, in case you get in a bad spot." The Kahangan grins.

No way I'm using this. I drop the drug into my cargo pocket. "Thanks, Mos."

"There he goes," Bilgi says.

The Leader moves from the series of interconnected ladders, across a narrow platform, and along a walkway that disappears behind the nose cone of the rocket.

Bilgi continues. "Listen to me now, people. Do not forget the strength of your hearts. Whatever enclave you hail from, this world is our home. We will not let the Gracile oppressors take it from us. Fight. Give your life to save the people you love. This is our last chance for survival. If you do not spend your life here, then you will lose it pitifully when the elites above steal it from you. The people of Etyom are counting on the boldness of the resistance. Let them remember us all as heroes this day!"

We all stand, screaming, and as if on cue, the command building explodes. We continue screaming, even louder now, thrusting our weapons into the air. The plasma shield flickers and fizzles out. By the hand of Yeos. Ghofaun's plan worked.

Mos pulls a loaded auto-injector full of yellow liquid from a side pocket in his pants, flips the cap, and jams the nozzle against his leg. He exhales forcefully, clenching his fists.

Work through me, Yeos.

"Fly, girl." Bilgi grabs my arm. "Go now!" The old man has an energy in his eyes: the power of belief. "Go and become the instrument of fate. You can do this."

I pull my satchel from my neck and press it to his chest. He takes it and gives me a wink. He knows the priceless tome lies inside.

I turn, calling out to the resistance, "This is it. Stay with me."

The mass of resistance fighters pours from the mouth of the

tunnel and charges out into the madness beyond. We barrel across the snow-covered landscape toward the perimeter fence. Beyond, row upon row of Creed soldiers await, poised to fight.

"Mos, get up here," I shout.

Breathing with labored gasps, Mos's heavy bulk pushes past me. As the Creed shift, focusing their attention toward us, Mos raises his laser cannon and fires. Like a beam of super-magnified sunlight, the laser blasts forward, searing the faces of the robots. One by one their lifeless mouths drop open, their optical circuits fried.

"It's working!" Mos yells.

"I know it's working. Run!" I yell back.

Mos drops his shoulder and plows right through the middle of the blinded Creed, cleaving their ranks like a heated blade through ice, but a lone robot strides forward and raises its rifle.

I shoulder my bag launcher, aim, and fire. The lead-filled bag rockets from the chamber, slamming into the visor of the Creed. Its head spins 180 degrees. The robot drops to its knees and slumps against the frozen ground.

"Go. Get to the suspension bridge," I scream.

Mos trains his laser, blasting and blinding the Creed as they converge. I chance a look behind and see Faruq strike a Ripper with the butt of his rifle. Denni takes out a Ripper with a precision shot to the head. Behind them, a group of resistance fighters perish under a swirling tide of death and destruction.

But where's Demitri? That fool. "Demitri. Where's Demitri?"

CHAPTER THIRTY-THREE

DEMITRI

Far off in the distance, through the smoke, sleet, and pockets of battling Robusts, the rocket sits in its subterranean hiding place. From what I can make out, it's a hybrid of the old space shuttle program and some kind of laser propulsion. This is what even our people sacrificed for. But where is he going? Just into orbit?

"Demitri, run." Mila screams, sprinting away into the fray.

Where am I supposed to run? All I can do is try and keep pace.

Mos fires his laser rifle over and over, frying the optical circuits of the Creed before him. He plows through them with his body—brute force and absolute doggedness are his tools, but it clears a path for the rest of us.

Snow explodes as bullets and bombs detonate around us. Covering my ears, I trudge forward, yelling for them to slow down, to wait for me. But they can't hear anything over the din of war.

A grenade explodes to my right, the force knocking me clean off my feet. I crash awkwardly into the slush, spread eagle and vulnerable. My head ringing and my senses compromised, I roll to my knees.

"Think fast, Gracile." Giahi slams the butt of his rifle across my face, sending me back to the ground with a thud. He spits on my head. "Poor little cloud prince, all alone. Do us all a favor and stay there. Even better, die there." He glances over his shoulder and

259

runs off into the fray.

Stay here and die, he said. Blood pours from my split nose, and my world spins. Would anyone even notice? I roll onto my stomach to search for Mila. She's gone. They left me behind.

Don't be pathetic, pidaras. *Let me out. Let me save us.*

I can't let Vedmak loose again. Not now.

Something horrible shrieks from above. I flip to my back. A lone Ripper stands there, wielding an ax above his head, his eyes wild. Instinctively I grab at the sick stick Denni gave me and plunge it into his stomach. The effect is instantaneous—he convulses and vomits over my legs, clutches at his abdomen, then collapses to the ground. I scramble to my feet and push off into a sprint.

Ducking and diving between blasts and the high-pitched squeal of passing bullets, I run and run, only to drive deeper into the conflict. Parts of Creed bodies pepper the landscape, jerking autonomously. The limbs of fallen Rippers bleed into the snow, soaking it a deep crimson.

Another Ripper comes screaming toward me, his spear held high above his head. I dive behind a nearby boulder and wait, my chest heaving. The crazed man hurtles toward me, screeching. Three steps from impaling me, he evaporates in a puff of gray powder. A Creed soldier stands in the distance, its energy rifle smoking. It glances at me as if deciding whether I'm a threat or not. Then, apparently uninterested in me, the Creed stomps off.

Let me out. Vedmak snarls again. *Let me do what I was born to do. This is no place for you. I can save us. I can make sure we survive.*

What choice do I have? I don't know what I'm doing. I don't know how to get out. Mila, Mos, Faruq. Even Denni. They all left me. They were never my friends.

I'm your only friend. I'm your only way out of this.

A silhouette crests the snowy hillock some fifteen meters away.

I know this shape, this person. "Bilgi."

But it's not Bilgi. My moment of relief is snatched away. It's a Ripper—the chieftain I saw outside Zopat. He recognizes me, his eyes wild with the desire for my blood.

There he is.

"No!" Forcing my tired legs once again into action, I push off the ground and tramp in the opposite direction, dodging a scrum of Robusts and Creed. But I only make it another hundred feet before finding myself, once again, face down in the freezing snow. Lying there, panting and exhausted both physically and mentally, my head fills with Vedmak's nagging to set him free—to let him save us.

Far off in the distance, the rocket is shuddering. Smoke billows from beneath it as a powerful laser burns away the launch plate, creating the plasma that will thrust it into space.

We're too late. I'm not a soldier. How did I ever think I could do this? I should just let them kill me. Or maybe I'll just succumb to hypothermia. Better than being ripped apart by a black hole. I roll onto my back, spread out in the cold sludge, and close my eyes to accept my fate.

Without warning, my right hand flies to the side pocket of my pants, pulls out one of the syringes, and pops the cap off. It's the Red Mist. "What the hell? Vedmak." With my left hand, I clasp my right wrist and fight back. "Vedmak, no!"

The Ripper chieftain yelps into the cold air like a wolf. It's enough to distract me, to give Vedmak a vital window. The needle pierces my chest and slides into the fibers of my heart. The pain is sharp, but momentary. My arms slump to the ground, my muscles tingle, and the world begins to darken. As the blackness closes in, Vedmak's maniacal laugh fills my skull.

Now ... we play.

CHAPTER THIRTY-FOUR

VEDMAK

I return to claim what is rightfully mine. In this body, I'm a machine built for war. A machine the Graciles never understood how to harness. I understand all too well.

Rising from the slush, where the weak Demitri fought my right to this corporeal shell, I take in the scope of the war. I'm not interested in the petty squabbles of men. Mine is a calling more primitive, purer than the snow that drifts onto this battleground.

Stretching and testing this biological engine, I move with stealth through the twisting masses. All too easily, I snap the neck of one of the Gracile's robotic puppets and snatch up its energy rifle. But it won't fire. Future weapons. Whatever happened to the efficiency of a sturdy bolt-action rifle, or the simplicity and effectiveness of a good hand ax? Those were true means of killing.

Throwing the useless rifle to the ground, I dodge the swipe of a short sword as a Musul attempts to remove my head. Ahh, that's more like it. I'll return the favor. I wrench the weapon from his grasp and fling him to the ground, removing his head with a single downward swipe. His eyes gape wide with the shock of my savagery. These are not terrorists. These are impostors, pretending to understand terror—to what end? They will all be slaughtered for their efforts. But it's not them I search for.

"Activate neuralweb connection."

My pathetic host did this a few times, and I've had plenty of time to watch. I hate this strange technology, but it has its uses. My vision springs to life with images and text, most of it useless.

"Filter all information. Show me only where the savages' chieftain is."

The images flicker and flash. The connection is weak down here. A single visual feed shows a large shadow moving heavily in the snow.

"Magnify."

There you are. You belong to me. I turn and match the image to reference points on the true horizon. There, the south corner of the launchpad.

Outside the perimeter fence, I run. As I come into the open atop a small snow-covered hill, my target comes into view, surrounded by his attendants. I raise my blade and point it directly at him, the way he did to me those few days before.

"You. Face me, coward. Face me if you dare."

My foe turns and locks his crazed eyes with mine, fury burning in his blood-smeared face.

"Yes. That's it. I challenge you. Face me—or run away like the dog you are." I continue to point my blade at him, tracking his movement as he paces back and forth, his face contorted in a snarl.

With a grunt, he shrugs off his animal-skin cloak and motions for his weapon bearer to hand him a spear. Four attendants appear, each holding a long stick with a syringe lashed to the end. They simultaneously stab his muscular back, the strange greenish liquid in the vials draining into his tissues.

"Yes, take your drugs. You will need them."

The chieftain screams with rage and comes for me, slowly at first, then faster and faster, a train of fury hurtling forward.

"Let's see what you're made of, savage." I rush at him, sword at the ready.

We clash in a ravenous lust for death. The chieftain lunges in an attempt to impale me. Rolling effortlessly to the outside, I spin inward to take his head with a single blow—but it's not to be. He blocks my strike, my sword notching the hard wood of his weapon. I swing to the rear, harnessing the fury boiling within me and fusing it to my empowered Gracile form. Again and again my blade notches his spear, and I grow careless of his strength. The brute kicks me squarely in the groin and follows with a sharp blow to my head. A cheap but effective play. Doubling over, my knees crash into the snow. My world spins and my stomach convulses. Mortal pain. I have not experienced it in so long.

It feels good.

The chieftain bares his teeth, raising his spear, but I grab it, yank it downward, and strike him in the face with it. He throws me from him. I flop against the snowbank but quickly rise, wiping the dripping cut across my cheek.

"Is that all you've got, cave dweller?"

"Stop your crying and find out," the chieftain taunts, the words barely understandable.

"As you wish."

Weaponless, I charge him again. He turns his spear on me and screams. Deflecting the iron point, my body slams against the shaft, shattering it at the blade notch. With a fierce blow under his chin, I simultaneously jerk the broken, jagged wood from his calloused hands, then spear him through the thigh, tear it out, and pierce him again through the gut.

The thug shrieks and grabs me by the throat, choking me to the ground. Not today, you mindless dog. I grab a handful of his fingers and break them. He shrieks again and releases me. I thrust him away with a kick, then slowly rise to my feet, hot breath puffing into the frozen air.

My foe appraises his wounds. With a swing of his arm, his Rippers run at me from all directions. An honorless move. He wants to deliver me some playmates. Very well.

Stepping into the center of their attack, I obliterate them with my bare fists. The sheer power of these hands—no, my hands—is astonishing. Nothing can stop me. And yet, my control over this vessel wanes, the muscles no longer as responsive to my will. Something is trying to get through. He is trying to get back in. No. Not yet, fool child.

The chieftain pulls the spear from his stomach with a scream and comes again. I knock the jagged shaft from his grasp and into the bloodstained snow at our feet. He strikes me again and again. There is no pain. No weakness. Nothing but hate, deep and endless, flows in these veins. I torque against him with my whole body and dislocate the brute's arm at the shoulder, and with a groan, I throw him to the ground. Dropping on top of him, I grab him by the throat and pluck the wooden spear from the crimson snow.

"Beg me for mercy."

Eyes wide, the chieftain groans.

"Beg!" I cry, centimeters from his blood-smeared face.

"Mercy."

"Not this time!" I scream with glee, and jam the wooden stake up under his chin and through the top of his head. I find my blade and swing it down, claiming my prize. As I hoist the chieftain's head into the air, his blood runs down my arm. The Rippers flee in terror. It is beyond glorious.

"I will rule the weakness of this world. It is mine to command."

A wave of sickness jolts through me. I falter and drop the severed head. Sudden pain racks my skull, pushing at the backs of my eyes. "No." The effects of the drug are fading fast. My descent will be painful. No, I must find a way to stay in control. I try to make my way forward, stepping over the bodies at my feet.

265

The cries of the puppet echo inside my skull.

Look at what you've done!

Fog creeps over my consciousness. Groaning and grabbing my head, I stumble on, no longer in control. And then, just as quickly as my freedom came to me, it slips away. A cold sleep descends to reclaim me as its own once again. Back to the hateful chains of purgatory that bind my spirit and inhibit my desires. I fade, until nothing remains but the uncompromising, swallowing blackness of my eternal prison.

CHAPTER THIRTY-FIVE

MILA

If this doesn't work, we're all as good as dead.

A plume of fire bursts a little too close, and I instinctively flinch. No second chances. I will myself forward, my legs shaking, nearly refusing to carry me farther across the creaking suspension platform. My lungs burn from smoke and exertion.

One of the elite's strike ships whines overhead, driving an atmospheric pressure change that makes my eardrums throb. Its massive engines rotate, and the gunship turns to face us. Its giant electrical weapon crackles.

"Keep moving." I scream to my comrades. Mos forges ahead, slamming the Creed from our path. "Get across the bridge. We have to make it to the cargo pad."

A rocket-propelled grenade screams overhead, slamming into the tail rotors of the Creed gunship, which then spirals past us and crashes into the mines in a mass of flaming wreckage.

I shoulder my weapon and fire the last beanbag—it knocks a charging Musul to the ground. No more rounds. I sling the weapon down onto the icy platform as we make it to the other side.

Mos screams and drops his weapon. "Mila, I'm hit!" A plasma burn blackens his right side.

"I'm here. Get behind me." Mos's goggles slide over my eyes, my hands clamping down on his weapon. Rising up, I crank the laser's exposure wide open—exactly what Denni said not to do.

The giant laser fires from my hip, and the beam sears across the last remaining lines of the Creed, setting the rubbery flesh of their faces on fire. Pivoting, I swing the beam across a mob of Musuls. They howl, cover their blistered faces and ruined eyes, and throw their own smoking bodies to the ground.

My flesh tingles. I feel sick. But better blind than dead.

Denni screams behind us.

She's still on the bridge, trapped with a few others. They're quickly swarmed by Rippers. Denni calls out, but I'm too far away. Her eyes flash wide as a Ripper's blades pierce her body.

"Denni!"

With eyes full of fear, she locks her gaze onto mine—and detonates her satchel.

The air is knocked from my lungs. My ears ring as I'm thrown to the platform's floor. Smoke and debris hang in the air like confetti. Nothing of the bridge, or Denni, remains.

Denni used the explosives. We can't destroy the rocket. We're all going to die.

The rocket's rumbling grows louder. From here, I can see everything. It isn't a rocket, at least not like I imagined. A huge central cylinder with a massive nose cone is flanked by two thinner ones. A separate vessel that looks like a huge black-and-white old-world airplane sits on the back of the central tube. A walkway leads to the side of the monstrous metallic bird. Ladders branch off to various doors in its side. Far below, a white laser beam streaks from deep within the pit, directly against the bottom of the largest cylinder. Glowing green plasma fills the old quarry.

Two pairs of arms yank me to my feet. It's Faruq and Ghofaun.

"Hurry, Mila. You have to go," Ghofaun yells.

"Denni just—" I cough.

Ghofaun grabs my shoulders. "I know. Mila, look at me. You have to get *in* the ship before it takes off."

"You're crazy."

Ghofaun points to a square hatch in the side of the vessel. "In there. We have to move, *now*."

"Inside it?"

"Yes. Mila, you must stop the Leader."

"But I won't know what to do. Where's Demitri?" I shout over the sounds of the rocket and gusts of snow.

"If he doesn't show, you'll have to leave without him. The mission is more important," Ghofaun yells back. "You have to go. We will protect you as best we can. Faruq."

Faruq nods and ushers me along the walkway.

Ghofaun spins like a dancer and kicks into a mob of knife-wielding Musuls approaching us from one of the bridges on the opposite side of the platform. Faruq jerks my arm and drags me backward across the metallic causeway toward the nearest hatch.

"Logosian." A faint voice makes its way over the din.

The wind stings my face and blurs my vision. But in the chaos, a man appears on the platform: Kapka. He stands, pointing an old Soviet RPG launcher at us.

"You filthy *kafir*." He holds up a single finger, the big weapon balanced over his shoulder. "Your way of life is dead, your enclave lies in ruins, and yet, *you* still live. I should have broken your spirit when I had the chance. You won't escape this time."

Faruq stands between the maddened gangster and me. "I stole her out from under you. If you want to have a problem, have it with me."

"What is your name, traitor?"

"You don't remember me?" Faruq moves toward Kapka. "My mother was worthy of your attention, until she fell ill. Then you cast her and her bastard children out."

Kapka narrows his gaze. "Faruq? You simple idiot, get out of my way. This Logosian is mine."

"Never." Faruq takes another step. I grab his arm.

He glances over his shoulder, his stare resolute. "I have to go. I have to do this."

"No, don't."

"We don't have a choice." Faruq pushes my hand away. "Get in the rocket, Mila. Finish this. Do it for *all* of us." He turns back to Kapka. "*You* murdered my father. We all have endured enough of you."

Kapka breaks into a wicked smile. "Oh no, boy. You have not even begun to know pain, to feel the weight of my boot on your spine—but you will. For this insult, I'll track down that wretched sister of yours and choke the life out of her with my own two hands."

"You would do that to your own daughter?" Faruq shakes with the words.

"I'll do it to *anyone* who gets in my way." Kapka spits. He raises the weapon and pulls the trigger.

The RPG doesn't fire.

Faruq sprints toward him. I move to run with him, but I'm seized from behind and pulled, flailing, away toward the hatch. "No. I have to help him."

"Mila. We have to go." It's Demitri. "We'll be incinerated. The rocket is taking off."

I struggle fruitlessly against his superior strength. He snatches open the sealed door to the hatch and pulls me inside.

I scramble for the door. "No!"

The rocket shakes. Time slows, every painful second dragged out. Demitri's arms snake around me, and he pulls the door shut. My arms outstretched, my body writhing, I can only watch through the closing gap. Faruq fights with Kapka over the malfunctioning RPG. It fires against the platform with a deafening boom. Everything flashes white.

CHAPTER THIRTY-SIX

DEMITRI

The immense power coursing behind us, an enormous wave pushing up and up, fills my consciousness to the exclusion of all else. The rocket shakes uncontrollably, as if in the jaws of some gigantic beast. I clasp my arms around Mila's body, her back to my chest, and hold tight. The acceleration presses us to the bulkhead like the hand of an angry god, determined we should not leave this world. My stomach convulses.

The initial thrust of the laser stops abruptly, and we're thrown forward. I curl up in a ball and shield Mila, but we clang against the hull, her head taking a hard knock. She goes limp, and then we're immediately slammed back against the rear bulkhead as secondary boosters kick in.

With my eyes screwed shut, I cling to Mila and wait. It feels like forever, but eventually the boosters cease. Gradually we lift away from the bulkhead and float in the dark. The fluids in my stomach rise into my gullet, burning the soft tissues of my throat. My legs kick outward, but I go nowhere.

"Mila?" I spin her around and hold her shoulders.

She doesn't respond, though she appears to be breathing.

"And now, what do I do?" Perhaps I'm asking myself. Perhaps I'm asking Vedmak, or a god I don't believe in. But no reply comes. Even Vedmak is silent. "Vedmak? Vedmak, I know you're in here." But he's not. "Vedmak?" There's no answer. Did he leave? Am I

271

free? The dark of space says nothing.

I am alone. Vedmak is gone, a freedom at the cost of so many lives.

Only Mila is with me now.

A loud clunk and the ship shifts. We float into the hull again. The thrusters must have fired. We're positioning ourselves? For what? I arrange Mila near the wall and shed my heavy coat. I push off the hull—just enough to get some momentum—and stretch my hands out to protect my head.

My fingers find the opposite wall, and I feel along rather than halt my ascent. There's a faint light a few meters ahead. Eventually I come to rest with my face centimeters from the thick glass of a small porthole.

A beautiful blue-green marble sits in the purple-black fabric of space. It's awesome in every sense of the word. My breath halts. Earth. My home. From up here I can see no lillipads. No slums. No Etyom. From here, our agendas seem insignificant. The war. The Leader's plans—all of it. Our little blue orb, tiny in the vastness of space. Does the universe care if we exist? I think not.

But we care. And perhaps we should. In the vastness of the cosmos, on this tiny speck of insignificant rock, was born an intelligent life-form that, for all we know, may be the only one like it ever to have existed. Our stint in this universe cut short because the Leader believes it is time. Even Mila's Yeos hasn't done that. If He exists, He's allowed us to play out our fretted reality without interfering.

You are more important than you know. That's what Evgeniy had said. Maybe I can stop the Leader. Maybe I can make the people of Etyom see what I've seen. Maybe I can stop their petty squabbling. I owe it to everyone. To Evgeniy. To Nikolaj. To Mila.

The rocket jerks again, and I cling to the edges of the portal. A huge metal structure comes into view. A space station. Is that …

Asgardia?

The structure resembles a humongous metallic insect. Long and thin, it has a glass biome at the far end of one arm. At the opposite end is a large boxlike structure that must be the living quarters, and maybe communications if that large dish on the dorsal side is anything to go by. But it's the huge structure in the dead center that commands attention. A giant disk, like an enclosed hamster wheel, easily more than thirty meters in diameter, and four meters thick. It's fixed by external axles to a support structure that sports two massive arrays of solar panels like huge wings.

Why would he dock here? Why not fire the accelerator from the rocket?

The enormous station hangs in space, the huge disk that would rotate to give the occupants at least some gravity unmoving, the massive glass dome once designed to house hydroponics, dark and lifeless.

Why here?

I fumble along the wall for a headlamp, remove it from its hook, pull it over my head, and switch it on. A narrow beam of light penetrates the dark. This isn't a service area; this is a cargo hold. I push off the wall and float to the opposite side, where a large square unit hums quietly. The self-contained computer and monitor embedded into the casing is a standard unit. With a few presses of the correct keys, I have the inventory pulled up. Seeds, grain and ... embryos. He's transporting fifty Gracile embryos? If it all goes wrong, he's going to start again. No wonder we haven't frozen to death; this hold is temperature controlled.

The Leader must need a backup plan. If it goes wrong—if he creates strange matter rather than a black hole—he'll want to continue the Gracile lineage somehow. To use Asgardia as a *new* New Etyom. He must have found a way to power it up.

Think, Demitri, think. He'll need time to set up the station and initiate the gravitational disk. He's probably using Nikolaj's fusion reactor to power everything, including the heating and electronics, so he'll need to install that first. Then he'll back the station away from low orbit and any chance of coming into contact with strangelets. Then he'll fire the supercollider. We need to sever his link with Earth—so he can't do that.

I push off again to the opposite side. There, fixed to the inner hull, is an array of tools. I grab as much as possible and stuff it into the pockets of my tunic. Perhaps, without Vedmak, this is who I am. Perhaps without his crushing personality devaluing me at every turn, I am a good person. A brave person.

The ship clunks, shudders, and comes to a complete halt.

CHAPTER THIRTY-SEVEN

MILA

Silence—a stillness like I've never experienced before. In Etyom there's always some racket: a generator running, screams in the streets, a bar fight. Etyom is not silent—ever.

My eyes open with great care, unsure if I'll be among the living or the dead, but I'm greeted only by darkness. I'm inside the rocket. If the rocket wasn't destroyed, and it launched … I'm in space.

Why does my head hurt? I must have passed out. Am I in a cargo area or a maintenance hatch? Is it safe in here? As I attempt to sit up, the strange sense of weightlessness pulses through my stomach.

"Demitri?" More silence. "Demitri."

"I'm here. Keep your voice down." As he glides toward me, the lamp on his head illuminates his blood-soaked clothing. His grisly appearance is out of place with his meek personality.

"What happened to you? Where'd you go?"

Demitri paws at the blood on his face and clothes. "I don't really remember. Vedmak took over. It was bad this time."

"Are you okay?"

"I'm a little sore, but yes, I think so. The people I came into contact with fared worse, I'm afraid."

"Are you in control now?"

"For now. He tricked me and used a drug to subdue my consciousness for a time. I think I'll be all right."

275

"Where are we?"

"I think it's the cargo hold."

"But we're in ..." I motion to his floating body.

"In space? Yes, with our dumb luck, we actually made it."

"I can't believe it. We just left everybody."

"We had to," Demitri says. "They're resourceful people. I'm sure Denni has some gadget to help keep everyone safe."

Denni. He doesn't know.

"What?"

"Denni. She didn't make it."

"Oh." Demitri's face grows solemn.

"I'm sorry, Demitri. She was overtaken by Rippers and detonated her satchel while she was still on the bridge."

He doesn't say anything for a long while.

"It's not your—"

"But it is, isn't it? If I hadn't abandoned everyone ..."

"We both abandoned them. We had to. We didn't have a choice."

"On the rocket maybe, but if I'd had control of Vedmak, Denni might still be alive."

There's not much I can say to that.

He turns and pushes off the bulkhead, floating away into the dark.

Can I live with myself? What choice do I have? Someone had to finish this. I didn't die. My dream was incomplete. There's still work to do.

"Demitri," I call after him, pushing off into the dark passage. "We can't bring them back. But we can make sure they didn't die in vain. You may not believe in Yeos, but He believes in you. He has a plan for us both. And right now, we are the best hope for everyone—Robusts and Graciles."

"I know. It just isn't fair."

"If life were perfect, Demitri, it wouldn't be."

"That's pretty profound. From the Writ?"

"My brother, actually. He used to say it to me. Didn't really get it myself until now."

He allows a gentle smile, but who knows if it's genuine.

Demitri believes my religion is a security blanket designed for weak-minded children, that without it I'm as broken as he is. In that regard, he's right. I am badly broken. But it's my acceptance of this brokenness, and my need for Yeos, that draws me back to life. For what he doesn't understand is the wellspring of hope that can be found in true faith. How the power of belief can triumph over even the worst of circumstances—that even when we're lost, and alone, and beaten, we are never truly these things because we rest in the knowledge that the hand of our creator is upon us.

How would I know about the love Yeos has for me if I hadn't been told about it? How would the gift of the Lightbringer be real to me? It wouldn't, and thus, I can't expect Demitri to understand, unless I choose to show him.

Demitri clears his throat. "You want to see something?"

"Sure."

"I figured out his backup plan. If it all goes wrong. If he creates strange matter. He's prepared to start over."

"Start over?"

"The cargo hold of this ship is full of Gracile embryos."

"What?"

"Genetically enhanced embryos. If he botches up the black hole, he can start over up here."

"He's trying to play God."

The Gracile nods. "The Leader is in the station now. I have an idea, but we may not have much time."

"The station?"

"Follow me." We propel ourselves toward a small window.

"Look." Demitri gestures.

Through the small porthole, I see it: we're connected to a huge space station. Behind it sits my home, my planet, glowing blue and white. I've never seen anything so beautiful in my entire life.

"Look here now." Demitri taps the glass. "That's Asgardia—or at least it was going to be."

"Asgardia?"

"It started almost as a joke, an experiment in how willing humans were to jump ship and create a whole new nation free of the bonds of tyranny, capitalism, and politics. It was laughed at—until the New Black Death took hold. Huge amounts of money were poured into building a long-term habitable environment for humanity to survive here. This is the result."

"What happened with it?"

"It was never fully realized. The NBD happened too fast."

"But this station is still operational?"

"Entirely," he says. "The Leader just had to provide the sustainable power source—my brother's miniature fusion reactor."

"Okay, what next?"

"I have an idea, but it's a little far flung."

I give Demitri a stern look, urging him to continue.

"The Leader needs to fire the supercollider under Fiori from up here," he continues, "probably using the ancient spacenet set up between Asgardia and Earth. You'll have to distract the Leader while I shut down his connection to the spacenet."

"Can we do that?"

"I think so, but remember—"

"You have no idea if this will work, do you."

He shakes his head slowly. "No. It's an assumption."

"Okay." I rub my hands together. "Where do we start?"

"We'll climb up into the cockpit and then into the equalization chamber. Hopefully we can do so unnoticed and make our way to the Leader."

"You know where he is?"

Demitri shrugs. "If I had to guess? The control platform inside the disk. It's the only place with gravity." He taps his fingers on his forehead.

"We need to split up. How do we communicate?"

"With these." He holds up a small circular plug.

"What's that?"

"It goes in your ear. It will allow us to talk to each other."

"Where'd you get it?"

Demitri looks flustered. "Here in the ship. What does it matter?"

"It matters. I'm not jacking myself up with strange tech."

"You're not jacking, it's ... You used Denni's radio to talk to Ghofaun, correct?"

"Yes."

"This isn't different. It's a miniature radio. Take it out when you're done. You're not jacking it in permanently."

I warily accept the small device. "A radio that fits inside your ear? Nothing else?"

"Nothing else."

"And I can take it out whenever I choose?"

"Yes. I don't see what the fuss is about. Try it."

I purse my lips and frown at Demitri as I push the small plug into my ear.

"See? Not so bad. Let's test it. Put your finger on the surface and twist like this to activate the transmitter."

Again, I follow his direction. A bleep sounds in my ear and makes me jump.

"That's just it turning on. Adjust the volume by tapping it." He turns his on. "Can you hear me?"

Inside my head his voice repeats the words with a short delay.

"Now you know what it feels like to be me." Demitri gives a little laugh, his small voice repeating inside my inner ear.

"Not funny."

"It is, though," he says with a smile that fades. "Mila?"

"Yes?"

"I never thought I'd say this to a Robust." He swallows. "Whatever happens, I want you to know how much I ... respect you. You have a strength and character I've never had. I'm glad you're not like me—or any other Gracile for that matter."

"You're not a bad person, Demitri."

He turns his head away, but I reach forward and turn his shoulders back toward me. "Whatever our great differences, I appreciate you for being here with me in this. I consider you a friend."

He looks flustered and quickly changes the subject, "Hey, uh ... look." He motions out the window. "The Leader has activated the artificial gravity. He's almost got the station completely powered up."

"I see it."

"I'm afraid the odds aren't in our favor, and we're running out of time. Are you ready?"

"I'm ready. The odds are irrelevant. We can do this. Are you with me, Demitri?" I take a deep breath and hold out my hand.

He accepts it with a firm shake. "I'm with you, Mila."

Up through the cargo hold, we float toward a closed portal. Demitri pulls on a lever and the hatch glides open. Before us is another chamber.

"What is this?"

"It's an equalization chamber. It's harmless. Get in."

I pull myself into the sterile chamber alongside Demitri. He secures the door and then cranks a lever on the wall. With a hiss, the pressure in the chamber equalizes.

"Okay, I'll head for the tech platform, and you—"

A green light registers on the wall, and the hatch to the station flies open. Anchored to the floor by magnetic boots are two Creed soldiers. They stare blankly at us—their heads twitching. "Intruder," one calls out.

I grab a support bar above the door's opening and kick the soldier on the right square across the front of his visor. To my surprise, Demitri thrusts off the wall, grabbing the other geminoid and wrenching its head around, disabling it with brute force.

Taking his cue, I wrap my legs around the neck of the Creed, pull a straight-blade knife from my waistband and drive it through the side of its skull. The robot spasms, then stills. Its internal processor silenced, it floats slowly away like a hunk of garbage. I kick it to create more distance and replace my knife.

Demitri is staring at his hands. "I didn't mean to … I mean, I did, but … I just did what came naturally, I didn't mean to kill—"

"Just go, Demitri," I shout, pushing off in the direction of the giant spinning disk. "Shut up and go." The Leader knows we're here.

CHAPTER THIRTY-EIGHT

DEMITRI

Blackness gobbles up the beam from my headlamp as I fly along the narrow corridor, barely avoiding cracking my skull on the pipes and casings protruding from the walls. Through the dimness, the shape of a hatch begins to form, round and metallic—a huge manual release adorning the front. Finally, an end to this horizonless trip down a rabbit hole. But what is that? Through the small window in the portal, something moves. The shadow passes over the glass. Then back again. It repeats this over and over, as if someone inside is pacing. A geminoid?

I extinguish my headlamp and float silently like a shadow to the hatch, then carefully peer over the lip of the window frame. Inside, there's a little more light—a dashboard aglow with dials and buttons. A Creed blocks the doorway, its back to me. Sard.

The robot jerks into action, turning to pace, its magnetic boots clomping away. As it reveals its face, my stomach lurches. Nikolaj.

It's him, and yet it's not him. The rubbery skin perfectly simulates every aspect of my brother's face—every crease and line. But the eyes don't burn with the ambition I watched with envy growing up. My heart aches. I'm sorry, Nikolaj.

"Demitri, can you hear me?" Mila's voice crackles over my earpiece.

Turning away from the door and ducking below the glass, I

swallow, take a breath, and tap the mic on. "I'm here, Mila."

"You any closer to shutting down that comms station?" she asks.
"I'm almost at the disk."

"I've run into another Creed. Not as easy to get in as we'd hoped."

"I just watched you nearly rip the head off the last one. Whatever you did before, do it again. We don't have much time." She's calm, but firm—and totally unaware she just asked me to murder my brother.

"Sure."

"When you're done, come to me. I need you."

The earpiece crackles again, and she's gone.

My chest is tight. The room spins, and my stomach swims for the thousandth time since this all began. I wish I were stronger, braver. Perhaps a god of my own would make me brave.

I tap my forehead again and again. Come on, think. There has to be some way out of this. But I just yearn to be back home with Nikolaj nagging me again.

You have no home. That's what Vedmak would say. And he'd be right. He'd also just want to break every limb of that Creed, simply because it looks like Nikolaj. How ironic now that you're gone, Vedmak, I need you.

Here goes nothing.

Forcing out a huff, I spin to face the window and turn on the headlamp. The cone of light streams through the glass. Within seconds, the lock clunks and the door opens inward, swinging effortlessly in zero gravity, to reveal the geminoid inside. My brother's face stares back, illuminated only by my light. In that moment, there seems to be recognition in his face—a flicker, a lingering memory.

I'm sorry.

Screwing my eyes shut, I grab the robot by the head. It fights back immediately, clamping its cold hands around my forearms. The pressure is excruciating, my flesh crushed by the force. I yelp and twist its head as hard as possible.

The Creed's neck snaps, and its spinal column severs with a loud crack. The robot freezes in its position—a toy without power. I yank my arms free, grab the open door as an anchor, and kick the robot directly in the chest. It uncouples from the magboots and floats away, back into the comms room, where it comes to rest against the wall. Trying not to look at it, I maneuver to the console, clasping at the walls, pipes, and other protrusions to gain purchase.

Several screens, an old-fashioned physical keyboard, knobs, and dials. Where the hell to begin? On the main screen, green letters flash: *PASSWORD*. Even if I crack it, I'll have no idea how to access the comms protocol. This tech is too old. There isn't even an intranet for me to access. We're screwed.

CHAPTER THIRTY-NINE

MILA

Releasing the hatch, I pull myself into a tunnel. Rung by rung, the steel cold beneath my hands, I reach the portal into the giant wheel. There's an opening like a doorway here. Around it are yellow-and-gray-striped markers and a simplistic picture of a stick man being cut in half by the rotating inner disk. My lips purse. Don't share the same fate as the stick man.

The portal opens for just a few seconds at a time. Inside the disk there's movement, but before I can analyze it further, the window closes and I must wait again. Not long enough to really see anything. I wait for the next opening, and when it arrives, I count out the seconds until it closes. Almost six seconds. I can make it.

I tap my ear. "Demitri, where are you on figuring that stuff out?"

The earpiece buzzes and I hear Demitri sigh. *"It's not good. I have no idea where to start with this antiquated junk."*

"I need you to figure it out. If the Leader fires that thing, it's all over. You have to shut down the connection."

"I know. I just have no idea where to start."

"We don't have time for you to figure it out. I'm about thirty seconds away from making direct contact with the Leader. He's probably going to kill me, so do it and get down here."

"Mila." He sounds exasperated. *"You're not helping."*

"I'm going in." I tap my earpiece again.

The disk is about halfway through the rotation. If I time this right, it could put me right on top of the Leader. What are my odds? Don't think about it. Just go.

The doorway slides open. I push off the wall to pass through the opening, but my momentum slows as my body crosses the threshold. Weight like a thousand pounds of water pours down on me. Every bone in my body, every fiber of muscle feels as though it's been filled with lead. "What's going on?" I gasp, and slump to the floor.

"Gravity," a voice echoes across the vast interior of the disk. "It's a little hard to transition back quickly, especially once you've been free from it."

Rows of glowing consoles line either wall. The pathway inside the disk arcs ahead of and behind me. I crane my neck to see yet more consoles on what to me looks like the ceiling – but to anyone standing there, I'd be the one who was upside down. Look forward, Mila. Focus on what you know.

Some three meters away, two pairs of Creed magboots face me. In this room the artificial gravity removes the need for them, and the sheer weight of the boots will slow the geminoids. My advantage. The robotic soldiers stand there staring, their faces perfect blank masks. They aren't armed. They didn't expect a fight up here, and even if they did, they couldn't fire their energy weapons in this place.

Behind them stands the tall silver-haired Leader, engaged at one of the consoles. He stops what he's doing long enough to remove a small translucent mouth cup from a pouch and snap it into place under his nasal breather. He checks that the nasal apparatus is secure and, otherwise ignoring me, continues tapping away at a frenetic speed.

"You can't do this."

A small laugh echoes in the vast space. The Leader speaks without diverting his attention from the console. "I will give you credit. You're bold for such an insignificant and inferior little creature. I don't know how you figured out what I was doing, much less that I was going to do it from up here. It took me a moment to realize you were the same one I saw in Kapka's dungeon. But what you don't yet understand is I can do whatever I choose, and you are nothing more to me than a resilient little insect."

"Not if we stop you." Come on, Demitri.

"We? Oh, you brought someone with you. That fool child, Demitri, perhaps? Where is the little coward hiding?"

"I'm not telling you anything."

"Don't waste my time, then. My Creed will make short work of you."

"I'm not afraid. We've destroyed hundreds of them by now."

"But not these. These two are my personal guard. You don't stand a chance, surface dweller." He nods at the Creed. "Squeeze the life out of this wretch. Then find the traitor. Try not to make a mess with them."

"Affirmative," the Creed chime in unison. "Initiating close-quarter combat and elimination protocols."

I jump to my feet and drop my strong side back slightly. They come for me, moving faster than I thought possible, utilizing some advanced protocol the others don't have. Pain compliance is useless here. I have to go straight for the kill shot.

The first Creed lunges in with a strike that attempts to take my head off. Sidestepping, I kick low, as hard as I can, to steal the balance from its front leg, then kick into its other leg and drive the full weight of my shoulder into its center. As it falls, I fall with it, ensuring the felled Creed is between me and the other one. Pulling my blade, I drop down upon the creature now flailing like a baby.

My knife pierces it through the eye portal, and the creature jerks to a stop.

I rise and deflect a thrusting kick from the other one. Closing quickly, it grabs for me. I leap forward and slam both knees into the Creed's chest, even as it wraps me in a crushing embrace. But I'm right where I want to be—front and center. Securing the back of the robot's neck, I look deep into the depths of the Creed's empty eyes and drive my knife through the floor of its chin and into its skull, silencing it. I ride the thing to the ground, execute a forward roll, and rise to my feet, casually spinning my knife back and forth in my hand. It took me less than thirty seconds to fell his best.

The Leader refuses to look at me. His gaze remains focused on the control panel—and yet his jaw is set, the muscles of his neck flexing as his breath hisses through pristine clenched teeth.

I touch my ear. "Any time now would be great, Demitri."

CHAPTER FORTY

DEMITRI

"Mila? Mila."

No answer.

There's no way to know how long I've been hovering here, tapping away, trying to hack the system. It's no use. There's no question this is the console for the spacenet—and I'm never getting in. The luminous green letters blink defiantly, mocking my futile attempts at access. I slam my fist on the console. The screen flickers. It's not so sturdy. What would Vedmak do? He'd tear it apart—with his bare hands.

For Evgeniy—adrenaline electrifies my every muscle fiber.

For Nikolaj—every buried emotion and memory floods to the surface.

For Denni—I raise my fists above my head.

For Mila—I slam them down like a hammer.

The console splits. Blue arcs of electrons spew out and fizzle across the surface. The images on the screens flicker. I roar loud and long, slamming my fists down again and again. With each attack, the console buckles a little more.

Fist-shaped marks now pattern the metalwork. My hands don't hurt, until I look at them. Then the throbbing comes.

The screens are now black. Metallic and plastic innards hang from the deep wounds like the entrails of a disemboweled animal. I yank at them, ripping wires, capacitors, and other components from within the belly of the console.

My shoulders heave with my heavy breathing. If nothing else, I may have delayed the Leader. I make for the door back into the corridor. My hands rest on the lip of the portal, but I pause and glance behind. Nikolaj's namesake lies perfectly still, its arm outstretched, against the bulkhead. It looks as if it's reaching out to me for help. I swallow hard and turn away, then power into the tunnel and toward the disk.

CHAPTER FORTY-ONE

MILA

Stepping away from the console, the Leader turns to face me. His face is darkened, not by shadow, but by something far more sinister. "You think you're doing something great? You think purpose, or some benevolent god, has led you to this point? Is that what you think?"

I steady myself, the knife gripped in my right hand. Maybe if I can get close enough …

"Tell me," the Leader continues, "do you really think you can stop the evolution of mankind?" He touches at the plastic cup covering his mouth.

Why is he always touching that thing? "This isn't evolution. It's extinction. And yes, I will stop it."

He laughs. "You're too late." He jabs his finger on a large red key. I hold my breath. A moment passes, then another. The Leader turns back to me, a terrible look in his face. "What have you done?"

By the hands of Yeos, Demitri did it. "I told you. We're stopping this."

The Leader steps forward, towering over me, a terrible fury pouring from his features. "You are all below me. I will no longer entertain a conversation with a creature that spends its life scrambling around in the filth." The rebreather under his nose shakes with the words. "You want to taste death? I shall offer it to you."

Moving faster than humanly possible, the Leader slams into me—jarring my organs against my ribs. I fly from the ground, flipping end over end, crash into the far console, and slump to the floor. There's a void in my chest where my breath used to be. My head spins. One blow. That's what he can do with one blow. He'll kill you if you let him, Mila. Get up.

I search the floor, but the knife is nowhere to be seen. As I climb to my feet, Mos's Hyper auto-injector shifts in my cargo pocket. *Just in case you get in a bad spot.* I grunt and pull it out. Damnation. I'm pretty sure this qualifies. Flipping the safety cap off, I jam the auto-injector against my thigh and feel the rush of the serum as it enters my system.

"Is that all? That's the best the resistance has to offer?" he says, stomping forward.

"No. This is."

Springing from my crouched position, I drive upward, slamming my fist under his chin, then back down again with a crushing brachial stun, followed by a spinning back kick that catches him square in the chest. Dance like a sparrow hawk. Capitalizing on the element of surprise, I press the advantage, striking multiple times while working my way to the outside of his guard.

The Hyper is working. For an instant, I'm unstoppable. The Leader, with all his sophisticated bioengineering, appears wholly unable to defend himself against my overwhelming offensive. He swings his arm in from the outside of my guard, but I intercept and counter. My fist slams right across the nose and mouth, sending his nasal breather and cup flying. His face is a picture of shock and disgust.

"How does it feel to be exposed?" I shout, spit flying at him.

He flinches, the crack in his discipline widening. I launch in and kick low to strip his front leg, but I may as well have kicked a stone pillar. Pain arcs through my leg and up into my back. Not wanting to lose my advantage, I deliver a series of hand strikes. But the Leader parries them as though he has trained in chum lawk his whole life. Frustrated, I drive harder, varying my attacks, but it's useless. He finds a gap in my defense and exploits it, slamming me across the neck with a hammer fist.

Everything fades. I lay on the floor, breathless. It's not possible. There's no way he could be this good. Ghofaun isn't this good.

The Leader leans over me, a few strands of silver hair falling across his furious face. "You're in trouble, now, little one."

CHAPTER FORTY-TWO

DEMITRI

The inner disk spins, and the corresponding opening aligns only briefly before sliding past for another revolution. Each time it opens I get a brief glance inside, a snapshot of Mila battling with the Leader.

Each time I hesitate, and fail to step through, I fail to help her. Each glimpse inside is a frozen image of my friend in pain—kicked, punched, thrown. The Leader is huge in comparison, towering over her with a psychotic smile on his face as she throws another onslaught of combinations, only to have the majority of them blocked.

I huff out my fear and coil in readiness, feet resting against the inner wall of the tunnel. The opening slides into position, and I push off as hard as possible. Immediately as I pass through the portal, gravity clasps my body and slams it against the floor of the disk.

My muscles ache, remembering how to move in gravity. But I'm nowhere near Mila. Where is she? Directly above, they come into view on the opposite side of the disk. Mila battles the Leader, but he's toying with her, knocking away each assault. Finally, he counters with a fist strike that sends her sprawling. He could just grab her by the neck and snap it. But he's enjoying himself.

"Mila!"

She glances up. Her face is split and smeared with blood, her chest heaving. But all I've done is distract her. The Leader kicks her squarely in the stomach, and she slides across the floor, wheezing.

"Mila, you can't beat him," I call into the radio. "He's learned your style already. Get away from him."

The Leader's laugh fills the disk, reverberating off the walls and consoles. "Stupid girl. What is it you think you can do? Infect me with disease? I am genetic perfection. And you—you're the genetic waste we cast off. You disgust me."

"C'mon." Mila dives and rolls, grabs something from the floor, and then rockets toward him. As they collide, she spins under his arms and flicks the gleaming steel of her knife across his solar plexus, the blade penetrating to the hilt and dragging through his flesh.

Did she do it?

Mila spins again and slices low across his abdomen, but he anticipates her move, grabs her wrist, and lifts her into the air. He squeezes until she drops the weapon, and he kicks it away.

Mila flails against his grip, but to no avail.

He flings her viciously to the floor. She hits the metalwork hard and slides to a stop.

The Leader cranes his neck to see me and points. "Meddling child. You die next."

What the hell is that? Gleaming from the wound Mila just inflicted are metallic innards. Buried among them is something more familiar: a miniature fusion reactor, much like the one Nikolaj created. The nanobots are already at work, sealing the gash.

"You're a geminoid? Is that why the gunship wouldn't lock on to you?"

"Don't be stupid, boy," he shouts. "I'm as human as you. But how would you expect someone could live so long? Even Graciles have an expiration date. I did what was necessary to survive and complete what I started so many years ago."

"You're jacked?"

He grins. "I enhanced myself, for the benefit of all of you. To ensure you all can live forever."

"This doesn't make any sense. Have you ever asked us what *we* want? If we want to be dissolved into information and stored on the event horizon of a black hole?" Even saying it out loud sounds crazy.

"I didn't need to. I know. The neuralweb is a wonderful thing—it tells me everything I need to know."

"You're not making any sense."

"You're a feeble-minded boy, Demitri Stasevich. I *am* the neuralweb. Every thought, every search, every use of our web passed through me. I have collated every conscious and subconscious desire of every Gracile in my long lifetime. You all want the same thing—immortality. You may not say it out loud, but this is the truth. You are afraid of death, of not existing. I am your Leader. Your savior. This is my destiny. To give you all what it is you crave. You're too afraid to pay the ultimate price for what you want."

We take death to reach a star.

"Just because people think something, it doesn't mean that's what they truly want. Trust me on this. You're mad."

"And you're out of time," he snaps back.

He steps to Mila, grabs her by the jacket, and lifts her into the air. "Say goodbye to your pet."

Mila's eyes open. She grabs the little fingers on each of the Leader's hands and yanks on them. It's enough to make him drop her. She rolls to the side and crouches in a defensive stance.

"Demitri. Do something."

Even if I run to her, the Leader will see me coming. And if I did manage to make it to her, what can I do against him?

"Demitri," she shouts.

"Mila, keep him busy." This is a long shot.

"Are you kidding me? What do you think I've been doing?"

"Just a couple of minutes."

"I don't have a couple of minutes," Mila yells back.

I drop to my knees and empty the contents of my pockets—everything I took from the Opor hideout. The second stim syringe is still there. I pull the cap off and empty the liquid onto the floor. Using a stripped piece of thick copper wire, I make a tight coil around the body of the syringe—as many loops as possible. Where are they? Yes. Two neodymium magnets.

Mila is using her small size to dodge and evade the Leader, bouncing from the floor to the walls and throwing anything within reach at his head.

"Demitri!" she cries again.

"Almost there!"

The last piece, where is it? Here it is. The firecracker Denni gave me. I slide it into the syringe, cap both ends with the magnets, and wrap either end of the copper wire onto them, leaving the fuse sticking out.

"Mila. Do you remember the gunship in Etyom? The one you took out?"

"I remember," she cries back, ducking another blow.

"Brace for impact." If this works, the magnetic field protecting the miniature fusion reactor will collapse. Of course, that will result in a chain reaction …

The Leader grabs Mila again. "Time to die, bottom feeder."

It's now or never.

I grab the small torch from the pile on the ground and tap it a few times. It snaps on with a brilliant blue flame and catches the fuse of the firecracker. The device in my hand, I squat deeply and shove off from the wall with all my might.

The reduced gravity pulls at my limbs, but its hold is not enough. My body powers upward through the air. With arms outstretched, and still clasping the fizzing EMP device, I soar past the midway point. Everything inverts. My stomach turns.

I slam down to the floor directly between the Leader and Mila. He stumbles back, but grips my arm to maintain his balance. His eyes glass over at the sight of the EMP. The Leader lets go of me to run, but it's too late. I throw the firecracker at him, and it bursts with a high-pitched squeal and a plume of red smoke.

"Fool! Do you know what you've just ... I'm ... I'm ..." He coughs through the smoke.

"You're finished."

I spin to face Mila. Her wide-eyed gaze meets mine as realization dawns on her. I give a knowing look, then step forward and envelop my small friend in my arms. There's a popping sound, followed by a blinding flash.

CHAPTER FORTY-THREE

MILA

Demitri turns to me with a sad smile. Oh, Yeos, no. "Demitri. It's going to—"

With a quick step, he pulls me close and wraps his huge arms around me. A pop precedes a blinding flash and a deafening sound like cannon fire. I flinch and hold tight to him. White-hot flames smother us, but Demitri takes the brunt.

The Leader just exploded. He just exploded, and I can't hear. And ... Demitri—

We fall to the floor. "Demitri." I roll his muscled torso to the side. Blood pools on the floor beneath him, but he's still breathing.

"No ... no, hang on, Demitri." I tear a section of my shirt and begin to pack the oozing wound in his lower back. This is bad, really bad. "Stay with me, Demitri. Don't you dare die on me." We've got to get out of here. From the floor of the disk, I peer through the chaos—strobing yellow emergency lights flash on the wall and wisps of smoke rise from the Leader's flayed body.

Slowly the ringing subsides, but it's replaced with the station's blaring alarm. What do I do? Demitri's been burned across the side of his face, his clothing scorched through to the skin of his back. I pat out the glowing embers and reassess his condition. The wounds are significant. Maybe I can stop the bleeding—

"*Attention,*" an automated voice echoes across the disk. "*Explosion detected inside the command disk. Disk compromised, breach fissure detected, artificial gravity systems failing, oxygen levels failing, reactor compromised. You now have eight minutes, thirty-seven seconds to reach minimum extraction distance."*

"Eight minutes?" How in the name of Yeos am I supposed to move a seven-foot unconscious Gracile? I scan the disk for something I can roll him onto and drag him with, but there's nothing.

"Attention," the voice begins again.

Artificial gravity systems failing ... That means stuff seems lighter, right? I can feel it, a strange creeping sensation of weightlessness. I've got to move.

I stand, grab two handfuls of Demitri's jacket, and give him a hard tug. His body slides a little. "We can do this, just stay with me."

"You now have seven minutes, sixteen seconds to reach minimum extraction distance."

I give him a pull and swing his body past me toward the portal. My grip on the floor is rapidly diminishing. Yeos help me.

Scanning the disk's interior, my gaze falls on one of the Leader's vanquished Creed leaning at an angle as the gravity fails—but its feet are stuck to the floor. Magboots. Pushing myself off the wall, I glide through the air to grab the Creed soldier.

"Attention. Explosion detected inside the command disk. Disk compromised, breach fissure detected, artificial gravity systems failed, oxygen levels failing, reactor failing. You now have six minutes, six seconds to reach minimum extraction distance."

The side of the disk begins to buckle. I fumble with the Creed's boots before hitting the glowing blue button on the side of each. The boots relax, and I yank the lifeless robot out of them. They're big enough for me to put on over my footwear. I tuck my feet in and tab the button on the side, and the boots automatically cinch against my shins. Straining, I lift one foot up and step

300

forward with a *shunk-clunk*, then the other, and again. Developing a rhythm, I approach the floating, unconscious Demitri.

I grab his jacket with one hand and drag him through the air toward the portal that leads out of the disk. We might be different. We might have nothing in common. We might not ever fully understand each other. But he's my friend and I'm not going to leave him here to die.

I wait impatiently for the failing disk to rotate, then align with the exit. "Come on."

"You now have four minutes, twenty-seven seconds to reach minimum extraction distance."

The disk stops, and the last of the gravity fails, the alignment with the exit incomplete.

"Damnation." The opening is just wide enough to squeeze through. I shove Demitri through the gap, then grip the bulkhead and pull myself through to the tunnel. Lights flicker. The station groans.

Demitri moans as I shove him down the cramped tunnel. A thin trail of red spheres leaks from his wound. Keep moving. Another tremor shudders through the station, and with the sound of steel tearing, I'm thrown against the wall. The air suddenly grows thin. I can't breathe.

"Attention. Explosion detected inside the command disk. Disk integrity failure, breach fissure critical, artificial gravity systems failed, oxygen levels failed, reactor critical. You now have two minutes, forty seconds to reach minimum extraction distance."

Straining, I seize Demitri and press off the wall toward the equalization chamber. We glide into the compartment, and I thump my fist against the red button on the wall. The hatch slams shut. There's a hiss as the pressure equalizes.

"Open," I shout to the opposite door.

"You now have one minute, thirty-eight seconds to reach

minimum extraction distance."

There's another terrible quake and the distant sound of something collapsing. The door to the cockpit flies open. I shove Demitri inside and slam the hatch shut. "Now what?"

"Above you." Demitri is conscious, but barely, his voice but a whisper.

A bright orange lever above my head reads, *Emergency Disengage.* No time for questions. I yank it down and feel the ship separate from the lock. The vessel floats, aimlessly bumping back into the crippled space station. Another shudder.

"You have thirty seconds to reach minimum extraction distance."

"What am I supposed to do? How do we get home?"

"Return to point of origin?" An automated voice speaks from the glowing command panel before me.

"Yes."

"The confirm key ...," wheezes Demitri.

I scan the console. There. I jab at the key to initiate.

The boosters ignite, and we swing against the back wall of the cockpit. Directional thrusters fire as the ship spins away from the station. Through the glass of the cockpit, the stars whirl across the blackness of space as we plummet toward Earth.

The shuttle quakes violently. I pinch my eyes shut and swallow hard, struggling against the force of our descent. I force my eyes open to see Demitri already halfway into one of the rear seats. I shove him down and pull the locking harness over his head with a clunk. Then I strain to reach the adjoining seat and pull myself into it. With one swift downward movement, I yank the harness across my shoulders and torso and snap it into the locking plate between my thighs.

Demitri slowly lifts his arm and clasps my fingers. With a sickening jolt, there's a flash of light through the cockpit window. The shockwave slams against the rocket and shoves it forward as we re-enter Earth's atmosphere.

"Yeos is here with us. His good hands are upon us. There is nothing to fear." I clamp my eyes shut and chant under my breath.

"Mila ... we're going to die, aren't we?" He sounds scared.

"Yeah, Demitri. I think that's a fair bet."

The shuddering intensifies, rattling us down to our bones.

"I don't believe in Yeos." He swallows, his lips speckled with blood. "What does that mean for me?"

"I can't judge your heart, friend. I can only offer you the truth and hope it's enough—that Yeos will hear my prayers."

He nods. "It's all right with me. Maybe He'll listen to you."

"*Warning,*" the automated voice says from the cockpit. "*Air brakes compromised, descent thrusters failing, recommended entry speed exceeded.*"

Demitri screws his eyes shut. "I'm sorry, Mila."

"We did the best we could, Demitri."

The ship shudders, and the atmosphere burns bright orange through the cockpit window as we plummet through the sky. As we shake violently, the autopilot struggles to maintain a normal entry trajectory. Steel rivets holding everything together pop and pull apart under the force. Finally, the impact rips through the ship. The squeal of steel tearing against earth pierces the air for a brief, sickening moment.

Then, only darkness.

EPILOGUE

MILA

"*Arrived at point of origin. Brrrrr …* " A crackle of static. Smoke hangs in the air. The smell of something electrical burning fills my nostrils. *"Arrived at point of ori—brrrrr."*

The ringing in my head is deafening, and it's difficult to see— or move. The restraints cut into my shoulders. I'm … sideways. The ship must have rolled during the crash. The crash. By the great hands of the creator, we're alive.

"Demitri. Demitri, we're alive."

He's not in the cockpit.

A harness hangs from the empty seat where my friend should be, and a hatch in the side of the ship is open. Wisps of smoke drift out and are stripped away by a cold, cutting wind. I unlatch my harness and fall hard to the opposite wall.

"Demitri? Demitri, where are you?"

Every muscle aches as I climb up and through the portal. A gust of icy wind rakes across my face. It's the most amazing feeling. I scramble from the cockpit and stand on the hull of the crushed vessel. The wreckage and the trench from the crash are remarkable. There's no logical reason we should have survived.

Sitting on the edge of the long furrow is Demitri.

"Demitri. We made it. We did it. I can't believe we did it."

He doesn't answer. Maybe he's still bleeding? I dangle back into the hatch to grab a bright-orange medical pouch that hangs precariously from the side wall. Pulling it free from its case, I hoist myself out, then quickly unzip the pouch. Rifling through the contents, my fingers eventually find an auto-injector labeled, "Medical Stabilizer."

"Okay, Demitri, I think this will help." I hop down to the ice-covered ground and trudge toward him. "Try this. It's a medical booster. It'll help."

Demitri takes the injector without looking up and presses it to his neck with a hiss.

Patting him on the shoulder, I step past to survey the distant ruins of Etyom. Back where the launchpad still smolders, there's an occasional pop of a rifle or the echoed concussion of an explosion.

"Please be alive, Faruq," I whisper. Is it possible he and the others survived? Maybe. But even if they did, what do we do now?

"Okay, Demitri. We're going to get ourselves fixed up, regroup, and then figure out what we can do to help everyone. We owe them that much. Right?"

He's on his feet now, holding his wound, his eyes cast down.

"Demitri?" Crossing to him, I smile and touch his wounded shoulder. "Let's find the others. We'll figure this out."

The back of his fist strikes me across the jaw like a slab of steel, sending me sprawling back into a snowbank. I clamber to my feet, my legs rubbery, my jaw throbbing. "What the hell, Demitri?"

He turns to walk away.

"After all this, you're going to ... attack me?"

"Stupid little bitch. You and your pathetic band of misfits better not get in my way again."

No. It can't be. "Vedmak. Don't do this—"

The demon laughs. "It's done. I'm free. And Hell will follow with me."

My dream. It was a warning, but not about the Gracile Leader or even Kapka. Famine, pestilence, and war we have survived, but no matter what I do, there's no stopping the coming of the fourth—the coming of Death.

Bile rises in my throat. My muscles tingle with shock and adrenaline. At long last, we freed ourselves from the tyranny of the Leader, but at what cost? I can only watch as Vedmak steals my friend's wounded body, limping across the wasteland of snow and ice toward the ruins of Etyom. His dwindling silhouette melts into the twisting pillars of smoke waving like long lazy arms into the sky. And then, in the distance, the emergency balloons holding the last lillipad give way, and it collapses in plumes of debris, crashing down into the enclaves beneath.

ACKNOWLEDGEMENTS

We would like to thank the following people for their help in making this book the best it can be.

Our beta readers: Larissa Büchi, Bilal Bham, Chris Curenton, Kelly Hambly, David Jones, Shelby O'Connor, Samantha Walford, Dominica Worthington.

Our editors: Jason Kirk for developmental editing, Irene Billings for copyediting, and Jonas Saul for proofreading.
Our agents: Italia Gandolfo and Renee C. Fountain at Gandolfo Helin Fountain Literary Management NYC.

Our cover designer and Etyom map creator: John Byrne.

And of course the crew at Vesuvian Books, especially Liana Gardner for all her support.